Forgive Us This Day

[Anniversary Edition]

Barbara Joe Williams

mani
ublishing, llc

Barbara Joe Williams

Tallahassee, FL

This book is published by [Barbara Joe Williams]:

Amani Publishing, LLC
P. O. Box 12045
Tallahassee, FL 32317
(850) 264-3341

A company based on faith, hope, and love

ISBN: 9780983366690
LCCN: 2014916415

.

Visit our website at: www.barbarajoe.webs.com
Email us at: amanipublishing@aol.com
Cover designed by: Adrienne Thompson

Other Titles from Barbara Joe Williams

Upcoming titles:
A Cup of Barbara Joe (January 1, 2015)
First Class Love Affair (February 14, 2015)

Current titles:
First Class Love (February 2014)
You Don't Even Know My Name (novella, January 2014)
A Writer's Guide to Publishing & Marketing
 (Volume 2, December 2013)
Double Proposal (August 2013)
Losing My Soul (March 2013)
The 21 Lives of Lisette Donavan: Anthology (2012)
A Man of My Own (2011)
A Writer's Guide to Publishing & Marketing (2010)
Moving the Furniture:
 52 Ways to Keep Your Marriage Fresh (2008)
Courtney's Collage (2007)
How I Met My Sweetheart: Anthology (2007)
Falling for Lies (2006)
Dancing with Temptation (2005)
Forgive Us This Day (2004)

All books are available on Kindle and Nook devices.

Please visit my website at: www.barbarajoe.webs.com

Prologue

(November)

Michael Wayne was the Chief Executive Officer of a million dollar business who was about to make the biggest mistake of his life. He didn't have any business in Lisa's house, let alone in her bedroom on a stormy night. Unfortunately, he was hypnotized by her sensual presence. After all, he and Lisa had history. They were once labeled the "cute couple" in college, even though that was almost twenty years ago. Right now, he was just trying to remember to breathe. The pounding of his heart was making it difficult to concentrate, especially with Lisa's soft lips trembling against his. Somehow, he had to break her spell and get out of there before the situation went any further.

"Lisa, please stop. I can't do this." That's what he wanted to say, only his mouth was betraying him by not opening. Her intoxicating fragrance was simply driving him mad. She was wearing her signature scent. Obsession.

"Michael, baby, just relax and let me help you release some tension," Lisa whispered, seemingly reading his mind. Then she tongued his ear in a smooth circular motion.

"Lisa, you—you know that's my weak spot," he responded, leaning away from her.

"Yeah, I know all your weak spots, Michael. I want to lick every one of them all night long."

She moistened an index finger, slowly slid it across his lips, and pushed him back on her queen-sized bed. While climbing on top of him, Lisa let her red silk kimono slither down, revealing her nakedness. She felt an electric sensation go through Michael's body from the top of his head all the way down to the tip of his toes. *I got you now, baby. You never could resist my sexiness.*

He still had feelings for her and she intended to capitalize on them tonight. With a slim body in perfect form, Lisa was prepared to please him in all the ways she remembered he liked. Lowering her head, so her long, reddish, wavy hair would cascade around her face, she wickedly smiled down at him. Her seduction plan was working perfectly.

Yes, Michael used to love her vanilla chocolate skin with the pretty freckled face, beaming brown eyes, and luscious lips. She would easily remind him of all of her feminine assets tonight and add a few tricks to the mix.

Michael's mind went blank. He finally relaxed, eased back against the black satin sheets, and succumbed to temptation. Obviously, he couldn't think anymore and his body had already made an executive decision. He didn't have any control over what was happening. The blood flowing to his manhood had drained all the guiltiness from his brain. Now the passion consumed Michael and took over his entire being as if he was having an out-of-body experience.

Lisa willingly helped him out of his clothing. Feeling him weakening against her tempting charms, she slowly undressed him, enjoying the sight of his fine brown frame, round piercing eyes, and silky smooth skin. He still had the six-foot, muscular, defined shape of the twenty-two year old man she had always loved. She even remembered the slight tickle she used to get from his barely there mustache on her face. Lisa loved the closely trimmed beard he had grown, and the way it connected to his mustache emphasized his full fiery lips. He was more handsome than ever, and his dark, neatly waved hair was sharply edged to perfection.

Tonight, she was his completely. Lying in his arms, they engaged in a fierce kiss. All the years they had been apart meld into nothingness. They were together again, the way they were meant to be. Only this time, she would do anything to keep her man. He would be hers alone. Forever. It didn't matter if he had a wife. Alese didn't know how to please him like she did.

Hell, I had him first anyway. Besides, I could easily replace her. Where is she in his time of sexual need? I'm what he needs at this moment. I'm going to make sure he's satisfied and comes back for more.

Pulling away from his scorching lips, Lisa gazed down at the engorged penis she gently massaged. She hunched her body against the grown man shuddering at her touch. *Clearly, he hasn't been stroked like this in a long time. Poor thing.*

"Oh, Lisa, please don't stop. Please don't stop what you're doing," he begged, using the sexy tone she craved.

Lisa straddled his torso, slipped his shaft into her wetness, and began working her usual magic. While licking his hard nipples, he moaned with pleasure. From the intense frown on Michael's face and his shortness of breath, Lisa surmised they were only seconds away from a blissful orgasm. Hoping their lustful night would never end, she slowed down her strokes.

As they made eye contact, Lisa murmured, "Don't worry, baby, I hadn't planned on stopping. We're just getting started."

1

Alese Dean Wayne

"Oh, no, it's morning already," I moaned, stretching my entire body and yawning softly before sitting up in our king-sized, Victorian mahogany bed. The sun was shining through the bedroom window directly on my face. I leaned over and kissed my loving husband, Michael, on the lips and said, "Happy New Year, baby."

He gently rose up on his left elbow and pecked me on the right cheek and said, "Happy New Year to you, too, sweetheart."

We hugged each other tightly, welcoming in the new day and the New Year together. I felt the sizzling heat of his body penetrate my whole being as I eased away from him.

"All right, that's enough of that. I better get out of this bed before you get some ideas," I said, teasing him. We enjoyed playing with one another like that.

"Yeah, you best do that because I'm ready. You tried to get me drunk last night, but I'm ready now," he joked in the same playful tone as I remembered the sweet taste of the Cristal champagne from our private New Year's Eve celebration.

Lying back slowly onto the pillow to entertain the idea of pleasing my man, the mood dramatically changed when the bedroom door flew open. Bianca, our two-year-old daughter, came running into the room and climbed up onto the bed. She rolled over until she reached the middle, lodging herself between the two of us. Obviously proud of her small accomplishment, she giggled with delight.

A typically playful child for her age, Bianca enjoyed watching cartoons, playing with stuffed animals and dolls, coloring, and drawing. Wearing her favorite pink and white flannel "Dora the Explorer" pajamas with attached footsies, she had her usual sleeping pal, Winnie the Pooh, clutched safely under her arm.

Once on the bed, Bianca was all over her daddy, jumping up and down and laughing as he tickled her belly and made funny noises. Those two were just unbelievably happy whenever they were together. No one would ever guess Bianca was not our biological daughter.

"My daddy, I want to watch toons, please," she said excitedly, making her childish attempts to form syllables sound cute and innocent. Michael had to make her say cartoons again in her childlike speech by pretending he hadn't heard her the first time.

"What did you ask your daddy?" Michael asked with a grand smile on his face.

"My daddy, I said—I want to watch toons, please," Bianca said louder, cleverly making a droopy face to win over her daddy.

"Okay, okay," Michael chuckled wildly at his baby girl. "Let's see what's on the Disney Channel."

He happily relented and reached for the universal remote control on the nightstand by his bed. Bianca clapped with glee and sat up in the center of our bed with her legs tucked underneath her.

Realizing that was the end of my luxurious morning, I slid on my pink terry cloth housecoat and headed drowsily to the bathroom. I decided to get washed up and do my morning stretches before breakfast. As I reached upward to stretch my arms, I surveyed my body in the full length mirror and wondered if Michael still found me attractive. Sure, I had gained weight over the last fifteen years of our marriage, but I was a size twelve when we met. Now, at a women's size fourteen, I still felt good about myself. I was healthy and that was one of the most important aspects of my life since I would be turning forty in the next four months. I contemplated for a second about the idea of throwing myself a birthday bash for the upcoming milestone in my life but, instead, I returned my mind to Michael.

Michael made it clear he loved my shoulder-length, caramel-colored locks. He often complimented me on my hair and how he loved having a natural woman without all that make-up. Michael held my hand when we watched movies together. He kissed me every time he entered a room, and he still begged me to make love almost every night of the week.

Oh yes, he loved him some me, and I was sure of that. I was just happy he was willing to adopt a child after so many unsuccessful attempts at pregnancy. I was also sure I'd never share the real reason why I couldn't have a baby with my husband. I was certainly thankful he had never suggested getting tested or seeing a fertility specialist.

After several minutes of introspection and self-assurance, I decided to head to the kitchen to prepare breakfast for my family. I passed the living room on my way to the kitchen but turned around and went back to admire my holiday decorations. Walking into my earth toned living room, I noticed the beautifully adorned Christmas tree. I had outdone myself this year by decorating the seven-foot pine tree with glittering peach, cream, and silver ornaments. I had handmade glitter ornaments with each of our names on them. I stood there staring at the sensational looking tree in front of the wide brick fireplace and debated about taking it down. Then, I decided to pass on that idea until after we had a nice breakfast together.

Admiring the seldom-used contemporary designed sofa covered in saddle-colored leather, I sat down in the matching chair and crossed my legs. Pleasant memories from the recent holiday flooded my mind for several minutes before I rose and continued my journey to the kitchen.

I wanted to start the New Year right, beginning with a well-balanced breakfast for my family. While I was in the kitchen making a breakfast casserole, I could still hear the laughing and the giggling of Michael and Bianca playing on the bedroom floor with the "SpongeBob" cartoon blaring in the background. I bowed my head, silently thanked the Lord for blessing me to see another year to enjoy with them, and recited the prayer of Jabez:

Oh, I pray that You would bless us indeed, and enlarge our territory, that Your hand would be with us, and that You would keep us from evil, Amen.

Just when the family was about to sit down to eat in the breakfast nook, the telephone rang. I looked at the clock over the kitchen counter to see it was almost eight-thirty and wondered who would be calling so early. Then, I glanced at the caller identification system and saw my sister's name. I figured Vivian was calling to be the first one to wish us a "Happy New Year" because she always got a kick out of doing that.

"I'll get it, Michael. You and Bianca go ahead and eat breakfast," I said, turning to pick up the telephone.

"Hey, Vivian! Happy New Year to you and yours," I said, greeting my sister in my merriest voice.

Vivian was my only sibling. I was always happy to hear from her. Even though she was five years older than me, Vivian and I were close. I enjoyed having a dependable "big sister" around to take care of me and now to take care of our mother since I lived so far away. I hated the long distance. I went home to visit as often as I could manage.

"Hi, sis," she said. "Happy New Year to you, too."

I could barely understand what Vivian said because she was speaking in a really low voice. Immediately, I perceived something was seriously wrong. My sister had never sounded this sad before.

"Vivian, what's going on? You don't sound too happy," I responded with great concern, trying to push any signs of negativity from my thinking. I didn't have time for that.

"Well, it's Ma Dear. She had another heart attack last night, and we took her to the emergency room. She was admitted to the hospital about four-thirty this morning. I just came home to get some of her things and decided to call you."

"What!" I shouted.

I could hardly think, much less speak. There were so many things going through my mind regarding all the times my mother had been hospitalized in the last three years.

Finally, I was able to gain enough composure to verbalize something. I stumbled over my words, trying to gather my thoughts and speak coherently.

"What is—what is her condition? What did the doctors say? Why didn't you call—call me last night?" I stuttered.

"Ah, well, she's stable for now, but it doesn't look good, sis. The doctors aren't giving us much hope this time. We're all headed to the hospital in a few minutes. I was too upset to call you in the middle of the night, but I think you need to come home. I really need you right now." Vivian sounded depressed.

"Oh, God!" I shouted. "I'll call the airlines to see how soon I can get a flight out. Vivian, you should ask the family to start praying and don't give up hope. Please don't give up hope, no matter what the doctors say. We've been here before, and we'll get through it this time, too. Ma Dear is strong-willed and determined to be with us. She always pulls through for her girls."

I wasn't sure if I was trying to convince my sister or myself. I just had to remain positive, knowing if my mother was still alive, there was still hope. I was not the one to give up easily.

"All right, sis," Vivian replied. "We'll all pray together before we head back to the hospital. Aunt Lucy and Uncle Clevell are here, too." She spoke with a little more pep in her voice.

"Oh, that's good. Please tell them I'll be there soon."

"Alese, I love you, and I'll do my best to take care of Ma Dear until you get here."

"I know you will, sis. I know you will, and I love you, too. I'll be home soon."

Slowly replacing the telephone on the receiver, I turned around to see Michael standing directly behind me with his arms outstretched ready to embrace me. I melted into those arms and tried to muster the courage to tell him what had happened. I had been in this position several times over the last three years, so I tried not to get too upset, but there was always that fear of losing my mother. It was the most dreadful feeling in the world.

"Michael, baby, it's Ma Dear. She's had another heart attack, and she's in the hospital. I told Vivian I would be there on the first available flight tomorrow. I'm calling Delta airlines right now."

I pushed away from him and reached for the telephone. I had the number to the airlines on speed dial because I had used it so often in the past.

"Oh, baby, I'm sorry to hear that, but, yeah, yeah, you go ahead and call the airlines to get tickets for the three of us. You know how much I love your mother."

"Yes, I know you do, and I know you want to come with us, but you have a huge project you're working on right now for your firm. I can't ask you to leave your business every time Ma Dear gets sick. You know Ma Dear will be fine because she's not ready to let go

[11]

yet. If the Lord wanted her this time, she'd already be gone. I'll call you when I get there. Maybe you can fly out there in a few days if things don't improve," I said, noticing some nervousness in my own voice. It was going to be hard even trying to fool myself this time.

Michael put his hands around my elbows and held me steady. "Baby, are you sure about this? I hate for you and Bianca to travel all the way out there alone."

"Yes, I'm sure, Michael. We'll be fine." I sounded more confident this time.

"I appreciate your understanding about this project, but my family comes first. Maybe I should just come on with you. Marty can handle this project alone for now."

"No, no, I'll just call you when I get there. I'll keep you up on what's happening and then we can decide what to do," I said, reassuring him regarding my decision. My mind was made up.

"All right, all right," he responded. "I love you, and I want you to be careful traveling alone with Bianca. Make sure you have your cell phone turned on so I can reach you wherever you are."

"Yes, Michael," I said, pressing the quick dial number for the airlines to make reservations for two.

My hands shook as I held the receiver waiting for an available representative. I hated listening to the automated system and just wanted to speak to a human being. I also wanted my husband by my side, but I was too riddled with guilt realizing how he had sacrificed and traveled with me so many times before. I just couldn't find it within myself to ask him to go this time. I whispered, "Ma Dear will be fine. Please God, save my mother."

After I completed my reservations for Wichita on the next available Delta Airlines flight for seven-ten the next morning, the telephone rang again. I was so edgy, I didn't bother to check the caller identification this time. I just snatched up the telephone and answered as calmly as possible, "Hello."

"Good morning, Mrs. Wayne. This is Jenny Riley."

"Yes, good morning. How are you, Ms. Riley?"

We hadn't heard from our attorney over the holiday season. I wondered why she was calling us now of all days. I guess some lawyers never take a day off work.

"I'm fine, Mrs. Wayne, thank you. I do apologize for calling you on a holiday, but I received a bit of bad news last night regarding your case."

Oh, Lord, not now. My heart dropped to my stomach. I really didn't need to hear any more bad news today, especially regarding the joy of my life, Bianca. I just closed my eyes and tried to brace myself for whatever news Ms. Riley wanted to share.

"That's okay. There is no need to apologize. I'm just anxious to hear whatever news you have."

"I've been out of town. When I got home last night, I had a message from the State Department of Children and Family Services regarding your case. I figured you'd want to know right away what was happening."

"Yes, I do, and I appreciate your calling me. So what's the word?" I asked, trying not to sound too perturbed. Lawyers sometimes take forever to make a point.

"Well, it seems Bianca's birth mother has a sister who has decided she wants to pursue custody of the child."

"Oh, no, this can't be happening," I gasped and almost dropped the telephone receiver. My head was spinning fast.

"Wait a minute before you get too upset, Mrs. Wayne. We're not just going to give her the child without a fight at this point. She'll have to pass the background investigation and submit all the documentation and paperwork you and your husband did to gain custody of Bianca. This will take some time because I'm going to do a full-scale investigation of her. In the meantime, you and your husband will still have custody of the child."

"Well, where has she been all this time? We've had Bianca for over a year now and were expecting to finalize things within the next month. We have become so attached to this child; I cannot bear the suggestion of giving her up. We made it clear from the start that we wanted to adopt Bianca and not be foster parents indefinitely."

"Yes, I know, I know, but we have to give the blood relatives ample time to claim their family. Believe me, once we get through this investigation, the time will have elapsed, and we can proceed with the adoption process."

"Ms. Riley, I know you're trying your best to reassure me Bianca will not be snatched from us, but the court system is so strange. This has been an eye opening experience for us, and we're just not comfortable with the process. I don't know if I can trust what's happening."

"Listen to me. I understand your concerns, and I'm on your side. I'll do my best to get you through this."

"It was our understanding that Bianca didn't have any family who were willing to take her, and since both her parents were killed, we would have an uncomplicated adoption. Now, this is turning out to be perplexing to my husband and me. Our court dates keep getting delayed because the investigations and paperwork are taking so long to complete. It just feels like a never ending legal process."

"Yes, it can be overwhelming, but that's why you hired me. I will keep in touch with you through each stage of her preliminary investigation. You have provided this child with a wonderful home, and the court will not take that lightly. This aunt will have to prove herself whereas you all have already done that. Just stay with me on this, Mrs. Wayne."

"Okay, Ms. Riley. I'm with you until the very end. Thank you for calling me today. I will try to be strong and continue praying for this to be over soon. We truly love this child. Thanks for all your help."

"Thank you, Mrs. Wayne. I'll get back with you in a few days. I'm sure it is going to be fine."

I was tired of the empty promises being made by our attorney, but I had no choice but to be patient with the court system. It wasn't going to change just for us.

"Oh, Ms. Riley, I was going to call you today, anyway. I have a family emergency in Wichita, Kansas. Bianca and I need to leave town for a few weeks. Is it okay if I take her with me without a court order?

"That's not a problem, dear. I'll take care of it."

"Thank you, Ms. Riley. My husband will be here, so please don't hesitate to call him if necessary."

"Yes, Mrs. Wayne," she said. "You all have a safe trip."

"Thank you, Ms. Riley. Good-bye."

After I relayed my conversation with the attorney to Michael, he became agitated and started pacing back and forth, shaking his head in disbelief. He wanted this to be over with more than I did. I could see the frustration all over his face and sensed how helpless he must have felt. Even though he had been enjoying the pre-game football shows on ESPN Sports Center, his concentration was now broken, and his mind seemed to be someplace else. Finally, he said he was going to his office for a while until he could calm down.

"Listen, babe. Marty called a while ago. He wants to set up for the meeting we have tomorrow. As partners, we're meeting with some new software developers for the upcoming project we're planning to bid on. I need to finish up some of the preliminary work while it's fresh in my head. It'll help take my mind off things for now while you're packing and everything."

"Okay, babe," I said. "I'll work on taking down this Christmas tree and packing for the trip tomorrow. I'll take Bianca next door to Shelly's house to play with her daughters while you're gone. She'll enjoy getting out and playing with the girls. It'll be good for her, and I'll have time to do some things around the house before we leave."

Michael just nodded his head at me, and I continued talking.

"I also need to call Mary Patterson about my classes and ask her to contact the principal for me tomorrow. I need her to let him know I won't be returning to work next week. I'm really not up to talking to him myself. They'll just have to call in a substitute teacher for all my business computer classes."

I noticed Michael was being silent. I reached over to hug and kiss him softly on his lips. My heart ached for him and his emotional stress right then. He had always been a sensitive and caring person. I trusted that he didn't want to lose Bianca any more than I did. He had been the perfect father for over a year now and losing his daughter would tear him apart. I honestly felt my husband's pain. We would have to comfort each other to be able to get through this latest setback together.

"Michael, we haven't come this far to give up now. It'll work out. I'm sure it will," I uttered.

[15]

"Yeah, I know it's going to work out, but it's just frustrating trying to deal with it right now. I just want this to be over." Michael sounded really agitated, but I was determined to be a rock for him.

"Don't you believe I want that more than anything myself," I whispered, reaching out to touch his hand. "But we have to trust in God and let Him work it out in His own time, and it will be done the right way. We just have to be patient and let Him work for us. I'm scared, too, but we have to fight and pray."

"You're right, babe. I promise not to be too long at the office. Marty is already there, so this shouldn't take long. I'll definitely try to be back before it gets dark."

Leaning over, Michael kissed me on the cheek. Dressed comfortably in a brown long sleeved shirt and blue jeans, he grabbed his brown suede jacket and quickly headed toward the double-sided stained glass front door. He picked up Bianca and kissed her on the forehead before walking outside with his black leather briefcase in his hand.

I know he felt horrible for leaving me at a time like this, but he needed to get away for just a little while. The day was starting to turn into a nightmare with the news about my mother and now this issue with the adoption. I wasn't sure how much more he could handle, and even though I was trying to put up a strong front, he had to feel how much I was hurting.

\#

His wife had been out of town a lot in the last year with her sick mother. While he wholeheartedly supported her traveling, it still left him feeling lonely on many nights, aching to feel her silky skin and smell the Obsession perfume she loved to wear. He would often closely hug her pillow to his face at night just to get a whiff of her scent before drifting into an erotic dream.

Michael decided to drive around in his copper Infinity sports utility vehicle. After starting the motor, he opened the power sunroof. Leaning back, he felt the cool leather seats through his jacket. He turned on the premium digital Bose stereo and popped in his favorite classic Maze CD mix. It contained all their greatest hits, including a live extended version of *Joy and Pain*. The soulful singing voice of Frankie Beverly always helped calm him down and stay grounded in reality. Being a millionaire co-owner of a growing business was not enough to help him get through his personal turmoil today.

When he arrived at his office, the parking lot was bare except for Marty's vehicle. Michael let himself into the building and made his way to his corner office space. He enjoyed being on one corner of the building while Marty, his partner, had the other corner side of the complex. They had been best friends since they were college freshmen and business partners for over eighteen years. Michael was primarily in charge of developing and securing software projects. Since Marty's major was Business and Finance, he was mainly responsible for operating the business side of the company, including planning out projects. All of the other major duties were split between the two of them and their staff of almost fifty employees.

Michael spearheaded the Alpha Team and Marty handled the Omega Team. Each team had four head program designers who supervised a staff of at least five people with competent administrative support assigned to each unit.

Michael wasn't really concerned about getting any work done; he was more concerned about having a quiet place to think and a friend to confide in. He had staff that could set up for the meeting. Still, he was glad Marty had called and given him a reason for leaving home. A lot had happened in the last six months. Michael had no idea which way his life was headed or the meaning of everything that was happening at this time. Placing his head down on his desk, he prayed silently for relief until he heard a voice.

"Hey, Mike, are you all right?" Marty asked.

"Yeah, come on in," he replied. "We need to talk."

2

Note to Alese

Standing at the closed door in a trance, it was several seconds after Michael left before I realized Bianca was pulling at my pants leg.

"Mommy, I ready to go play, please."

"Okay, baby."

Fighting back tears, I bent down towards Bianca. I hugged and held my precious daughter just a little bit longer than I ever had before. I was determined not to lose our only chance at having a child. Michael and I had tried to have children the natural way. But after that failed to happen, we decided to trust in God, and He sent us a beautiful daughter to adopt. Nothing would shake our faith now.

I called Shelly Anderson next door and asked if it was convenient for Bianca to come over and play with her daughters for a while. Of course, Shelly was always willing to have Bianca over to play with her daughters: six-year old, Angela, and ten-year old, Macy. They enjoyed playing "big sisters" to Bianca and watching cartoons with her. I appreciated their being such good role models for my daughter because that was important to the development of a young girl.

I was grateful to have Shelly for a good friend and neighbor for the last ten years. Even though Shelly was divorced, she believed in the sanctity of marriage and often prayed for married couples. We all attended the same church and had attended many functions at each other's homes over the years as close neighbors often do.

Our middle class neighborhood had certainly changed over the years, but the homes in Meadow Bay East were nice sized houses and in the perfect location—near our jobs in downtown Jacksonville. We had won the "Best Neighborhood Contest" at least three times in the ten years we had resided there. The single-story homes were much closer together than I liked, but the neighborhood was unusually clean and quiet.

Michael and I had often talked about buying a larger house, but we both loved our older but contemporary styled, three-bedroom home and decided instead to keep it well-maintained and updated. Recently, we had the roof redone, upgraded to granite countertops in the kitchen, added stainless steel appliances, and bricked three sides of our wooden home. We dreamed of retiring early and someday traveling all over the world with our daughter. But for now, we were content to stay in this community, keep our vehicles while they were running well, and not spend all our money on extravagant jewelry and designer clothing. However, we did enjoy taking a well-planned vacation whenever Michael managed to tear himself away from his work between major projects. We'd toured the Bahamas, Hawaii, and Puerto Rico, among other places.

Not all millionaires flaunt their wealth. Michael said he'd been poor once, and it wasn't happening again. He was going to be a good steward of his money, and that he was. He not only saved a large portion of his income, but he made some wise investments in the stock market. I didn't complain because I hadn't worked since Bianca had come to live with us, and we were comfortable enough.

Florida was certainly beautiful and sunny this time of the year. Even though the temperatures were cooler than usual, it seemed like a typical day for Floridians to be outside enjoying the weather, walking their dogs or jogging through the neighborhood. I had always wanted to live in the warm Florida climate, so after graduating from Wichita State University in Kansas, I accepted a job offer and moved to Jacksonville that same year. Although it was lonely at first, I was outgoing and made friends quickly. Once I met Michael Wayne that was absolutely the end of my loneliness.

I helped Bianca put on her pink puffy jacket and walked her next door to play with Angela and Macy. As we crossed the lawn going to the house next door, several motorists passed by and waved at us. The drivers seemed to be amused at the full-sized trampoline taking up a major portion of the small front yard. The girls had gotten it set up for Christmas, and it had quickly become one of Bianca's chosen daily activities.

I was about to knock above the Christmas wreath on the front door when Shelly opened it smiling. She always looked her best

[19]

whenever she opened her door and today was no exception. She kept her petite frame in tip top shape by walking at least two miles every morning before going to work at Jacksonville State University as a Financial Aid Coordinator. Even though she had on a black and white Nike jogging suit with athletic shoes to match, she wore Fashion Fair make-up in the matching shade for her creamy cocoa skin along with the chocolate raspberry lipstick she loved. Her "Halle Berry" hairstyle was layered and curled to perfection.

"Hey, girl, how are you doing? Happy New Year," she beamed, looking at me and reaching out to give me a friendly hug.

"Well, the same to you, Shelly. You look great today as usual."

"You're too sweet, but listen. I'm really sorry to hear about your mom. I hope you all have a safe flight tomorrow."

"Yes, I'm still a little afraid to fly, but I have got to do this. Our flight leaves at seven-ten in the morning, and we'll probably be gone for at least two weeks."

"Well, be sure and call me and let me know how it goes."

"Sure, I'll be back to get Bianca before it gets dark."

"Don't worry, Alese. She'll be just fine with us. They have lots of toys to play with."

"Well, I can see that, Shelly, but thanks again," I replied, kissing my daughter good-bye and heading home.

I entered the house running to answer the ringing telephone. Feeling my heart pumping rapidly, I took a deep breath and allowed the caller to speak first.

"Hello, Happy New Year! How are you doing today?"

Thank goodness, it was my best friend and pastor, Karema Wright, calling this time. I didn't know if I could take any more bad news today. As a deep sense of relief flooded my body, I answered sounding as friendly as I could considering the day I was having so far.

"Hi, Happy New Year. I'm doing well enough." I replied, mustering some energy.

"What's wrong? I've heard you sound better."

"Yes, I know. It's Ma Dear. Vivian called this morning to let me know she's back in the hospital."

"Oh no, I'm sorry to hear that. Is it her heart?" Karema asked.

"Yes, it is. She's stabilized for now, but the doctors aren't giving us much hope," I mumbled. This was the one person who I could let down my guard with. She was my best friend long before she became my pastor.

"We'll just have to pray like we always do and then turn it over to Jesus."

"I know that's right. I've been praying all morning."

"Have you made flight reservations for you all yet?"

"Ah, yeah, Bianca and I are leaving out first thing in the morning."

"Michael's not going with you?" Karema asked.

"No, he wants to go, but I talked him into staying this time. He has a major contract he needs to handle after the holidays."

"I see. Well, be careful while you're traveling alone with Bianca."

"I will, Karema," I said, pausing. "I received some more disturbing news today, too. Our attorney called with some news regarding the adoption."

"What? You mean she called you on a holiday with bad news?"

"She wanted to let us know what was going on right now. Apparently, the biological aunt has shown up and wants custody of Bianca."

"That's ridiculous. Where has she been all this time?"

"Well, that's the same question I asked the attorney, but I didn't receive a satisfactory answer. So, we'll just have to wait and see about it when I return."

"I'm sure it's going to work out fine. If she hasn't shown any interest in all this time, I doubt if they're going to take her serious."

"I'm just ready for this to be over, Karema."

"I understand how you feel. Just stay in prayer. The Lord is working for you as we speak. I can feel Him working miracles right now. Just don't let go of your faith."

"Oh, that will never happen. I've seen too many miracles performed to let go of my faith now. Listen, I just took Bianca next door to Shelly's so I can get some packing done. I'll call you when I get to Kansas tomorrow."

[21]

"That's fine. I'll be praying for you and your family. Have a safe trip."

"Thanks, Karema. Good-bye."

I clicked off the cordless telephone, feeling almost as well as I did when the day started. Remembering I had some packing to do, I headed to the bedroom in search of a suitcase.

#

Hours had passed and I had taken down the Christmas tree. I carefully packed all of the Christmas ornaments away in foam containers. I had the huge box with the artificial tree neatly secured and waiting for Michael to place on the top shelf in the garage.

I'd also completed the packing for our trip. I was passing by the spare bedroom we used as a home office and heard a fax coming in. Just as I had suspected, it was the travel court order required for me to take Bianca out of state that I had requested from Ms. Riley. It didn't make much sense for us to have to get a legal document to take her out of state since we had legal custody, but that was Florida's law.

I would definitely have to go visit our attorney when I returned from Kansas to get more information about this latest development in our adoption case. I glanced up at the clock and saw it was a little past five and thought Michael should be home soon. I also figured it was about time to go retrieve Bianca from her fun in the sun.

They were still outside taking turns jumping on the new extra-large trampoline. Macy was having her turn and she could really soar, doing all types of flips, twists and turns high in the air. Both Macy and Angela had been taking gymnastics for years and they knew the proper way to jump and fall. They were trying to teach Bianca since she was afraid to jump too high, but she had fun with it just the same. They were all clapping and laughing like they were at the circus watching the clowns jump on that thing. Shelly was standing there watching them and enjoying herself as much as they were.

I called for Bianca and she came running to give me a hug. After they all said their good-byes, I took Bianca by the hand and was turning to leave when Shelly called my name. I turned to see her pointing over at my mailbox.

"Alese, did you see that the flag is up on your mailbox?"

"No, girl, isn't today a holiday? I know Michael didn't put anything in the box before he left."

"Well, I saw a brand new white convertible that looked like it was leaving your house earlier today, and immediately after that, I noticed the flag was up on your mailbox."

"Really? Did you see who was driving the car or notice any other details?" I asked, trying to think of anyone who Michael and I identified with a brand new white convertible, but no one came to mind. All of our friends had children and drove full-sized vehicles or minivans.

"No, I didn't see who was driving the car, but I noticed the tag was purple and gold like the colors for Jacksonville State University. So I just figured it was one of you all's associates who were dropping off a package for you guys."

"Well, thanks, girl. I'll check it out before we go in the house."

I walked towards the mailbox with a creepy feeling. My curiosity had been piqued regarding the red flag being lifted on a holiday. Approaching the mailbox, my eyes quickly surveyed the neighborhood for strange cars or anything that seemed out of order.

I opened the tall bricked mailbox and peeped inside. Then I lowered the red flag on the side. There was a long plain white envelope lying in the mailbox labeled:

"Personal for Mrs. Alese Wayne"

The line was typed across the center without a return address or any indication of who might have placed it there. I looked around again to see if anyone was watching me before I grabbed the envelope and proceeded to the house with my daughter.

Bianca's tiny two-year old body was tired because she hadn't had a nap all day. She went straight to her room, beautifully adorned in all pink with white trimmings, and climbed into the twin canopy bed by herself. I sat on the side of her bed, gently stroking her small hand, and sang her to sleep. Within a matter of minutes, Bianca was sleeping soundly. So, I silently tipped out of the room and headed back to where I'd placed the envelope.

There it was, right on the kitchen counter where I'd left it when I came into the house only minutes ago. I walked towards the den while opening the envelope. I'd definitely had a long day and needed to relax. My mind was racing with curiosity after I opened the envelope to see it only contained a couple of sentences:

Dear Mrs. Wayne,

I am sorry to inform you that your husband, Michael, is having an affair with Lisa Bradford, one of his employees. I just thought you might want to know.

Signed,

A concerned person

I stopped before I could reach the tan cloth sectional sofa in my cozy den. I read the note again before the meaning of it registered accurately in my mind. I asked myself, "What in the world is this? What insane person could have left this in my mailbox?"

I had to reach the sofa quickly because my legs were beginning to weaken. I felt like I had suddenly gained a hundred pounds. I had to think about this. How could anyone have the audacity to leave this note in my mailbox? There was no way this could be true of my husband. I was sure about that. But why would someone do this?

I could not get that idea out of my head. Whoever sent this message even had the nerve to name the woman with whom he was supposed to be involved.

"Wait a minute!" I remembered Michael had told me about hiring Lisa Bradford over a year ago. He came home one evening while I was in the middle of making a seasoned pepper steak, roasted potatoes with garlic, and seven-up pound cake for dinner. I could tell he had something on his mind from the way he kept hanging around the kitchen offering to help with this and that, watching my every move. He was trying to pick up on whether or not I was in a good mood. He always did that when he had something serious to share with me. Normally, he went straight to the bedroom and changed or went to the den to watch television with Bianca. I kept going through my regular routine, waiting for him to spring it on me.

"Alese, I have to tell you something, sweetheart."

"I already know—I'm beautiful, right?" I turned and smiled at him, trying to remove some of the pressure so he would continue sharing with me. That's how well I know my man.

"Yes, yes, you are beautiful," he said, giving me a light kiss on the lips, "but I have something to tell you about work. I want to be the one to tell you because I don't want you to hear it from anyone else, especially office personnel." Michael kept his eyes on me, trying to choose his words carefully from that point on.

"Well, I'm listening. You have my undivided attention."

"I hired a new software consultant today. She recently moved here from Washington, D.C. She has a lot of designing experience and some great contacts we can use to increase our revenues. I studied with her in college, but we haven't seen each other since graduation." He paused, rubbing his hands together in front of him, trying to figure out what to say next.

I listened carefully to Michael as he spoke. I figured there had to be more to this story than the fact that he had hired a new employee from D.C. with whom he went to college. I waited patiently for the punch line.

"Anyway, her name is Lisa Bradford, and we dated in college. Well, we lived together for a while in college during our senior year. We were serious, but we broke up after she decided to move to D.C. She wanted to leave Jacksonville to take a good job offer from NuWay Software Design Corporation. Back then, they were the hottest company in the field and everybody was trying to get to D.C. But, I wanted to stay here and make it on my own."

"I see—and why is she moving back to Jacksonville if that company is so hot?" I asked, eyeing him suspiciously because I could tell when he was lying. I really could.

"Well, they had to downsize the company earlier this year, and she moved back here to be closer to her family in Lake City. Her aunt who lives here in Jacksonville is also gravely ill, and Lisa wants to be nearby to help her out. Anyway, she came to see me about a job today and since we had an opening available, Marty and I decided to offer her the job. We were all classmates and we used to talk about working together someday."

[25]

"So, what you're telling me is that you lived with this Lisa in college, she left you, and now you want to give her a job," I stated, using a questioning tone over crossed arms.

"Baby, baby, this was strictly a business decision. Our personal relationship is history. I just wanted to be open with you about the situation. I would never do anything to jeopardize our marriage. You can trust me on that," he said, making direct eye contact with me, showing his sincerity. I could tell he wasn't lying.

"Michael, I do trust you," I commented, reaching out to hug him, feeling certain he had been honest with me.

Bam!

I jumped when I heard the front door slam and my mind snapped back to the present when I heard Michael approaching the den. Looking down at the note and envelope still in my hand, I quickly stuck them in an *Ebony* magazine I picked up from the coffee table.

"Hello, baby—you okay? Why are you sitting here like that?" he asked, sounding really concerned about me. I guess I had a scared look on my face. He slowly moved towards me but remained standing. "Did you hear any more from Vivian? Is your mom worse?" he persisted.

"No, I haven't heard any more from Vivian about Ma Dear. I was just sitting here in the quiet trying to relax while Bianca is napping," I replied, trying to sound like my normal self.

"How did it go today? Did she have fun next door?"

"Yes, they had a ball. Did you get everything set up for your meeting tomorrow?"

"Yes, it's straight."

He was already headed toward the bedroom while he spoke. I stood and followed behind him watching his movements. Had he been out to see his lover? Was that the reason he claimed he had to go to the office on a holiday? All these questions clouded my mind. I was feeling suspicious whereas I had never had any doubts before.

I watched my husband get undressed, place his clothes in the hamper, enter the master bathroom, and close the door. I heard the water from the shower pouring down full blast and the shower door snap shut. I hesitantly walked toward the laundry hamper pondering whether I should check his clothes or not for evidence of infidelity.

[26]

"Mommy, mommy, I wake up." Bianca entered the room, startling me.

"Oh, baby, I see you're wide awake."

"Mommy, I hungry," she said.

"Well, let's go find you something to eat."

I led Bianca out of my room and towards the kitchen. I pushed those ridiculous ideas out of my mind. I wasn't about to resort to smelling dirty underwear based on a stupid note.

#

Later that night, as we cuddled in the darkness, my mind went back to the day when I'd first met Michael. It had been near the beginning of the school year almost seventeen years ago. I wasn't interested in going to the local software conference at the downtown Holiday Inn, but my friend, Mary Patterson, had persuaded me to go. Mary was a middle school math teacher and her room was across the hall from my computer lab.

"Come on, girl. What else do you have to do? You're single and you don't have a man to go home to. Wouldn't it be fun to go down there and see what new technology they have to offer for our classrooms?"

Mary was almost ten years older than me and a little on the thick side. She was married with two young daughters. Mary was always ready to go somewhere, especially if there was food and free stuff available.

"Yeah, right, like Bayshire Middle School can afford to replace those outdated computers we're using," I responded, shaking my head at Mary.

"Well, we might be able to get some free sample programs and persuade the principals to help us write a grant proposal or something. We just have to get creative and try whatever we can to help our kids."

Mary did make a good point. We decided to meet downtown after work and spend a couple of hours at the conference. There were several presentations in various rooms showing educators the latest technology available for use in their middle school classrooms. We decided to split up and attend different presentations so we could compare notes later.

As I strolled down the corridor, it seemed one presenter had a crowd of female teachers clamoring to get into their room. I bet money it was a man.

Umh, let me see what's going on in here. I stepped in to determine what was so interesting about this particular presentation.

Well, the male presenter was so fine I almost fainted when I walked into the room. He was definitely a tall drink of water; actually, a tall glass of chocolate milk might be a better description. Anyway, the blue striped suit he had on draped his towering body like it was especially made for him, and his tie looked like it was pure silk, imprinted with a colorful tropical design. His Stacy Adams crocodile leather square toed shoes were the same shade of blue as his suit. Yes, most would agree the brother was spectacular!

Standing at the front of the room doing his slide presentation, the gentleman was talking about this software packet his company had developed to help instructors be more efficient with calculating and processing grade reports. I watched in awe as he captured everyone's attention with his graceful gestures as he pointed at the slides.

My mind didn't really focus on very much of what he said because I was too hypnotized by the soothing sound of his voice. He spoke in a balanced even tone, showing he was sure of himself and confident in the product he was selling. His thinly trimmed mustache seemed to dance across his lips with each word that radiated out of his mouth. Needless to say, all the women, including me, had their eyes glued to his tall athletic frame, creamy brown skin, fresh wavy haircut, and sexy bedroom eyes.

It looked like the name of his company was M & M something or another, but I thought the only thing they made was candy. Well, he looked like he came straight from the chocolate factory himself.

He walked around the room introducing himself, shook people's hands, passed out brochures and business cards, and asked for individual input regarding his presentation. Of course, all the female instructors happily gave him positive feedback for his product along with a telephone number slipped in here and there.

I waited patiently for him to make it to my side of the room. I wanted to be ready for him when he introduced himself to me. But I would have to play it cool because I didn't want to seem overly eager like the other females smiling in his face, trying to make light conversation. He had been all about business, only entertaining their professional comments and moving quickly around the small room.

When he made it to me, he extended his hand and said, "Hi, I'm Michael Wayne. How did you enjoy the presentation today?"

"Hi, I'm Alese Dean, and the presentation was great," I replied, smiling and extending my hand in return. "I'm working with a group of teachers at Bayshire Middle School, and we're in the process of writing a grant proposal for the business technology department. Our instructors would love to sample your products, and I was wondering if you might be interested in letting us reference your latest software program for one of our grant projects."

"Wow, that's a great idea. I would certainly be interested in helping you all write our company into your grant proposal. We definitely would like to help out middle school kids."

"I see, well, this would be a great opportunity for your company to make a contribution to a struggling school."

"I agree with you," he said. "I'll give you my business card with my cell phone number so you can call me at any time. I'm in and out of the office so much it's hard to reach me."

All eyes were on me when he pulled a business card from his pocket and wrote his personal telephone number on the back. I politely took the card and walked out keeping my calm demeanor the best I could. As I searched for Mary, my heart thumped. She was not going to believe this!

Anyway, the rest, as they say, is history. That was nearly seventeen years ago, and I was still madly in love with Michael. He had never once raised a hand to me in the heat of an argument. He only spoke kind words to me and was a master love-maker. Michael was an excellent provider and made sure all the bills were paid on time. Even though we lived on a budget, Bianca and I never wanted for anything that he was not willing to provide for us. He supported me emotionally, financially, physically, and spiritually. What more could I want?

[29]

He had been a faithful, caring and supportive husband.

"It was probably some hot young thang he turned down at the office," I surmised.

I had never had any reason to doubt him. My faith would not be shaken now when I needed my husband more than I ever had before. I had always believed some jealous women would do anything to break up a decent marriage.

Looking down on Michael's peaceful face sleeping so soundly beside me, I felt he'd love me past eternity, but someone had to have a reason for leaving me that note. I was going to find out who and why real soon.

I wasn't about to approach Michael with this until I had more information about this allegation. First, I had to get to Wichita to see about my mother. Ma Dear needed me right then more than anyone else in the world, and I would not let her down.

Laying my head affectionately on Michael's chest, concentrating on his calm breathing, I remembered my mother's comforting voice while falling asleep.

"Baby, no matter what problems you have today and no matter how hopeless life may seem, just always remember that tomorrow will be another day. You can always try again."

I was determined to save my marriage.

3

Michael Leron Wayne

"Good morning, Mike. What's going on, man? How about lunch today?" Martin Carlisle asked, swaggering into Michael's office close to noontime. He had his flashy Christian Dior gold tone suit fitting his small muscular frame just right. Marty was sporting a freshly faded haircut and a new pair of alligator leather shoes.

Michael had taken off his charcoal gray suit coat and hung it across the back of his chair.

"Nah, man, I've got too much work to catch up on, but you go ahead. I'll see you later today," Michael replied, glancing up at Marty and then returning to his work.

"Mike, it's such a warm, bright day outside. Let's go have a leisurely lunch outdoors somewhere we can sit on a patio and enjoy ourselves. How about we go to the Applebee's Restaurant on Atlantic Boulevard today?" he asked, taking a seat in the armchair directly in front of Michael, rubbing his stomach after it lightly growled.

"Marty, do you see all this work I have in front of me?" Michael asked, pointing to a stack of papers on his cluttered glass desk.

"Yeah, I see it, but you still got to eat, don't you? It'll do you good to get out."

"Like I said, I can't make it today. Maybe we can go later in the week. I just need to get caught up on a few things in this stack of paperwork."

"Mike, man, what's up with you? You've been moping around here every day like you lost your best friend. Is Alese still out of town with her mother?"

"Ah, yeah, she's still in Wichita with her mom. I'm just trying to keep myself busy until she returns," Michael responded. He glanced in Marty's direction and then went back to reviewing the papers in his hand.

"Yeah, I can understand that, man, but you got to have a life. Why don't you come hang with Tina and me tonight? It'll be great to spend some time with my boy again. We haven't hung out together in a while. Besides, you look like you need some cheering up. What do you say?"

"Thanks for the offer, Marty, but I'll pass. I'm just not feeling too sociable lately. Can you just leave me alone and let me finish my work here, please?" he replied, unbuttoning his shirtsleeves and rolling them up.

"Man, you got to stop beating yourself up over this Lisa situation. I know you're still troubled by your 'indiscretion,' but like I said before, you need to get over it. The deed is done. There's nothing you can do to take it back. You just need to get it together and concentrate on your marriage."

"I just—I just can't believe I let myself get into a situation like that with Lisa, man." He dropped the papers in his hand on the glass desk and looked up at Marty shaking his head from side to side. "I shouldn't have taken her home that night. I should have called her a cab, but no, I had to be Mr. Nice Guy and offer her a ride home. Then, I had to be Mr. Smart Guy when she invited me in from the rain."

Michael closed his eyes, took a deep breath, slowly exhaled, and eased his head back against his plush black leather high back office chair.

"Well, you're going to have to let it go. Mike, I mean it. You have to let it go. I mean what else can you do? You're not going that route again. So move on."

"Yeah, that won't ever happen again. That's why I'm thinking about confessing to Alese. We've always been so open with each other I just don't think I can keep living with this and not tell her about it. I know she'll forgive me," Michael said, looking directly at Marty for sympathy, hoping his friend would encourage him to come clean with his wife.

"Man, have you lost your damn mind?" Marty shouted, jumping from his seat. He frantically paced around the room but tried to keep his eyes on Michael. "You know good and I know well," he continued, "Alese would never forgive you for this! No, no, not a black woman, there is no damn way! You best—you best keep your mouth closed and live with it until you can deal with it. I can't—I

[32]

can't even believe you would entertain that crazy idea because that's crazy right there!" Marty was talking so fast he started stuttering.

"Well, thanks for sharing your opinion, my brother—so much for hoping my best friend of twenty years would back me on this one. And would you please watch your mouth. This is our place of business."

"Mike, I hear you, but I'm telling you to listen to me," he pleaded, calming down. "Don't do it. Don't let your guilt fool you into confessing. Alese is a kind, Christian woman, but she is not going for that. Now, that I know!"

"Oh, so you know my wife better than me now?" Michael widened his eyes and stared at Marty, waiting for a response.

"I—I didn't say that, man. I'm just saying, you—you need to keep this to yourself, if you want to stay married, that is. Besides, I do know something about black women. I've been married to one for sixteen years myself," he responded quickly.

"Marty, I truly believe Alese would forgive me because she knows my spirit. She knows I would never intentionally do anything to hurt her or destroy our marriage. If I confess now, we can move on together and be stronger together. We are soul mates."

"Well, I truly believe you're out of luck if you tell your wife about Lisa. Your marriage will be over for real. But look, man, I'm going to lunch, and I'll see you this afternoon before I leave." He went over to Michael and slapped hands with him before turning to leave. Marty glanced back at his former college roommate before opening the door. "Don't do it, Mike. I'm telling you, again. Don't do it. Do not confess to something you have not been accused of. Read my lips, man, don't do it," he said, walking away.

Pressing back on his chair, Michael reviewed the conversation he'd just had with Marty. He was bitterly torn about how to handle this moral dilemma concerning Lisa. Priding himself on being a strong Christian man, he had never even thought about cheating on Alese in all the time they had been together. She was the epitome of womanhood to him and represented all that was right in his life. Even when Michael first found out they wouldn't be able to have children, it didn't matter because she was all that mattered to him. They had discussed the numerous advanced medical procedures available but had discarded all of them. Both of them felt like God had put them together for a reason, and only He could reveal it whenever He was ready.

Michael believed Alese would be a good mother whenever the time came, and he was right. Alese had proven herself to be an outstanding mother and an excellent role model for their daughter. She had Bianca involved in several activities outside of preschool, including African dance, ballet, gymnastics, and swimming. She spent a lot of time with Bianca teaching her letters, colors, numbers, and shapes. Alese made sure Bianca was always clean and well dressed. Bianca was a jubilant child and Alese was primarily responsible for that.

He especially enjoyed the African dance class Alese and Bianca took together. They loved coming home and showing him the dance routines they had practiced in class, moving to the sound of the different drums from the compact disc player. Bianca would say, "My daddy, watch this. See what I can do," as she danced around the room wearing her African printed skirt.

Finding it difficult to concentrate on work today, Michael's mind kept drifting back to that rainy November night over two months ago when he slept with Lisa. That was the first and last time they had made love since they had lived together in college.

Most of his Alpha team members worked late that night and Lisa had volunteered to help with the research on their major development project for the Maxwell Corporation. With the progression of the evening and the increasing rain, everyone discreetly disappeared, leaving him and Lisa sitting at the table in the main boardroom alone.

"Hey, you, where is everybody?" Michael asked Lisa, looking over at her. He quickly scanned the empty space.

Lisa couldn't help but laugh as he gave her a curious stare. He was so engrossed in his work that when the last person said good night a half hour before, he hadn't noticed.

"What's so funny?" he asked Lisa without smiling.

"Michael," she said, "the last person left about thirty minutes ago, and you told her good night."

"Oh, I did? It must really be late, and I must really be tired. You should go home, Lisa. Thanks for all your help, but I'm closing up for tonight." Michael stood and clicked a button, shutting down his Mac laptop computer while tossing papers in his briefcase.

"Michael, do you think it's too late to call a cab?" she asked innocently, with her head tilted to the side, looking up at him. "My car is in the shop," she added, making it appear to be an afterthought.

"You don't need a cab, Lisa. I can give you a ride home tonight."

"Great, thank you," she responded with a cunning smile. This was going to be easier than she had initially believed.

#

Lisa made light conversation with him for the entire twenty minutes it took them to make it to her place. She definitely wanted to keep him in a jovial mood in order to successfully execute her plan of seduction. She was over-skilled at manipulating men and had used those powers for all of her adult life. Lisa had perfected her craft while she was a college student with many boyfriends and one night stands. She found the college professors had been the easiest to persuade in giving her academic leniency. Even the hint of sex meant an instant passing exam grade or whatever she needed to complete the course.

Lisa and Michael arrived at her place around ten that stormy summer night. It was pouring down rain like the bottom of the sky had fallen out. When they made it to Lisa's duplex, Michael offered to walk her to the door with the extra-large umbrella he had in his car. They were both still soaked by the time they got to the door, and Lisa insisted he come in for a minute to dry out. Since Michael didn't want to hurt her feelings, he obliged her by going in and having a seat in the small living room.

She wasted no time in carrying out the next stage of her plan. Lisa hurried to the refrigerator and got the Sutter's chardonnay wine she left chilling earlier in the day. She reached up to the see-thru glass cabinets above the sink and retrieved two hand painted wine glasses. She strolled back to the living room, placing them on the table in front of Michael. Then, before he could utter a word, she told him to help himself and headed for the bedroom.

[35]

Lisa undressed and carefully took off the red lace teddy she had been wearing underneath her soaked work dress and threw on the matching red silk kimono laying across her bed. She quickly freshened up her make-up and checked her appearance in the dresser mirror before returning to the living area.

"Hey, are you okay?" she asked, entering the room while tying the sash on her robe.

"Yes, I'm fine, Lisa. But, ah, it's late, and I need to get home," he responded, rising from his seat.

"Oh, that's right. Your wife is probably home waiting up for you."

"Well, actually, she and my daughter are out of town right now."

"Really, well, then there's no need for you to rush out in this stormy weather. I mean—I wouldn't want to be responsible for you having an accident or something. Why don't you just take off your shirt and let me place it in the dryer until the weather clears up some? Besides, I can't drink all this wine by myself," she added, pouring two semi-full glasses of chardonnay.

"Ah, it is coming down pretty bad out there," he said, standing at the window holding back the textured silk curtain and looking outside. "I probably should wait a little while longer in case some of the streets are flooded," he said, releasing the curtain to unbutton his shirt. He handed Lisa his wet shirt to put in the dryer before taking a seat on the edge of the sofa and reaching for the glass of wine. Michael took several sips before placing it back on the coffee table.

Returning to the room, Lisa sat down beside him, poured a little more liquid into both their glasses, and slowly leaned back on the sofa next to Michael. She sexily eyed him while she sipped the tasty wine from her glass.

She pretended not to notice that her robe had parted to reveal her baby smooth legs. Lisa slowly reached over and took his long hand into hers and cupped it over her small breast so he could feel her pounding heart.

Leaning gently into him and tasting his sweet warm lips, she slipped her flaming tongue into his mouth. Lisa held his hand while they rose and seductively led him into her boudoir.

"Lisa, please stop. I can't do this." That's what he wanted to say, only his mouth was betraying him by not opening. Her intoxicating fragrance was simply driving him mad. She was wearing her signature scent. Obsession.

"Michael, baby, just relax and let me help you release some tension," Lisa whispered, seemingly reading his mind. Then she tongued his ear in a smooth circular motion.

"Lisa, you—you know that's my weak spot," he responded, leaning away from her.

"Yeah, I know all your weak spots, Michael. I plan to lick every one of them all night long."

She moistened an index finger, slowly slid it across his lips, and pushed him back on her queen-sized bed. While climbing on top of him, Lisa let her red silk kimono slither down, revealing her nakedness. She felt an electric sensation go through Michael's body from the top of his head all the way down to the tip of his toes. *I got you now, baby. You never could resist my sexiness.*

He still had feelings for her and she intended to capitalize on them tonight. With a slim body in perfect form, Lisa was prepared to please him in all the ways she remembered he liked. Lowering her head, so her long, reddish, wavy hair would cascade around her face, she wickedly smiled down at him. Her seduction plan was working to perfection.

Yes, Michael used to love her vanilla chocolate skin with the pretty freckled face, beaming brown eyes, and luscious lips. She would easily remind him of all of her feminine assets tonight and add a few tricks to the mix.

Michael's mind went blank. He finally relaxed, eased back against the black satin sheets, and succumbed to temptation. Obviously, he couldn't think anymore and his body had already made an executive decision. He didn't have any control over what was happening. The blood flowing to his manhood had drained all the guiltiness from his brain. Now the passion consumed Michael and took over his entire being as if he was having an out-of-body experience.

#

[37]

Suddenly, Michael shook his head, bringing his mind back to the present. He could not bear to remember any more of his adulterous evening with Lisa Bradford.

"Well, that night was certainly the biggest mistake of my entire life," Michael mumbled to himself, picking up a wedding picture of Alese and him encased in a gold frame setting on his desk.

She was wearing a gorgeous white gown with a sheer overlay and free-flowing, naturally curly hair. Alese was radiant, but he adored the lovely locks she sported now even more.

He had on a black tux with his arms wrapped around her waist as they posed in front of the old-style, pristine church. Not even the bright sunlight made them squint on that beautiful day.

It was certainly the happiest moment of his life thus far. Michael smiled from the memories of that day as they flashed through his mind. He remembered the small wedding they'd had fifteen years ago. They had agreed only to have their immediate families present for the religious ceremony. His father and his brother had been there to stand with him. Alese's sister stood with her while her parents and brother-in-law proudly observed the momentous occasion.

Michael laughed out loud when he remembered how jolly Reverend Johnson had been when they first met and the kind advice the pastor passed to him. He could still repeat the words in his mind.

"Son, that's a fine woman you're marrying. I've known Alese all of her life. If you be good to her, she'll be good to you," he laughed, firmly gripping Michael's hand.

Well, Reverend Johnson was partially right. He had been good to Alese, but she had been even better to him.

Michael also recalled when he first met Alese at the software conference almost seventeen years ago. He noticed her the second she entered the room wearing a beige linen pants suit hugging her ample bust and fitting her round hips. She carried herself with such a sense of confidence and earthiness that he was instantly drawn to her enticing smile. He was always attracted to the sexiness of a natural woman, and she sported an awesome looking short afro that day. A woman had to be really bold to wear her hair so close cut, and it was quite appealing to him.

He waited to introduce himself to her last, making sure she got his personal digits before leaving the conference room. Alese was so nonchalant when he wrote the number on the back of his business card, he didn't think she was going to call. Although he recalled she mentioned something about writing a grant with M & M, Inc. for some middle school project, he wasn't sure what she had said.

Anyway, he concluded within a matter of months that Alese was different from any woman he had ever known in his life. She was so intellectual. They would sit and talk for hours about everything, including sports, politics, and family. Alese was more knowledgeable about the history of basketball than he was. They played sports trivia all the time and she actually won some of their games. He even took her out on the basketball court a couple of times to show off his skills, and she definitely handled the ball well.

They had similar family backgrounds and admired each other's values and work ethics. They both came from two parent homes and each had a sibling of the same sex. She was talkative and outgoing and so was Michael. They were both southerners and enjoyed the simpler things in life. Michael was raised in Tampa with his parents and his older brother. His father, Jeremiah, still lived there. He worked as a plant foreman at a juice processing plant where he had been employed for the last thirty years. His mother, Margaret, and brother, Reuben, were both deceased. Michael understood Alese's desire to help her mother. He had watched helplessly as a child while his mother suffered through many bouts with cancer before succumbing to the deadly disease.

He had never been so open and honest with anyone in his life. Alese made it easy to share his soul with her because she was never judgmental about his humble past. She encouraged him to follow his dreams and supported him in furthering his business plans. Alese even helped him and Marty research the business proposal for the expansion of M & M Software Development, Inc. She also volunteered to assist with office work during the summers while school was out.

They enjoyed many of the same things like gospel, jazz, soul, and reggae music. They both loved spicy Italian food, sports, and traveling. They shared a passion for reading and had many of the same books on various topics, including historical black leaders, poets and philosophers. They were so compatible with each other, Michael felt Alese was an extension of him.

Yes, he strongly felt she was "The One" for him. They were best friends, but the most important thing was that she had strong Christian faith and values. Michael had just gotten saved three months before meeting Alese, and she helped affirm his spiritual awakening. She quoted the Word and shared it freely with him. Alese always spoke her mind. He didn't have to guess about where he stood with her, and he liked that. He had prayed for a woman with her outstanding qualities since he had vowed to maintain celibacy until he was an honorably married man.

Michael had to put her one-carat round diamond solitaire ring on the lay-a-way plan at Friedman Jewelers' about three months after they started dating. It took him almost eight months to pay for it. He wanted to be debt free before asking her to marry him on the Fourth of July holiday. Alese was so excited when he proposed that night on his knees. They had just returned from eating dinner at Red Lobster Seafood Place. It was time for him to say good night before he summoned the courage to propose to her. When he showed her the brilliant shining stone, she couldn't control her excitement. They were married exactly two months later.

Michael had been so absorbed in his thoughts that the telephone ringing on his desk startled him. He pushed the speakerphone button and quickly answered.

"Hello, Michael Wayne," he answered, addressing the caller in a deep professional voice.

"Mr. Wayne, I'm headed to lunch." Tracy, his receptionist, was on the line. "Would you like anything before I leave?"

"No thanks, Tracy. You have a good lunch," he replied.

"Okay, I'll check with you in about an hour, Mr. Wayne."

"Thanks again, Tracy."

Michael clicked off the speakerphone. Then, he looked around his office at all the reminders of his life with Alese. There were limited edition pictures by African-American artists she had bought for his office walls. There were framed photographs of them together and many mementos she had given him for his desk over the years. Every item related to a time or year during their marriage that reminded him of a happy and loving relationship. He especially loved the solid wood engraved nameplate s with the company logo on it that she gave him when they first got married.

They had overcome so much together during their marriage that it was almost unbelievable. Even though his mother had died from breast cancer when he was a young boy, he vividly remembered how Alese had comforted him after the death of his older brother, Reuben, from prostate cancer three years ago. That was really the lowest point in his life. He didn't know this type of cancer was most commonly found in men and accounted for nearly forty percent of all cancers diagnosed in African-American men. Still, Michael was too stricken with grief over his brother's death to think about getting himself tested.

Four short months later, Michael had his own cancer scare. Alese had insisted he get an annual checkup and take a prostate-specific antigen (PSA) blood test at his primary physician's office. It was almost a week before Dr. Carter's nurse called and asked him to come in for a meeting with his doctor. Nurse Wilson refused to disclose the test results over the telephone, which led him to suspect the worse. When Michael shared his fears with Alese that night, she prayed the "prayer of faith" and praised God for their many blessings all through the night.

Fortunately, Dr. Carter just wanted him to come in so that he could review his medical history with him personally. He had no signs of cancer, but the doctor wanted to be sure he was aware of the dangers of this type of disease, especially after losing his mother and brother to cancer.

Yes, he was blessed to have a good wife. Then, how was it that he could have feelings for Lisa? He didn't know what he felt for Lisa, but he had to feel something for her to be vulnerable enough to sleep with her even once. He believed it was partially the loneliness and longing for his wife that made him accept attention from another woman. Lisa made him feel needed, and he always had her undivided attention whenever they were in each other's presence.

[41]

Lisa had always had the uncanny ability to make him feel that way, as if he was the most special man in the world, and she absolutely adored him. The first time they met during his junior year in college, he was smitten with her. Michael was at the first basketball practice for the season in the school's gymnasium while Lisa and her squad were having their initial cheerleading practice session in one corner of the building. All of the players found it difficult to concentrate on making plays and passing the ball with the attractive girls cheering and jumping in the background. He noticed Lisa right away because even though she was the smallest woman in the group, her mouth could be heard above all others, and it seemed she was cheering especially for him. Every time he glanced in that direction, her eyes were glued to his; she only had eyes for him.

Michael was immediately attracted to her small shapely figure, long wavy hair, and effervescent smile, which she proudly displayed upon locking eyes with him. He remembered she was wearing one of those really short uniform skirts because all of the guys were checking to see if they had on something underneath those minis. She would shake her pom-poms in his direction and move those hips as they were turning around in circles, making sure he was watching her behind and giving him a little extra shake. He wanted to get to know her better right away, beginning with her name, telephone number, and address.

When the coach blew the whistle signaling their practice time on the court was over, the fellas didn't waste a minute scrambling to meet the new cheerleading team. The two head cheerleaders from the previous year, Monica Carter and Tasha Green, introduced the players to the newest members of the cheering squad, including Lisa Bradford. When those beaming brown eyes shined up at him with admiration, and he felt those soft warm hands during their initial handshake, he thought he would be hooked on Lisa for a lifetime.

Most of the players hung around the gym after practice that day. The girls' basketball team came in after the guys' hour was up, and the fellas wanted to see what their female counterparts had to offer.

"You don't have to rush off, do you?" Michael asked with a gleam of hope in his eye.

[42]

"No, not really, some of the girls were talking about going to celebrate after practice. Why?" Lisa asked.

"Well, I'm going to hang around and watch the girls' team practice. I was hoping maybe you could stay here with me and talk. But I understand if you have something else to do. I know this must be a special occasion for you to share with your friends."

"Ah, let me go talk to my girls, and I'll be right back." She flashed another smile, turning away from him.

"Sure, I'll be right here," he responded as she walked away.

Michael took a seat in the stands away from his teammates in case Lisa decided to come back and join him. A few minutes later, she climbed the steps and sat down next to him.

"What happened with your celebration?" he asked, smiling.

"Most of the girls said they were tired or had to study for classes tomorrow. We decided to celebrate at another time when we could all really enjoy ourselves."

"Yeah, I know most of the cheerleaders, but I've never seen you on campus before."

"I just transferred here from Lake City Community College. I just decided to try out for the cheerleading team so I could get to know more people, and I love basketball. How long have you been playing?"

"I've been playing basketball all my life. I've been a starter on the team here since my freshman year."

"Wow, that's great, Michael. I'm looking forward to seeing you play then. What's your major?"

"My major—I'm majoring in Computer and Information Systems."

"Hey, that's part of my major, too," she beamed. "I'm majoring in CIS with a minor in Business Administration.

"We'll probably be having some classes together next semester. What brings you to Jacksonville?"

"We don't have a university in Lake City, and I want to get a higher degree. I have an aunt who works on campus in the library. She invited me to move here and stay with her while I finish up my education. Are you from Jacksonville?"

"No, I'm not. I'm originally from Tampa," he replied, staring into those enchanting brown eyes. They talked on like that for almost an hour, gazing into each other eyes as they spoke to each other.

About an hour later, the girls wrapped up their practice session and people started filing out of the gymnasium. Not wanting the evening to end, Michael offered to give her a ride home in his used Chevrolet Chevette. Of course, she accepted. Since he wanted to stretch their first evening out together even further, he suggested they stop at a burger place for a bite to eat before taking her home. Lisa readily agreed.

From that day until the day of graduation, they had been almost inseparable. In fact, that was their theme song, *Inseparable*, by Natalie Cole. Michael would listen to the song whether he was with her or not. He bought a one-hour tape and recorded that song at least twenty times so he could listen to it over and over again whenever he lay in bed at night thinking of her. Michael had never known anyone as beautiful as Lisa.

They coordinated their schedules so they could have as many classes together as possible. With Michael's basketball practice and part-time job, he needed to stay in school. They didn't have a lot of time to spend with one another. During the following summer, they decided to move in together. They had a blissful school year attending social activities and sporting events. But then, shortly after graduation, Lisa was gone from his life as suddenly as she had come into it.

She accepted a job in Washington, D.C. with a well-known software company for a hefty salary. Michael was heartbroken, thinking Lisa would never leave him. He was aware of the fact that she had applied for jobs all over the country and had gone on interviews for many of them, but he never imagined she'd actually accept a job somewhere far away. While Lisa was searching for employment, Michael and his best friend, Marty, were working on a business plan for their future company, which included Lisa working with them. He was hoping she would have a change of heart and join him and Marty on their creative business venture.

Even though Marty's fiancée, Tina, was a business major like him, she wasn't interested in working with them because she wanted to own a natural hair salon. At least she was willing to stay in town to be close to Marty. He wondered why Lisa couldn't do the same for him but, like she said, she had to follow the big m-o-n-e-y, which was in Washington, D.C.

Now she was back in Jacksonville and a part of his company. He was wondering if he had made a major mistake in hiring Lisa Bradford and welcoming her so readily back into his life. She had managed to turn his whole happy world upside down in less than six months. The day Marty and he made a decision to offer Lisa a position with their company, he had no idea they would ever become intimate with each other again. Now, she was invading his thoughts, his life, and his marriage, but he would have to turn that around instantly.

He would have to avoid her at all costs because he was committed to keeping his family intact. He would never allow himself to be placed in that position again with her, or anyone else for that matter.

Man, I got to get out of here. I'm not doing any work anyway. Grabbing his car keys, Michael headed out of his office.

Michael wanted to get somewhere secluded where he could call his wife and have a private conversation with her. Michael hoped Ma Dear was doing better by now because he yearned for his wife and daughter to come home soon. Michael missed Alese and Bianca more than he had realized.

4

Lisa Laraye Bradford

Relaxing across the bed in her two-bedroom, brick front duplex, Lisa was alone again on a Saturday afternoon. She hadn't even gotten dressed for the day. In fact, she was still wearing her white housecoat, trying to decide which black designer gown she wanted to wear out this evening. Lisa had just washed her long hair and put rollers in because she was planning to go out somewhere tonight. It didn't matter where she went as long as she was away from the drudgery of her abode. Lisa just needed to get out of this place and have some fun. What she really wanted was something to take her mind off Michael.

One of her best friends from college, Ranetta, had invited her and another friend from college, Jolene, to go out tonight. Ranetta wanted to check out this happening new jazz club on the west side of town called Jazzie's Blues House. They featured live musicians and fresh talented singers on Saturday nights. Sometimes they even showcased some of the well-known jazz and blues singers. The way she was feeling today, Lisa could really use some soothing rhythms right about now.

Things had not gone exactly the way she had planned since moving back to Jacksonville. Oh, she had succeeded in getting Michael to sleep with her once, but he seemed determined to not let it happen again. Not that he told her this. Oh, sure, he was still pleasant with her when she encountered him at work, but he wouldn't allow himself to be alone with her or hold a lengthy conversation. He turned down all her lunch invitations, her offers to work late and even refused her a ride home. Michael had even insulted Lisa by offering to call her a cab when she tried that trick a second time.

Well, I'll just have to come up with a better plan.

Rolling over on her green floral printed comforter, she tried to hatch another strategy. After all, she didn't move all the way from D.C. just to lose her man again. She was confident he still had feelings for her, and she needed to strike again while his wife was out of town. He had to be lonely because that witch was always gone to Iowa, or Kansas, or wherever the hell she was from. She certainly didn't deserve to have a man like Michael, if that was all the sense she had.

"He needs to be taken care of by a real woman, and I got just the thang to do it," she mumbled under her breath with a nasty attitude. "That trifling wife he got, don't even know how to dress, let alone please a fine man like Michael. What the hell does he see in her anyway?"

Lisa picked up the cordless telephone and dialed Jolene's home number. They had all been good friends in college but had lost touch several years ago. Anyway, she had called Ranetta and Jolene the first week she arrived in Jacksonville to reconnect with them. They were both pleased to hear from her and ready to arrange an outing together since they had so much to catch up on. Lisa was surprised to find out they were both still living in Jacksonville and single.

As she walked to the living room, she remembered how they were so tough back in the day, they had been notoriously known as the "Triple Threat Team." They were always together and on the prowl for new meat. No brothers stood a chance if they came across these fine sisters' path because they were known for being uninhibited seductresses. None of their classmates wanted them around their men and with good reason. They had no qualms about sleeping with anyone else's so-called man. Every man they came in contact with was fair game to them, whether he had a wedding band or not.

Yeah, the three of them had it going on. Ranetta Chadway was the tall, sexy one with the honey colored skin and the mesmerizing hazel eyes. Jolene Dixon was chocolate, short and curvy with the alluring smile that drew men to her. Lisa was the medium height diva with the vanilla chocolate skin and beaming brown eyes, long wavy hair, and super slim figure, which she still had, by the way. They had all become acquainted by being roommates their freshman year in the college dorm. Ranetta and Jolene were both born and raised in Jacksonville, so they were ecstatic about showing her all of the happening places around town. By Lisa being the new kid on the block, they were eager to indoctrinate her into the nightlife of an urban city.

They didn't have to worry about transportation whenever they wanted to go partying or shopping. One of Ranetta's main boyfriends had a nice car, a super black Cutlass Supreme with burgundy leather seats and a moon roof. She could sweet talk him into letting her borrow his ride almost every day of the week. That Ranetta was something else when it came to men; Lisa calculated she would definitely be able to learn a few new tricks from her. Jolene was fine, but she didn't have as much street smarts as her hometown girl, Ranetta.

Lisa wondered if her two friends had maintained themselves as well as she had because she was still a perfect size six. It had been at least five years since the last time they had seen each other at one of JSU's homecoming events. They were all still about the same size then, but Jolene was starting to gain some weight.

From the few conversations they'd had, Ranetta's personality had probably not changed much at all. She was still undoubtedly the slut she had always been and proud of it. On the other hand, she noticed Jolene had changed since their outrageous college days at JSU. She was Ms. Buck Wild and "let's get freaky deaky" back then. Now, she was acting like "Ms. Saved, Sanctified and Filled with the Holy Ghost." But Lisa wanted to see just how long that would last. Jolene was always falling for something.

Jolene picked up on the third ring sounding out of breath.

"Girl, what's wrong with you? Are you getting it on with somebody over there?" Lisa asked jokingly.

"Honey, please, I'm on my exercise bike. I'm trying to lose some pounds," she responded, breathing heavily into the telephone receiver.

"I was calling to see if you wanted to check out that new jazz club on the west side tonight with Ranetta and me." She heard Jolene stop pedaling and paused for a second. "They have live music, and we could catch a table in the back and talk while we listen to plenty smooth sounds," Lisa said, hoping her friend would say yes.

"I'm saved, and I don't much listen to anything aside from gospel music."

[48]

"Jazz music is soothing and good for the soul. You can listen to that. It's not like we're going to some hip hop booty shaking place."

"I hear what you're saying. I used to really like jazz."

"See, it won't hurt you for one night, I promise."

"Well, that sounds good then. What time would you like to meet?" Jolene asked.

"Let me call Ranetta and see what she wants to do. I'll call you back later today. Maybe we can all ride together."

"That would be great," Jolene responded before they said their good-byes.

Leaping off the plaid cloth sofa, Lisa excitedly ran to her bedroom. She hurriedly opened the double glass closet door to pick out a hot, tight, clinging number for tonight. She zoomed through several outfits before deciding on the right one for her entrance back into the nightlife. Yes, she needed someone to tide her over while she was devising a plan to bring Michael Wayne to his senses. But right now, she was yearning to captivate some strong brother man just for the night.

Just for the night. Michael won't be able to resist me much longer. I know him and what he likes. That's why he's afraid to be alone with me.

Lisa took her time getting dressed and applying her Clinique make-up. She took the rollers out of her hair and finger-combed her fine wavy curls. But no matter how she tried, she couldn't get Michael out of her mind. She could still feel the touch of his warm fingers cascading across her breast. Just the thought of his lips against her throat caused her to quiver with high emotional intensity. No man had ever replaced him in the bedroom or in her life. Lisa felt she was a fool for leaving Michael here while she went off to make a fortune at some well-established company in D.C. But she couldn't wait for him to start a business so they could build a life together. She was just too ambitious to scrape and save while he poured their money into some company that might not ever get off the ground floor.

Anyway, that was all behind her now. Lisa was ready to be a part of the glamorous life they could have together. She would make up for all those years they had been absent from each other. If she could just come up with the perfect plan to get him away from Alese, her life would be wonderful again.

"Girl, this place is packed. I'm glad that brother let us have this table." Lisa's eyes swept the dimly lit room for desirable men as she spoke. She was in the mood to get her groove on tonight.

"Yeah, he'll be back with our drinks in a minute," Ranetta commented while bopping her head to the smooth music.

Just as Lisa had suspected, Ranetta was still almost as fine as she was. Jolene, however, looked to be about a size sixteen, which was huge to Lisa. Coincidentally, they all wore black outfits and black high heel evening shoes. Ranetta wore an above the knee, Donna Karan crepe dress with a wrap front and long sheer sleeves. Jolene had on a long skirt suit with sequins on the front of the jacket that made her look like the reincarnation of a church mother.

The five-piece "Rhythm Street" band played an excellent style of jazz, characterized by a rhythmic and harmonic complexity with brilliant execution. The group consisted of a piano player, percussionist, bass player, trumpeter, and tenor/soprano saxophone player. All of the brothers were exceptionally fine, especially the tall strikingly appealing saxophone player. His skin was so dark it was glistening under the tinted blue spotlight shining around him during his solo performance. He was a Wesley Snipes-looking brother playing a scene from the movie, *Mo Better Blues*.

When he was finished, he thanked the crowd for their applause and announced they were taking a five-minute break. He slowly looked around the club and commented on the fine looking ladies there tonight. Strolling past their table and leading the band members to the back dressing room, Lisa tried to catch his eye but failed.

"Hey, did you see that fine specimen?" Ranetta commented as the waiter, sporting tiny cute dreadlocks, returned with their drinks. He undressed her with his eyes.

"I sure did, and he is not just fine; he is F-I-N-E, and I want me some of that," Lisa remarked, ignoring the waiter as she rubbed her palms together and puckered her golden bronzed lips. "Girl, the saxophone is the sexiest instrument on the planet," she added, flashing a sinister smile.

[50]

"It's even sexier when you have a debonair brother with tasty looking lips playing it for you," Ranetta added, laughing wickedly. She winked at her girlfriend.

"You two need to stop lusting after men," Jolene interjected, using a condescending tone.

"Well, look here, Mother Teresa, I don't know what your problem is, but you need to get a grip," Ranetta said, rolling her eyes at Jolene with much attitude. She was not in the mood for being preached to this evening. Jolene had a way of turning every event into a religious convention, and she was tired of it.

"Both of you need Jesus. Y'all are coming to church with me tomorrow," Jolene stated sternly.

"Well, what we don't need is you chastising us tonight, Minister Farrakhan. We came out to have a good time. Anyway, when was the last time you had a man?" Ranetta snapped.

"Don't you worry about that now," she said. "You just worry about being ready for church tomorrow at ten-thirty in the morning. You hear me?" Jolene asked, stretching her eyes and placing her hand on Ranetta's shoulder.

"Yeah, yeah," she replied. "Right, we'll be ready." Ranetta waved her hand at Jolene, closed her eyes, and jerked her head back toward the bar. She was done with this conversation.

The crowd started cheering as the band made its way back to the stage. The saxophone player strolled to center stage, proving he was ready to do his thing again. Gradually, the lights dimmed and the spotlight rose on him as the club waited quietly for this man to raise the instrument to his sensuous lips and start blowing their minds. Everyone in the club seemed to be in a trance when he started to play a slightly upbeat, entrancingly sweet melody.

Lisa couldn't restrain herself any longer. She swayed her body to the music, dramatically making her way to the band's stage. She slowly climbed the steps and stood beside the saxophone player with her back to the spectators seductively moving her hips. Lisa started smoothing her hands over her bust and on down to her hips and knees before extending her arms upward. She crossed her arms in the front and caressed her shoulders while she deviously slid her delicately thin dress straps off her shoulders. She turned toward the

[51]

audience and extended one leg, then she slowly bent down to touch her ankle and began raising her slinky black slip dress up to show her upper thighs. She never stopped rotating her hips, doing several turns before stopping with the music.

"Girl, you worked it, you worked it up there!" Ranetta boasted, standing while Lisa returned to their table and held up both of her hands waiting for high fives.

Lisa glided through the audience feeling like she was on wheels until she reached her table and quickly grabbed Ranetta's hands and pulled them down to their sides. They were both bent over laughing uncontrollably and fanning themselves.

"Honey, you must have been a stripper in a former life!" Ranetta joked between their laughter.

"I'm leaving. I've had enough." Jolene gave them both the evil eye before she abruptly stood up and angrily pushed her chair under the table. She turned and marched out the door without looking back at their laughing faces.

#

Lisa could barely sleep all night because she was so hyped after returning from Jazzie's Blues House. She looked at the large red digital numerals on the clock displaying two-thirty in the morning as she slipped off her evening dress and fell naked against the fluffy cotton down comforter on her bed. She was disappointed the saxophone player didn't give her more play, especially after her sensual dance routine. Of course, after reflecting on the past evening, Lisa determined he had to be married or gay if he passed on her sexiness.

However, Morris, the piano player, was ready to play her tune. He was almost as sexy as the saxophonist but not quite tall enough for her taste. At least he would get her through the night. When he whispered in her ears, she heard Michael. When he touched her breasts, she felt Michael. When he kissed her lips, she tasted Michael. Then, when she closed her eyes, she imagined it was Michael Wayne inside of her, filling up her trembling body with pleasure. Raising her hips and following his rhythm, she matched

[52]

his thrusts stroke for stroke. They rode the waves to Fantasy Island as she quenched her desires, just for the night.

Once she was satisfied with Morris, his presence was nauseating. He was snoring loudly on the other side of her bed, unaware of Lisa's scowling eyes burning into his wide back.

She hadn't meant for her friends to see the sultry side of her, especially Jolene with her patronizing, religious, holier-than-thou-self, but it had been too tempting to resist. Lisa could not believe how much Jolene had changed and that she had the nerve to walk out on them at the club—and with an attitude.

Yeah, she definitely needed to get a real brother man in her life and stop hating on the players. Lisa's mind drifted to the love of her life and her reason for living, Michael Wayne. She couldn't wait for the day when she would be Mrs. Michael Wayne and give him his own children.

"What can he possibly see in a woman that can't even have his children?" she uttered to herself. She would definitely take care of him sexually and give him two babies right away. Since Lisa was already forty years old, she planned to have a tubal ligation after the second child.

Visualizing a profitable future with Michael, Lisa looked forward to living the grand life in a beachside mansion in one of the exclusive gated communities, exotic island vacations, mountains of expensive jewelry, several luxury automobiles, and all the trendy designer clothes her selfish heart desired. She would never have to work anywhere for anyone again.

There would be maids and butlers to take care of all the mundane housework. They would have live-in nannies to take care of the children while she stayed beautiful. She would relax by the pool all day waiting for her man to come home. They would also hire a professional chef to prepare the finest cuisines. She would never have to see the inside of the kitchen.

#

Lisa fondly remembered her childhood growing up in Lake City, the dreams she had back then, and how she always liked playing "Princesses" with her older sister, Jenna. They would march around

[53]

the house for hours adorned in their frilly dresses with scarves hanging around their heads, pretending they had long blonde hair, and wearing their mother's high heeled pumps. They wore their mother's old costume jewelry, hats, stockings, and anything else they could find to play dress up.

Her father had even bought her a silver magic wand to carry around with her on one of his infrequent visits to their house. Since James and Sadie Bradford were divorced from the time she turned four years old, Lisa hardly ever got to see her daddy. It seemed his visits were becoming fewer and fewer, but when he did show up, he treated them like princesses. He would pick them up in his big bear arms and tell them how they deserved to be treated like royalty. He boasted that someday they would be the queens of their own castle, and they would each have a handsome king to fulfill their every desire.

Sadie provided for her daughters as well as she could on her secretarial salary. James stopped sending child support payments after he remarried. Taking him to court and threatening him with the possibility of not seeing his children didn't faze him; he was barely seeing them anymore by that time anyway, especially since his new wife had become pregnant. However, Sadie was determined for Lisa and Jenna to be a part of whatever status-climbing events and organizations they desired to be associated with. They were parade queens and school event hostesses; they also participated in the Jack and Jill Club, ballet and tap dancing classes and the Delta's Debutante Ball in high school. Lisa and Jenna were willing participants in anything having to do with the society pages.

Lisa observed her mother struggling to make ends meet, but once she started having various gentlemen suitors come by to visit her on the weekends, life became a lot easier for all of them. Most of the men paid Lisa compliments on her pretty light skin, giving her money here and there after she had grown up enough to learn how to flirt with them behind her mother's back. Lisa stayed in the mirror often enough to realize that, because she had her mother's coloring and petite size, she was a beautiful girl. She soon discovered some of the men were watching her, and she liked it. In her preteen years, she'd noticed them staring at her on more than one occasion. Believing she was pretty and smart, Lisa had developed a fondness for manipulating the opposite sex during her teenage life. Utilizing her persuasive skills, there was never a shortage of money in her pocketbook.

Even one of the local high school teachers had been seduced by Lisa's charms. On many nights when Sadie thought she was supposed to be at a dance or some school event, she was at Mr. Carter's place. Lisa was just a first semester junior when she starting dating Ronald Carter, her social studies instructor. She didn't stop seeing him until the first semester of her senior year. He would pick her up from whatever event she had initially attended and take her to his place. They never went on any official dates or anything like that. All of their dates were in the confines of his home, which was fine with Lisa because that meant she wouldn't have to share him with anyone else.

She didn't have a lot of friends at school, so they were able to keep the affair on the down low for most of the year. However, they spent so much time together over the summer break cooped up in his apartment that tongues began to wag about them dating. After one of the female instructors living in the same building as Mr. Carter observed Lisa leaving his place on more than one occasion, gossip quickly circulated regarding their close relationship. Ronald, being a young second year teacher, feared for his job security and broke Lisa's heart shortly after the first semester of her senior year began. He continued giving her money on a weekly basis until she graduated from high school; she had threatened to expose their romance to the school board unless he did so.

After spending her entire adult life trying to make the fairy tale a reality, Lisa was ready for it to happen. Although it hadn't materialized in the last twenty years, she believed it was right around the corner. Every time she got involved with a wealthy prospect, something would occur to blow her out of the water. The first serious relationship she had after leaving Michael was with her supervisor, Anthony Tyler, at NuWay Software Designs. Even though she understood he was married when they first met, she supposed he would eventually divorce his wife and marry her. After three years of being his mistress and trying to break up their union, he finally broke it off with Lisa after his wife became pregnant and suspicious of his extracurricular activities.

From then on, there had been a parade of rich men she'd tried to snap up and who had managed to avoid taking her on a trip to the altar. However, she did succeed in getting them to take her on trips and cruises all around the world whenever and wherever she wanted to go. Lisa had learned a valuable lesson from Sadie: romance without finance didn't stand a chance.

Ever since she first laid her eyes on Michael Wayne that day at the cheerleading practice session, she wanted him to be the one to love and take care of her forever. Lisa had told her teammates she would join them later at the restaurant after Michael asked her if she wanted to stay with him and watch the other team practice. Understanding the importance of seizing the moment, she made an instant decision to remain at his side for as long as possible that night. Playing to his inflated male ego, they ended up staying at the restaurant until almost two o'clock in the morning on their first encounter.

Even though it had taken ingenious inventions to deceive him when they lived together, Michael never suspected her infidelities. Even on those few occasions when he dared to question her whereabouts, her two partners in crime, Jolene and Ranetta, were right there willing to vouch for her. That was how she'd been able to play him for two whole years. She could have been his wife then, if only she had been more patient and understanding of his dreams.

She had been foolish to leave him and run off to D.C. just for the love of money. No other man had ever compared to the love she had felt for Michael, regardless of how handsome or wealthy he was. None of them had treated her with an ounce of the kindness and warmth that Michael had shown her in the precious two years they spent together. Certainly, she had cheated on him with some of the other players she thought were going to the professional arena, but he was so in love with her, he was totally blind to her indiscretions and dismissed any gossip floating to his ears.

Soon, she would finally have the status and the riches she had spent her life longing to achieve. She always believed she was much too pretty to live the less than fabulous existence that her daddy had always talked about. Although she'd had many men in her life, she'd only loved Michael. It was time for them to live the rich and fabulous life just like Kimora Lee and her man.

Well, why not? He had the money. Lisa didn't know why they were living the common life now in that middle class neighborhood, driving regular cars and wearing plain clothes.

It must be that pathetic wife of his. I bet they don't even take decent vacations together since she's so busy running to Kansas to see her family, leaving that man alone like a damn fool.

Suddenly, she was completely annoyed by the man snoring in the bed next to her and proceeded to wake him up.

"Morris! Morris!" she shouted, hitting him in the back.

"What? What's wrong with you, woman?" he asked, sitting up in the bed and searching her face for a hint as to why she would be waking him from slumber.

"I can't sleep because you're snoring. It's time for you to go anyway."

"Ah, baby, come on. I always snore loud when I get my groove on like we did tonight. Don't you want some more loving?" he asked with lustiness dripping from his voice.

"No, thank you. Now if you don't mind, please get dressed and leave so I can get some sleep tonight."

"I know you can't be serious. It's after four o'clock in the morning. Why can't I just stay the night?"

"I don't care what time of the morning it is, it's time for your snoring ass to get out of my house," Lisa growled at him.

"Damn, you're one cold bitch," he mumbled as he shifted to the side of the bed and pulled on his pants.

"Yes, I am, and proud of it," she said, turning over in bed. "Lock my front door on your way out."

5

We Are Family

Three weeks had hurried by and I was praying Ma Dear would be discharged from the Kansas Heart Hospital in Wichita today. I had spent the last two nights by Ma Dear's side constantly praying for her recovery and calling on the name of Jesus. I made frequent visits to the hospital chapel and asked God to please give me more time with my beloved mother. I needed the advice only a mother could give at this time in my life. Even though Ma Dear was still in good spirits after having open heart surgery, she barely weighed in at ninety-seven pounds, and she had always been a pretty healthy sized woman for her short stature.

It was just past seven o'clock in the morning and the sun was just beginning to peek through the closed window shades when Dr. Goldstein entered Ma Dear's room. Doctor Goldstein was a short and pudgy middle aged man who wore round gold frame glasses, a long blonde hippie ponytail down the center of his back, and a casual smile. He was also wearing a stethoscope around his neck and had Ma Dear's hospital charts on a grayish clipboard in his hand.

Sitting up in the worn recliner, I stretched my arms and yawned. I glanced up to see the doctor coming in. Looking down at my ragged appearance, I tried to smooth out the wrinkles in my cotton pullover top and Levi jeans. I ran my fingers through my locks, trying to present a believable smile for Dr. Goldstein.

I hoped Ma Dear would be able to go home today. She was doing much better and was more than ready to "get back to her shack" as she put it. Ma Dear was tired of the bland hospital food, the nurses poking her every hour, and all those darn pills and tests she had to take every day.

Judging from the glint in Dr. Goldstein's blue eyes, I surmised he had good news for us, so I really perked up.

"Ms. Ruby," he began, "all of your vitals look normal today. Are you ready to go home?" he asked, grinning and flipping through her hospital charts.

Ma Dear sat up in bed the best she could and responded in a weak voice, "I sure am, Dr. Goldstein. Can I go home today?" she asked, observing him with a halfway smile.

"I think we can manage that since you've been such a good patient for us, Ms. Ruby. All the nurses told me that you have been very cooperative with them," he responded with a gleaming smile. Then he swung that smile in my direction. "Are you ready to take your momma home, young lady?"

He stood up straight, tucking the notebook under his arm. Dr. Goldstein reached out and touched my hand. I said a silent prayer before responding.

"Yes, doctor, I sure am!" I replied, radiating with joy and patting the doctor's hand in return. "I truly thank you all for taking such good care of my mother. How soon does she need to see you for a follow-up office visit?"

"Well, I need to see her in my office about a week from now."

"Yes, sir. That sounds fine. I'll make sure she's there. Thanks again, Dr. Goldstein."

"No problem. You just take good care of your momma. Please, make sure she eats right and takes her medicine at the same time every day. That's really important."

He spoke as he turned to leave the room. He glanced over at Ma Dear's happy face and gave her the "thumbs up" sign before swishing through the door.

Ma Dear and I hugged each other, laughing proudly like we had just won the state lottery. We praised God while holding each other until I finally pulled away to call Vivian. I shared the good news and asked her to come and pick us up from the hospital. I took my time getting Ma Dear dressed for the ride home because we lived almost an hour outside of the city limits.

While we waited for my sister's arrival, I helped Ma Dear get dressed in a pink duster prior to going to the check-out station and signing all the release papers. When I returned to the hospital room, Ma Dear was leaning back against the propped up pillows on her bed and scanning through a *Redbook* magazine.

"Ma Dear, are you feeling better?"

"Yes, baby, I'm feeling fine," she said, looking up from the magazine. "And I'm ready to go home. I'm so happy that doctor is finally dismissing me from this place."

"I know you can hardly wait to get home."

"Yes, I just wish I could do some of the things I want to do around my house. There's so much work that needs to be done, but I'm just not able, and that bothers me."

"Well, you just tell me what all you want done, and I'll see what I can do."

"I don't want you doing my work. I want to be able to do it for myself," Ma Dear grumbled.

"I know you do, Ma Dear, but you have to learn how to relax and allow other people to help you sometime. We want you to be with us for a long time, so that means you have to stop working so hard every day."

"Well, I guess I don't have much of a choice now. This old heart of mine is about to give out on me."

"Ma Dear, please don't talk like that," I begged, lowering my voice. I wasn't prepared to hear this speech, but I didn't doubt that it was coming.

"I'm just glad I've lived long enough to see both of my daughters grow up, get married, and have children of their own. Vivian and Darnell have been having some problems lately, but they're hanging in there, and I believe they're going to make it, too. And I can't tell you how proud I am that you and Michael decided to adopt a beautiful little baby girl. I've been praying all these years for you to get pregnant. Now, I'm just delighted to see you with a baby. I just wish you'd done it five years ago so I'd be well enough to help take care of her."

"Thank you, Ma Dear. I've always wanted to be a mother like you. But I was ready to accept whatever the Lord intended my fate to be."

"I never doubted for a second that you would be a mother someday. Don't you fret none over losing your chile. I believe in my old piece of heart that baby was meant for you."

[60]

"I hope and pray for that everyday myself, Ma Dear. Something always happens when you start thinking you just can't get any happier."

"Yes, that's true. I still think it's going to work out though. There are some things a mother can feel, and I feel this baby was meant for you and Michael."

"Are you all ready to go?" Vivian asked, entering the room glowing in her yellow printed pants suit and wearing bright red lipstick. One of the older nurses came in behind her pushing a wheelchair.

"Yes, goodness," Ma Dear replied, sitting up on the side of the bed. "I'm ready to roll out of here."

#

"Hey, Ma Dear! Hey, Ma Dear! Hey, Ma Dear!" Bianca and Vivian's two children, Denise and Dennis, were all clamoring to hug Ma Dear to welcome her home. Steadying herself using the walker, she carefully entered the den through the back door of her house. Her frail body was barely able to stand, but she was determined to make it in the house alone. Vivian and I were on each side of her with our arms slightly stretched out so that if she started wobbling, we could break her fall.

Ma Dear's white wooden five-bedroom house with the wide front porch had been built by her late husband, Nathaniel Dean, almost fifty years ago. Vivian and I affectionately called our father Daddy Nate, because he loved the sound of that name combination. He was a kind man, and he was generous with his wife and us. Although mama said he had longed for a son, he treated my sister and me like royalty. Daddy Nate was from the old school where no one and nothing ever came before family. He raised us to look out for one another and to take care of each other. Daddy Nate took his small frame and glistening ebony skin to work at the Columbus Shoe Factory six days a week and then took us all to church every Sunday. He believed in going early for the Sunday school lesson and then remaining for the regular service. If the church held evening programs, we had to go back after eating a full course meal.

[61]

Vivian and I had to sit up late on Saturday nights helping Ma Dear prepare Sunday dinner. All of the food had to be cooked before we went to bed so that after church, all we had to do was heat it up and fix our plates. Sometimes Daddy Nate would sneak in once all the food was wrapped up in the refrigerator and get him a taste of something, especially sweets. That fun loving man would give his right arm for a big slice of Ma Dear's special chocolate coconut layer cake. He would get downright angry if she didn't make that for him at least once a month.

The front porch on Ma Dear's white house was her favorite spot in the whole world. She had hosted many family gatherings, receptions, and celebrations out there. She would get up early on clear mornings and sit in her rocking chair or on the hanging swing, look out at the paved country road for hours as she listened to her collection of wind chimes dancing in the wind. She waved at every car that passed by whether she recognized it or not. Ma Dear cherished the country life, especially living in the Balm Road Community. Most of the people who lived there were related or either close family friends who had known each other for generations. The twelve acres of land the house rested on had been a wedding present from her late in-laws, Cecil and Althea Dean. She had kept most of the tall pine trees on the land in the back, but the front was mostly cleared so she could have a nice view of the road.

All the children were happy to see their grandmother back at home. Since she was still alive and talking in her right mind, they were elated. Ma Dear had barely sat down on the brass daybed in the family room before she was showered with hugs and kisses from her family. Everybody was there to welcome her home, including Aunt Lucy, Uncle Clevell, and Ms. Sue, her best friend since childhood. Even though they grew up together, Ms. Sue was about four years younger than Ma Dear. She was still in good health and working two or three days a week at the nursing home. Whenever Vivian had business taking her away from home during the week, Ms. Sue generously volunteered to be Ma Dear's companion for as long as she was needed. That way, they could watch their usual soap operas together all day long.

Ma Dear's face shined with happiness; her eyes darted from face to face.

"Oh, Jesus! I am so glad to be back in my own house," she exclaimed, sounding out of breath.

Glancing around the area, she made sure everything was just the way she'd left it. She smiled brightly as her eyes scanned the wall covered with family photographs from days gone by. Ma Dear ran her hand over the worn blue and white checker quilt she had made over twenty years ago. It was her thinnest cover, yet she kept it on the daybed in the den for when she napped during the day.

Ma Dear looked over at her Singer's cabinet-style sewing machine in the corner that Daddy Nate bought her thirty years ago. That was still her pride and joy because she was the first one in her sewing club to get the new model. Ma Dear thought she was too old and sickly to use it now. But she liked to keep it there as a reminder of her happy sewing and quilting years.

Bianca had certainly enjoyed staying at the "Big House" with Vivian's twelve-year-old daughter, Denise, and sixteen-year-old son, Dennis. They loved her to pieces and played with her constantly when they were not in school. Denise and Dennis were proud to show their cute little cousin from Florida to family and friends. Of course, Bianca loved being the center of all that attention.

Vivian and her husband, Darnell Smith, had moved in the "Big House" with Ma Dear about twelve years ago when Denise was just a cuddly infant. Vivian had decided to stay home and take care of Ma Dear and the baby while Darnell continued working at the Columbus Shoe Factory on the outskirts of Wichita. They were able to make ends meet because Ma Dear received a social security check for herself and a retirement pension on behalf of Daddy Nate. Since the house had five bedrooms, they each had their own room and a guest room for out-of-town visitors. I loved staying in Ma Dear's guest room with the white Early American styled furniture and the old-fashioned vanity table with a fold-down mirror on top.

Vivian was taller than me, but we were about the same size. Vivian was always happy to see what clothes I had brought her from the city shops whenever I came home to visit them. Both of us had the same taste in clothes, except Vivian liked a more colorful

[63]

wardrobe than I did. I preferred the natural colors like different shades of brown or either casual black attire. We both wore our hair natural but Vivian liked to keep hers braided in cornrows going up into a bun or hanging down in a ponytail. Neither one of us cared that much for makeup, but we always dressed our best.

Darnell would fit the typical description of a big black man, but he wasn't close to being six-feet tall. He was handsome, though, with a terrific outgoing personality. He was always making jokes and making everybody laugh, even during the toughest of times. Darnell particularly loved teasing Ma Dear whenever she was feeling well. He loved bragging on his mother-in-law and how well she fed him. Darnell let everybody know Ma Dear had been the recipient of many cooking awards, and he had been the first to sample each of her original recipes.

"Listen, you guys. I'm going to take a long hot shower. I haven't seen water on my body in over two days," I announced, heading down the long hallway to the bathroom.

"Take your time, sis. I'll go fix Ma Dear and the kids some lunch while you're doing that," Vivian said, bending over to kiss our mother's wrinkled forehead before heading towards the kitchen.

While I was enjoying my steaming hot shower, I remembered I needed to call Michael and let him know Ma Dear was finally home. I would also call the principal, Mr. Harper, to ask for a "leave of absence" for the rest of this semester. I hated to call him at home on a Saturday, but I wanted to inform him immediately since I had made a decision not to return to work right away. I needed time to get my personal house in order before dealing with that place. Now that Ma Dear was finally home, I could think about the adoption situation and how I would get to the bottom of that note about Michael that I received before leaving. I still couldn't believe someone had left a message in my mailbox. This was 2014. Why didn't they email me or something?

I have to trust Michael. I have to have faith in my husband. I know he loves me. I tried to reassure myself because a mustard seed of doubt had been planted in my mind.

I had an overwhelming feeling to hear Michael's voice. I had missed him so much it was almost unbearable. I dialed the number hoping he would be home.

"Hello," he answered after the fourth ring.

"Hi, baby. We miss you. Guess what?"

"What's going on, Alese?"

"Ma Dear came home today."

"Oh really, that's great! How's she doing?"

"She's okay, although she's lost some weight."

"Yeah, well, that's understandable. When do you think you'll be coming home?"

I hesitated, thinking for a second. I heard the longing in his voice. I didn't want to disappoint him, but I was needed here.

"Well, I need to be here at least a couple more weeks to make sure she's recovering properly and see her through the first two follow-up visits with her doctor."

"Yeah, yeah, that's cool. I just miss you both so much."

"We miss you, too."

"I miss you and Bianca more because there are two of you," he said, laughing.

"Well, speaking of Bianca. Have you heard anything from Ms. Riley regarding the aunt she told us about?"

"No, baby. I haven't heard anything from her, but I plan on giving her a call first thing Monday morning. This is just ridiculous."

"Yes, it is. But I believe it will be over soon, and it'll be like none of this ever even happened."

"I hope that's true. I really do." Michael sighed.

"How is our business doing? Is everything okay?"

"Oh, yeah, you don't have to worry about that. You just concentrate on getting back home unless you want me to fly out there."

"No, sweetheart, I told you. It won't be long now that Ma Dear is home. There's no need for both of us to be here right now."

"All right." He relented. "If that's what you want to do, but please call me every day. Don't miss another day like you did yesterday. I couldn't even reach you at the hospital."

[65]

"Yes, I know. I unplugged the telephone in the room so Ma Dear could rest, and then I fell asleep and forgot to call you. I'm sorry about that."

"Well, you're forgiven for your small indiscretion. Just don't let it happen again," he said in a loving tone.

"Sure, sure," I said. "I love you. Good night."

"I love you more," Michael replied, reluctantly hanging up the telephone. He always hated saying good-bye.

#

The following day was Sunday and I enjoyed attending my home church whenever I was in town. Bianca and I, dressed in our long burgundy velour dresses, piled into the Dodge Grand Caravan minivan with Vivian and her two children and headed to the New Hill Chapel Baptist Church at ten-forty-five in the morning. We only lived about a mile-and-a-half from the church so we didn't have to rush to get there. This was the fourth Sunday of the New Year and we were all looking forward to hearing Denise and Dennis sing in the young people's choir. Darnell volunteered to stay home with Ma Dear so we could enjoy ourselves.

The New Hill Chapel Baptist Church was a long standing institution in our small community. They had recently spent over five thousand dollars renovating the inside of the building with new paint, a new floor foundation, beige carpet, and gold cushioned pews. The outside of the building maintained its original structure. It had just been pressure washed and was gleaming in the sunlight with a roof layered in architectural shingles.

Reverend Johnson was in top form as he preached about the "Spirit of Giving," and the choir sang all of my favorite gospel hymns, including *Take My Hand, Precious Lord*, *Prayer Changes Things*, and *Amazing Grace*. I was so happy and thankful for my many blessings until I couldn't control the tears flooding my face towards the end of the service. Sister Johnson came and sat down beside me, wiped my face, and placed her arms around my shoulders. She understood what I was going through with my mother, but she didn't realize that was only a third of my problems.

[66]

Arriving home about two hours later, I noticed a green Ford Explorer parked in front of the house. I figured someone in the neighborhood had dropped by on their way from church.

"Vivian, do you recognize the car parked in front of the house?"

"No, I don't," Vivian replied, looking at the license plate on the new vehicle. "But somebody we know must have a new truck."

"I guess so. Let's go see who it is," she replied, exiting the van and watching the kids run in the house with Bianca trailing behind them.

The second I entered the family room I recognized the familiar scent of my man. Nobody could ever smell better than Michael. He was wearing the strong woodsy cologne, Drakkar Noir, which I had bought him for Christmas. *Oh, my God, Michael's here!*

Dropping my purse on the sofa in the den, I headed down the hallway, and saw Michael carrying Bianca in his arms walking towards me. My heart stopped and dropped at the sight of them.

"Michael, sweetheart, this is a nice surprise!" I exclaimed, hugging my husband as he released Bianca.

"I just thought I would fly out and surprise you guys. I figured three weeks was long enough to be away from my girls. I have to leave tomorrow, but I couldn't resist the temptation to spend one night with you all."

"Well, I'm happy to see you," I said, planting a mushy kiss on his lips as he wrapped his arms around my waist.

"I also wanted to see how my favorite mother-in-law was doing."

"I know she was overjoyed to see you. Come on down to the den and have a seat while we finish cooking." I grabbed his arm and tugged him forward.

By this time, everybody was in the family room watching television and waiting on Vivian to heat up the Sunday dinner. According to our tradition, we had prepared on Saturday night the baked turkey wings with yellow rice, green beans, macaroni and cheese, black eyed peas, cornbread, and vanilla pound cake. Darnell, Michael, and Dennis were really into whatever professional football game they were watching, so I decided to set the table. Approximately thirty minutes later, all of the food was placed in white ceramic containers and platters and then set on the oval-shaped wooden table. As soon as the dinner call was given, the dining room was filled with joy and laughter.

As the day progressed, Michael and I were able to fit in some quality time together between football games and family visitors. Bianca hung on to her daddy as if he was the tree of life. She fought taking a nap most of the day. But finally, late that evening, she fell asleep in Michael's arms. He carried her to the bedroom and placed her slumbering body on the bed in Denise's room. She had been delighted to share a room with her older cousin.

Slipping into our bedroom while the rest of the family was in the den, Michael and I squeezed and hungrily kissed each other. We could barely lock the door. The bed was so high Michael had to lift me up on the side of the bed, putting me level with his pelvis, while I had my arms wrapped around his neck, sucking the last drop of juice from his tongue. He hurriedly pulled up my long dress and pulled down my satin panties before unzipping his pants and dropping them to the floor.

Breathing heavily and pawing one another's body, we remained as quiet as possible. Ma Dear's room was right next door to ours and we certainly didn't want to disturb her with loud moaning sounds. While Michael was tracing liquid kisses up and down my throat, I consciously tried to stifle my lusty groans by biting down hard on my lower lip. Michael was still standing at the side of the bed as I leaned back on my elbows, wrapping my legs around his muscled thighs. Leaning his sweaty body over mine, we reached our peaks together.

Minutes later, we were both out of breath lying side-by-side on the bedspread. My bottom lip was throbbing in pain, but my body was tingling from pure satisfaction.

That was worth a one night trip. I heard Michael exhale deeply. Then, he snuggled up next to me as we drifted into sleep.

#

The next day, Michael had to leave on an early afternoon flight. I yearned for him to stay longer, but he had several meetings and presentations scheduled for the next day on two of his largest business accounts. I wanted to return home with him, but he encouraged me to remain in Kansas with Ma Dear and see her through the first two follow-up visits like I had already planned to do. As much as Michael loved me, I imagined he would never be able to forgive himself if something dreadful happened to Ma Dear and he had convinced me to change the plan because of him.

Ma Dear had only been out of the hospital for one full day and seemed to be doing fine. Still, I understood the importance of watching a patient the first few weeks they were home after a lengthy hospital stay. That was the most critical time of all because most people would start feeling better and do too much too soon and end up regressing. I had seen my mother do that before and I was determined for that not to happen this time. I surmised, *It's not just Vivian's responsibility to take care of Ma Dear. I'll just have to remain a few more weeks as planned.*

6

We're Still Family

"Ma Dear, you have your initial follow-up appointment with Dr. Goldstein scheduled for tomorrow morning at nine-thirty. Vivian and I will both be with you."

I was helping Ma Dear put on her pajamas while she sat on the side of her twin-sized bed. Ma Dear had insisted on getting a twin bed set in her room shortly after Daddy Nate passed. She just didn't want to be in a big queen-sized bed by herself.

"That's fine with me." She looked up at me and smiled. "Now, when are you going to tell me about what's going on between you and my son-in-law?"

"Ma Dear, I don't know what you're talking about." Ma Dear picked up on everything. Although I had tried to be careful and not show any signs of distress in my marriage, there was no fooling this psychic woman.

"Chile, please. I'm your mother. I know you better than you know your own self." I sat down on the other twin bed facing Ma Dear, looking down at her hands folded on her lap.

"Ma Dear, it's nothing for you to worry about. We're fine. I'm just worried about this adoption thing."

"I can tell it's more than an adoption that's bothering you. Besides, we've already talked about that. We know that's going to work out. Alese, you're my chile and I love my son-in-law. He's a good man and he's treating you right. I want to know what's wrong and don't lie to me. I can tell when you're lying. You were always a bad liar even when you were a little girl." Ma Dear laughed lightly, rubbing her arthritic knees and shaking her head at me.

"Ma Dear, you are so crazy." I laughed, feeling like a teenager again.

"Chile, don't call your momma crazy. Tell me what's going on right now," she demanded.

"Well, the day before I left to come here, someone left a note in my mailbox about Michael." I took a deep breath and exhaled. I looked at Ma Dear's concerned expression and continued. "The note did not have a return address or anything on it. It just had my name on the front of the envelope. Anyway, the anonymous note said Michael was having an affair with one of his employees and they wanted me to know." I was still looking in my mother's eyes.

"Chile, please. Is that it? You can't let that little note put doubts in your mind. You have been married to Michael for fifteen years. Has he ever done anything to make you doubt him?"

"No ma'am. But why would someone send me a note like that for no reason, Ma Dear?"

"Chile, I don't know—but I know you have a good man. Don't go stirring up dirt now. He takes care of you and he don't beat on you like some of these crazy men."

"But, Ma Dear, I have to know if it's true. I have to find out."

"Well, you do what you want, but I'm telling you to let it go and trust your husband until you know for sure—for yourself."

Ma Dear lay back in the bed, like she wasn't worried about us. "Well, I know you well enough to know you're going to investigate your husband and track down the source of the note if it's the last thing you ever do. But chile, you is stubborn and just asking for trouble."

"I can't help it. I have to know."

"Before you make a final decision, it's time I told you the truth about my marriage to your daddy."

I looked confused, wondering what Ma Dear was talking about. As far as I could tell, my parents had a great marriage. I shifted my body and scooted a little closer because she lowered her voice.

"Alese, your father wasn't always a good husband," Ma Dear whispered. She was trying not to upset me because I practically worshipped the ground my daddy walked on.

"Ma Dear, what are you talking about?"

"Well, when your daddy and I first got married, we moved to Topeka. This was long before you were born. Vivian was a baby and your daddy started running around on me while we lived there. One night, I asked my neighbor, Ms. Berry, to watch Vivian while I went out to find Nate. I had heard about the woman he was seeing and knew where she lived. Well, I went straight to her house and banged on the front door until she answered." Ma Dear paused before she continued. "Anyway, Nate took off out the back door and I beat that woman all over her own house before I left that night. After that, I made Nate move back to Wichita and then we had you."

"Ma Dear, I don't believe you," I said in bewilderment. I stretched my eyes, opened my mouth, and glared at my mother. This was the first time I had ever heard about my father's unfaithfulness.

"You don't have to believe it. It's the truth," Ma Dear stated firmly. "As a matter of fact, he continued running around for a long time after we moved back here, too," she added. "I just got tired of trying to beat up every woman he ran with and decided to stop chasing behind him before I got myself killed and guess what? He finally stopped running around. Doesn't that beat all?" Ma Dear turned to see if I was still listening to her before she went any further.

"Ma Dear, this is—I just don't know what to say." I honestly couldn't imagine my small frail mother beating up anyone over a man, even if it was over forty years ago.

"Well, I know what to say, baby. All men are dogs. But, some are good dogs and some are no good dogs. Now, the difference is this—even a good dog can fall, but a good dog will only fall down one time; a no good dog will fall down every time he gets up."

"Ma Dear, do you think we have a chance at staying together if this note is true?"

"Baby, all I can tell you is that whatever happens is between you and your husband. Now, the devil is busy, so don't let nobody outside your marriage influence your decision. If you two really love each other, put God first and He will help you through anything," she said slowly, emphasizing key words. "I prayed for Nate and God changed him in time. That's all I can tell you."

Ma Dear reached over and tapped the gold plated touch-lamp on the nightstand between the two twin beds to turn it off. She scooted down in the bed and pulled the quilt up snuggly around her shoulders. She had said her piece and was done with the conversation.

I kissed her good night on the cheek and slowly backed out of the bedroom. I gently pulled the door tightly closed behind me.

[72]

There was nothing else to say because Ma Dear always had the last word.

"Oops, I'm sorry Darnell." I jumped when I bumped into Darnell coming down the hallway still wearing his dark navy uniform.

"That's okay, Alese. No problem."

"Well, how is my favorite brother-in-law doing?"

"Ah, I'm doing fine. I just had a long day today, that's all," Darnell looked down at the floor, as if he was trying to avoid talking to me.

"Hey, I've missed being around here and having you to make me laugh," I said, playfully clapping my hands and laughing.

"Yeah, well, I can't always be the life of the party. Darnell spoke with a straight face. He entered the bathroom and closed the door behind him.

I stood there for a second wondering what was wrong with Darnell. Then, I shook the thought out of my head and walked on toward the den.

#

"Vivian, hurry up. We're going to be late for Ma Dear's appointment with the doctor this morning," I said, fussing at my older sister. She was always the last one ready to leave.

"I'm coming. Is Ma Dear waiting in the car?"

"Yes, she's waiting. I also have Bianca strapped in the back seat and I'm ready to go." I turned and walked through the doorway but left the door open.

Vivian grabbed her blue suede coat with the white fur collar and hurried to the van. Ma Dear and Bianca slept most of the way in the back seat to the doctor's office while Vivian and I reminisced about our past together. It felt great to be able to talk to the one person who shared so much of my life. I had dreamed of moving home and sharing my life with close family. Since Michael's business was doing so well, that would have to remain a dream for some time.

We arrived at Dr. Goldstein's office just in time for the appointment. Dr. Goldstein never liked to keep his older patients waiting. We were only there for about two minutes before Ma Dear's name was called.

[73]

"Ms. Ruby Dean! Right this way please!" the young nurse called out.

Ma Dear stood and balanced herself between the handles of the walker before moving. I stood to help, but Ma Dear waved for me to sit down while she made her way down the hall to the examining room. She told us to stay in the waiting room while she was with her doctor and we reluctantly agreed. There was no use arguing with Ma Dear once she had her mind made up about something. Though her body was frail, her mind was still sharp as a new knife. She handled all of her personal affairs with only occasional input from either one of us.

Bianca strolled over to the play area and picked up several toys before she sat on the floor to play. I looked around at the other patients in the almost bare waiting room before whispering to Vivian.

"Girl, what is going on with you and Darnell? He hasn't been his usual upbeat self at all. He hardly speaks to anybody when he comes home in the evening. Is everything all right with you two, sis?" I asked out of concern.

I had definitely noticed a rift between Vivian and Darnell over the last three weeks but had decided to keep quiet about it until now. I could sense my sister's unhappiness. Vivian crossed her arms and shifted in her seat like she wasn't sure if she should talk to me.

"Girl, we are sisters. We can tell each other anything. What is up with your man?" I asked again.

"Alese, Darnell and I have been having problems since early last year. You see, I don't know how to say this, but—but I cheated on him," she admitted, shamefully dropping her eyes to the floor.

"What?" I looked around to see if anyone else was listening. "Why would you be foolish enough to cheat on a good man like Darnell? Has he ever cheated on you?"

"I don't think so. No, I'm sure he hasn't," Vivian replied, shaking her head.

"Well, why in the world would you be unfaithful with another man?" I asked, glaring at her like she had just gone insane. Darnell had been a good faithful husband for twenty years. "How could you do this?"

"Well, first of all, I wasn't unfaithful with another man," she responded.

"What the devil are you talking about?" I was about to explode, but managed to keep my voice down. I glanced around the waiting room to see if anyone was watching us. There were only a few people across the room reading magazines or engaged in conversations.

"I slept with Paula, a female friend of mine, and told Darnell about it."

"I don't even want to know when it happened. Just tell me why the devil you did something like that," I demanded.

"Alese, please try to understand. It wasn't intentional. I went to a Christmas party at her house. Most of the people there were gay, but Paula and I had been good friends for a long time. So, of course, I didn't see any harm in attending the party. We were all dancing, drinking, having fun telling jokes, and that kind of stuff. Well, I must have had too much to drink and we ended up in bed together. I didn't get home until the next morning. Needless to say, Darnell was quite upset, and I was so confused that I confessed to him about what happened," she said, blinking back tears. "We're trying to work it out, but it has been hard for us. Darnell says he has forgiven me, but we haven't had the closeness we had before," she added, beginning to weep.

"How did you explain that to Darnell? I mean—just being drunk is not a good excuse for sleeping with another woman."

"Well, I've known Paula a long time and she's been gay for as long as I've known her. Maybe, I was a little bit curious. Anyway, I know it was wrong. I explained to him that I'm not like that."

"Vivian, I don't know what to say. I admire the man for staying with you. God knows he loves you. I can understand why he hasn't been his usual happy-go-lucky self," I stated, dropping my head.

"And I love him. It was just a terrible, terrible mistake. I'll never forgive myself."

"You have to forgive yourself and ask God to forgive you. There is nothing that He will not forgive."

"You're right and I know that, but it's so hard," Vivian replied. I reached over and hugged her right there in the waiting room. No matter what, this was still MY big sister and she had just confided in me by sharing her deepest, darkest secret.

I could feel Vivian's angst and shame as I held her for several minutes. I tried to imagine what I would have done in Darnell's shoes. I wasn't a violent person, but if Michael ever flat out confessed to me like that, I would probably try to stab him to death. Thank God Darnell didn't feel that way.

When I raised my eyes, I saw Ma Dear staring at us from the hallway. She never opened her mouth or let on that she had heard what we were talking about, but Ma Dear always knew everything.

#

Over two weeks later, I decided to take Bianca and Denise with me to visit Aunt Lucy and Uncle Clevell before leaving Wichita. Aunt Lucy was Ma Dear's younger sister and she lived in the same community. She and Uncle Clevell had been married for over forty years and resided in a three-bedroom, ranch-style brick home. They had one daughter, Colleen, who was a year younger than me. We had been best friends and playmates during our childhood but had only talked occasionally in the last few years. Colleen was a high school science teacher living in Topeka. She was still single and looking for love in all the wrong places.

Aunt Lucy was a short woman like Ma Dear, but she was about twice the size of Ma Dear. She would be considered pleasingly plump by any standards. She loved to cook and whenever I called her, she was always in the kitchen trying out some new recipe she had found in the *Home and Garden* magazine. She had been a hairdresser most of her life, but she didn't do perms. She still believed in the good old press and curl. Aunt Lucy did her own hair and kept it colored in a dark auburn hue with tight Marcella curls.

Uncle Clevell was a tall, average size man. He was a year younger than Aunt Lucy and was proud of it, even though he didn't look it. He sported a bald head and walked with a slight limp from a hip injury he sustained in the Army. He talked with an accent like a northerner, even though he was born and raised in the south. Uncle Clevell was also a good cook, comparable to Aunt Lucy, but he didn't prepare their meals on a regular basis. However, when it came down to barbecuing, he was the prized country chef.

"Hi, Aunt Lucy and Uncle Clevell." I hugged my aunt and uncle immediately upon entering their spacious living room. Aunt Lucy collected everything; she had nice ceramics, statues, bottles, and other fine collectibles on every table and shelf in the house. I had sent her mementos from every place I had ever traveled, including Italy and Japan. She also loved to read home improvement magazines and kept a stack of the most current issues in the magazine rack beside the sofa.

"Hey, baby. How have you been and where is that handsome, rich husband of yours?" Aunt Lucy asked, sounding in good spirits.

She was usually in a pleasant mood whenever she greeted someone, especially her relatives. Aunt Lucy took our coats and hung them up in the hallway closet. Uncle Clevell spoke and went back to watching television in his oversized recliner.

"I'm fine and Michael is home running the business. He sends his best to everyone, though," I responded with a smile. I was happy to be inside so I could feel the heat from the roaring fireplace. Uncle Clevell always kept that fireplace going and we certainly needed it this time of year. I enjoyed visiting my family in Kansas, but I had gotten used to the warm Florida weather. I wasn't prepared for the cold and ice they had here.

"Well, come on in here and have a seat."

Aunt Lucy invited me and the two girls to come in the living room and get comfortable. Bianca and Denise sat on the multiple-striped couch in front of the brick fireplace and watched the big screen television in the corner of the room.

"Aunt Lucy, how have you and Uncle Clevell been doing?"

"Oh, we're doing fine. We're just both trying to retire. It's about that time."

"I didn't know you were trying to retire, Auntie. You're tired of doing hair?"

"Yes, goodness. I am tired of hair. I'm ready to stay home and rest."

"How is my cousin, Colleen? Was she home for the holidays?"

"Yes, she was. She was here for over a week. We really enjoyed ourselves," Aunt Lucy responded in a stronger voice with laughter. She was definitely proud of her only child.

I followed Aunt Lucy into the kitchen and stood leaning on the bar counter. I glanced over at Aunt Lucy standing in front of a brand new stainless steel General Electric smooth-top stove.

"Hey, Auntie. I like that new stove you got over there," I said, pointing in that direction.

"Yeah, I got this a couple of months ago, baby, and I love it. This thing has everything. Look here."

She pulled the oven door down and motioned for me to come over and look at her newest gadget. Aunt Lucy demonstrated all the functions she was proud to have on her new oven.

Auntie had a cozy square shaped glass top table with four taupe colored chairs in the center of the kitchenette. She poured us both steaming hot cups of coffee in two tall mugs before she sat down to start a conversation with me. Auntie always spoke her mind explicitly when it came to family and tonight would not be an exception.

"Alese, you're my niece and I love you dearly. But I'm worried about you leaving your good-looking husband alone so much. Believe it or not, a good looking man is a magnet for women—and it doesn't matter if he's rich or poor." She paused, making sure she had my full attention. Aunt Lucy took a long sip of her coffee and cleared her throat before she continued. "I know you love your mother and everything, but you have your own family to think about now," she said, softly. She made sure the children and Uncle Clevell didn't hear us.

"Aunt Lucy, I appreciate your concern, but Michael and I are fine. We have an understanding," I responded.

"Oh, yeah," she said. "What kind of understanding do you have?" she asked, giving me a suspicious look with raised eyebrows.

"Well, he knows Ma Dear is my main priority right now and it's important for me to be here with her whenever I can," I said calmly, massaging my forehead with both hands when I spoke. I felt a headache coming on and I wanted to avoid a confrontation with my aunt at any price.

"Baby, I understand, but you been here more in the last year than you been home with your husband," Aunt Lucy continued, stressing her words. "I know I had some women calling my house about my husband back in the day. So, I know what these young hussies will do for a fine rich nig…Negro, like the one you got!" Aunt Lucy remembered I didn't like her using the "N" word, so she changed it fast.

"Ah, I don't think I've been here that often, but I do get your point, Aunt Lucy," I replied, nodding my head and running my fingers down the length of my locks.

"Alese, believe me, somebody's got their eye on your man and just waiting for you to slip up. Chile, the devil is busy. You hear me?"

"Yes, and thanks for your concern, Aunt Lucy, but I know what I'm doing."

"Chile, I sure hope so. I sure hope so," she repeated, before continuing to speak. "I'm not trying to get in your business. It's just that I've been around a lot longer than you have. I hate to see people make senseless mistakes, especially my own blood."

"Yes, I understand, and I'm listening to what you're saying, Auntie. But don't worry about me because we're fine."

"I'm done with it then. I'm just happy your uncle turned his life around or we wouldn't be together today. He's been going to church with me now on a regular basis for years." Aunt Lucy giggled, rising. "You want another cup of coffee?" she asked, heading to the stove.

"Yes, that sounds great," I responded.

I wanted anything that would take my mind off of the increasing unsettling emotions that were being aroused in my mind. The last thing I needed tonight was to be reminded that I had a very handsome and very wealthy husband at home alone.

#

That was it for me. Ma Dear always told me, "Baby, when you don't know which way to turn in life—just look for the signs and make sure you follow them. God will never lead you wrong."

In the last three weeks, the three most important women in my life had shared their hearts or witnessed to me. I deduced exactly which way to go. I was heading home.

"Hi, baby. I'm calling to tell you that I love you, I miss you, and we'll be home soon," I cooed into the cell phone.

"Oh, yeah," he said. "Well, that's wonderful news. I can't wait to see the two most beautiful women in the whole wide world. I love you and I miss you, too," Michael said, softly. "How is my baby girl doing?"

"She's doing great and she's already sleeping. I'm calling the airlines tonight to get a flight home for tomorrow, if possible. I'll call you with the details later tonight."

"That sounds like a plan to me. I'll be sitting here by the telephone until I hear back from you," Michael happily stated before they said their good-byes.

I quickly called the airport and was able to get a flight out for the next afternoon. I would have preferred to leave in the morning, but there were no more flights available at such short notice. The agent informed me that I was extremely lucky to be able to get anything, especially on a Saturday. So, I promptly called Michael again to let him know we would definitely be seeing him tomorrow.

Once I had taken care of the personal business for tomorrow, I needed to secure a ride to the airport. That meant I would have to ask my brother-in-law to drive me since Vivian would have to stay home with Ma Dear. Hesitantly, I walked down the hallway and knocked on their bedroom door, hoping they hadn't gone to sleep.

"Vivian, are you guys still up. I need to talk to you and Darnell."

"Yeah, sure, come on in." I eased the door open and stepped in the room to find Darnell sitting on the far side of the queen-sized bed watching television with Vivian on the other side propped up reading a book.

"I've made arrangements for Bianca and me to leave tomorrow."

"When did you make that decision?" Vivian asked.

"I just think it's time for me to get back to my life in Florida. I've done all I can do here for now."

"Well, I'm just thankful you were able to make it here this time. I don't know if I could have made it through this without you. I really don't. This time was different, though, sis."

"I know what you mean. Listen, I need a ride to the airport for tomorrow afternoon. My flight leaves at twelve-thirty-five. Darnell, do you think you can take me to the airport tomorrow?"

"Of course, I can. What time would you like to leave?" He glanced over at me and then turned back to the television set. He was watching a professional wrestling match and acting as if he didn't want to miss a thing.

"We need to leave around ten-thirty since it'll take us almost an hour just to get to the airport. I'll need at least an hour to check-in once we're there."

"No problem. I'll be ready."

"Good night. I'll let you guys get some rest while I go break the news to Ma Dear," I said, hugging Vivian. I tipped out of their bedroom.

Ma Dear took the news of me leaving the next day quite well. She was happy we had been able to spend some time together again.

"Baby, you have a husband to get home to. I've got plenty of folk here who can take care of me. You go on back and see about your husband."

"Yes, ma'am, that's exactly what I intend on doing," I replied before kissing Ma Dear good-night and exiting the room.

#

The next morning, Bianca and I were all packed and ready to go. We settled into the Dodge minivan with Darnell after saying our good-byes to the family. It didn't take long for Bianca to fall asleep in the back seat, which left me feeling uncomfortable in the car with Darnell, who was still unusually quiet. We listened as the gospel radio station played some of the old time songs we still sang in our country church. During a commercial break, I decided to make light conversation with my brother-in-law.

"Darnell, how are things between you and Vivian?"

[81]

"We're fine. I know she told you about the affair she had with another woman."

I was surprised Vivian had told him about our conversation. Since he had opened the door, now was a good time to enter the room.

"Yes, she did mention that to me when I asked her about you acting strange lately. It's none of my business, but I don't think she had an on-going affair with the woman. It was just a one night thing, right?"

Darnell deeply exhaled before speaking. "She told me that was the only time and that's what I have a problem believing. How did it just happen one time if she's known the woman for all these years?"

"She was drinking at the party and things just got out of hand. It doesn't mean that she doesn't love you or she ever meant to hurt you. Vivian made a mistake which she deeply regrets."

"I deeply regret it, too. I'm still hurting and trying to recover. I agreed with her going to the party, thinking she needed to get out and be with her friends for a while. Then, when she ended up staying out all night long, I had a feeling something was wrong. I've never trusted Paula, but I've never tried to stop Vivian from being her friend. Right now, I find it difficult to talk to people because I feel like everybody in this town knows what happened, and they're all talking behind our backs."

"Well, it is a small town and most people here are overly nosey. But you all are probably old news by now. Besides, your marriage is your business and you don't have to explain your decision to remain with your wife to anybody. If you still love her, and you have forgiven her, then the rest is up to you and Vivian."

"That's exactly what the pastor said," Darnell stated, glancing over at me. "It's just easier to say than it is to do. I never thought after twenty years of marriage I'd have to worry about Vivian cheating on me like this. You never know what you're going to do until you're faced with this situation."

That statement touched a nerve within me, prompting me to inspect my own marriage stability. *Good Lord! I pray that Michael is never unfaithful with another woman, and the image of him being with another man is utterly ridiculous.*

"I'm still there because I love her," he continued. "No matter what happened, I still love my wife and I'll never leave her. With prayer and a lot of help from the good Lord, we'll eventually get through this."

"I'm sure you will," I managed to say, hoping I would never have to walk a mile in his shoes.

7

While She's Away

Jennifer Riley arrived at her north side law office early Monday morning to prepare for her first meeting with Varnisha Grant, Bianca's biological aunt. She was surprised Ms. Grant had asked to meet her without an attorney present considering she was supposedly opposing the adoption. Jennifer was almost certain there was a hidden agenda and she was determined to find out what it was.

She had reassured Mr. Wayne she would handle this situation expeditiously and promised to call him whenever this interview was over. Jenny had completed her preliminary background check on Ms. Grant and learned she had a local arrest record for a misdemeanor crime. This, however, was not enough to prevent her from adopting her niece.

Jenny was anxious to meet with Varnisha in person so she could feel her out and determine a course of action. She had been an adoption attorney for almost twenty-five years and she had a keen sixth sense about these things. She pulled her straight light brown hair from her face and tucked it behind her ear before she thumbed through the Wayne's case.

Arriving about thirty minutes late, Varnisha gave some excuse about having trouble finding a ride downtown. She sat down in front of the attorney. Varnisha looked older than her twenty-nine years even though she tried to present a younger picture with her long blonde micro braids, heavy make-up, and metallic red artificial nail tips.

"Well, Ms. Grant," Jenny began the conversation. "Thank you for requesting to meet with me today. Do you have an attorney yet?"

"I guess. I met with some fat guy for a few minutes last week," Varnisha responded, shifting in her seat. "He didn't seem to know much about the case though."

"Okay, then, how can I help you?"

"After talking it over with my boyfriend, he told me I should come in and talk to you and see what you had to offer before we go any further, if you know what I mean."

"I'm not sure I do, but let's proceed. I just need to ask you a few questions for the record and then you can be on your way," Jenny said, smiling at the young lady. "Why do you want custody of Bianca?" Jenny asked, using a casual tone. She wanted Varnisha to let her guard down and expose her real agenda.

"She's my blood relative. Ain't that enough?" Varnisha replied, flashing gold teeth, glaring at Ms. Riley.

"Ms. Grant, this child has been with a foster family for over a year now. Where have you been during this time?"

"I, ah, I been trying to get myself together," she stammered, pulling up her strapless spandex top. She tugged on her denim mini-skirt as she crossed her legs, displaying a pair of high platform sandals.

"I see. Are you employed, Ms. Grant?"

"Yes, of course, I work. I just started working part-time at the Big K-mart store on Lem Turner Road," she said, lifting her arms, causing the numerous gold and silver toned bracelets to jingle.

"Ms. Grant, I don't believe working part-time will be enough to provide for yourself and a child."

"Well, don't the State give you a check every month for adopting a child? Won't I be able to get food stamps and Medicaid or something for taking her in?" she asked, stroking the multiple chains around her neck. The huge gold earrings dangled with each move of her head.

"Yes, that's all true. But it could take a long time for any of those benefits to kick in. The social worker will have to come out for an initial inspection. Where do you live?"

"Ah, I got me a two bedroom in the South Hills Apartment Complex on Hudson Street."

"Well, there is a tremendous amount of paperwork to be completed, several home visits will have to be conducted by the social workers, and other documents must be supplied to the State before you can be scheduled for a custody hearing. In addition, the State will have to conduct an extensive background check on you

[85]

which could take months to complete." Jenny slid a manila folder across the desk containing a list of the required documents with sample copies.

"Yes, ma'am. My social worker told me about that," Varnisha said, responding nervously, picking up the folder without looking through it. "She also told me that I was entitled to a visit with my niece. How soon can I see her?" she asked, staring at Jenny.

"Well, I'll have to speak with her foster parents about that and get back with you. It will have to be scheduled at their convenience."

"Yes, I understand. How soon will I be able to get a check?"

"You won't be able to receive any money until she is in your legal custody. All documents must be secured and the investigation completed before you may file for benefits."

"How long will all of that take? I wasn't expecting it to take too long."

"Ms. Grant, there is a process we have to go through. Just because you're a relative does not alleviate you from complying with the process. As I said, several home inspections will have to be done. It could take a year or longer to start receiving anything."

"I guess I need to talk with my, ah, social worker again. She sounded like it wouldn't take that long for me to get my niece. I mean my sister is dead and I'm her only relative."

"Your social worker or attorney should have advised you regarding that when you notified the State that you wanted to oppose the adoption."

"Oh yeah, maybe they did say something like that, but I didn't think it was really important. Anyway, what can you tell me about this family who adopted my niece? Are they well off?" Varnisha asked, inching to the edge of her seat.

Click, now we're getting to the real issue here. She's all about the Benjamin's. She wants to get paid for relinquishing the rights to her niece.

Jenny decided to be nonchalant. "Well, I'm not at liberty to discuss my client's personal life or finances. But why would you be asking about that?"

"Oh, no particular reason," Varnisha shrugged, trying to play it off. "I just thought if they were rich or something, we might be able to reach some type of custody agreement or something. Anyway, I guess I'll be waiting to hear from you."

"I'll talk with my clients and get back with you in a few days," Jenny responded calmly.

"You do that." Varnisha stood, tugged on her mini-skirt, and strutted toward the door.

Jenny watched her until she disappeared. She didn't plan on letting some derelict come near that innocent child. Jenny would have to conduct a more thorough background search on Ms. Grant herself. The State had a serious backlog and would take too long to perform their own investigation.

In the meantime, she would have to call Mr. Wayne with the information she had for now. Although Attorney Riley could stall the custody hearing, the aunt was still entitled to a supervised visit with the child.

#

"Girl, get in this car! I've been waiting out here almost an hour for you. What took you so long? Are they going to give you the kid or not?" Tyrone Miller, Varnisha's boyfriend, asked through the opened window of his older model Cadillac Seville. Varnisha opened the door and quickly jumped inside, not wanting to upset Tyrone any further.

"No, that attorney lady says it's going to take some time before I can get the child and start getting the money for her every month. She also said I have a lot of paperwork to complete and they have to conduct several home visits before I can even see my niece."

"Ah, damn. Why you got to do all that? Why can't they just give you the kid and the money right now?" he asked, licking his dry chapped lips.

"I don't know, Tyrone. She said something about them having laws and procedures and that just because I'm a relative, I don't have any special privileges."

"So, how long did she say all of that would take?"

"She didn't give me a time frame. She just said it could take several months. I have to pass some stupid inspections before I can get the kid or a check."

"Did she say how much money you would be getting every month for taking her in?"

"No, she wouldn't even talk about that with me. She was too busy looking down her pointed little white nose. She just kept saying how the social workers would have to come to my apartment and do a few home inspections. I guess they want to make sure I have a good place to bring the little rugrat."

"You shouldn't have any problem getting the kid. I mean you are the only living relative that's willing to take her in."

"Yeah, I thought that since my sister and her boyfriend were dead it would be easy sailing for me getting the kid. I didn't know they would put me through all of this. But then again, I didn't even think about getting this child until all the money ran out that my sister left me. I'm glad them hoodlums who robbed and killed them didn't get their greedy hands on the money. If it wasn't for that big check, I'd leave them crazy folks alone."

"I know that's right. But I was counting on that money right away. One of my home boys told me they would give you over a thousand dollars a month for taking in a relative like that from the State's custody."

"Well, it won't be anytime soon. She also said something about them doing a background investigation on me."

"You don't have to worry about them doing no background check on you. You don't have any felonies in the State of Florida. That little petty crime you have on your record won't amount to nothing as long as you don't have any felony charges. I know what I'm talking about. I've been in and out of jail enough times to know how this so-called justice system works. They'll give anybody a child for foster care. As long as you have the place cleaned up good when they come for their little inspections, we'll have the baby and the money in no time." Tyrone paused, glancing at Varnisha with a silly grin on his face, showing more gold teeth than she had. "So, I guess you'll just have to keep making me money the way you've been doing, baby, until you can get your hands on that little brat, that is."

Varnisha didn't answer him. She just pulled out a cigarette, placed it in her mouth, lit it up, and then took a long drag before letting the smoke float out. She looked over at Tyrone and smiled, "Yeah, baby, whatever you say."

She didn't let him in on Plan B. Hopefully, whoever had her precious niece would be willing to pay some serious money to keep their little darling. Then, Varnisha could have a fresh start in a new city, far away from Tyrone.

#

Stretched out on his comfortable tan cloth recliner in the den, wearing torn jeans and a gray Dolphins sweatshirt, Michael enjoyed watching ESPN-Two on their sixty-inch Sony flat screen television set. He had cleaned the house the best he could in anticipation of his family returning today. Discerning that Alese would love to come home to a tidy place and a hot delicious meal, he also decided to cook. Michael wasn't a gourmet chef, but he could pull a dinner together.

They all enjoyed the taste of seafood, so he had prepared a wonderful platter combination of coconut shrimp, deviled crab cakes, fried cod fish fillets, and hush puppies. He was about to doze off when the telephone rang on the end table beside him.

"Hello," he answered, sleepily.

"Hello, Mr. Wayne. This is Jenny Riley. How are you?"

"Oh, Ms. Riley, hi," he replied, sitting up. He was alert now. "I'm fine, thank you. Do you have any news for us?"

"Yes, Mr. Wayne. I've met with the child's natural aunt. I'm sorry to inform you that she has been granted a visit with the child."

"What? How is that possible? I don't understand why she should be able to see the child."

"I know, and I'm sorry, but we'll have to arrange a time for her to visit the child at my office or one of the State buildings."

"Ah, man, I don't believe this," Michael said, disgusted. "Well, my wife and daughter are still in Kansas due to a family emergency. They should be home later today and I'll have my wife call you sometime tomorrow."

"That's perfect. Just call me whenever they return. Believe me, there is no hurry on this."

"I'll call you later. Thanks for getting back with me, Ms. Riley."

Michael had known for almost two weeks that telephone call was coming, but it still didn't ease his pain. He hadn't told Alese about this latest development because he wanted to spare her a little grief. Michael couldn't bring himself to tell her over the telephone while she was away, but he would have to somehow tell her tonight, for sure.

At least he had managed to avoid Lisa Bradford, except for that one incident. He kept himself occupied by working overtime almost every day of the week. He had even instructed his assistant, Tracy, not to let anyone enter his office unless they had an appointment until further notice from him. By the time he got home most evenings, he was too tired to think of anything except hitting the sack.

Michael had gone out with Marty a few times while Alese was away, but he didn't want to monopolize all of Marty's time since he was a married man, too. When he did socialize with Marty, Tina and their two sons, Malique and Jordan, it made him miss his family even more. Although he enjoyed spending time with fourteen-year old Malique and ten-year old Jordan, and they admired Uncle Mike, he wasn't up to being their buddy tonight.

Well, I won't have to wait much longer. My baby will be on her way home soon.

Michael clasped his hands together. Now, if he could just get Lisa Bradford out of his mind, he could relax.

#

"Hey, I'm sorry I'm late. Have you all been waiting long?" Lisa inquired, rushing to take a seat at the table with her girls.

She believed she was looking exceptional today in her body-hugging, lime green Lycra pants suit. Lisa and Ranetta had decided to treat Jolene to lunch today at her selected restaurant, Genghis Grill, to make up for their behavior at the jazz club last week.

"That's okay. We both just got here a few minutes ago," Ranetta replied, glancing up at her. Jolene and she were both perusing the colorful four-page restaurant menu.

"Hi, Lisa. It's nice to see you, again. I appreciate you both inviting me to lunch today. Let's just try to forget about the other night." Jolene smiled and then glanced down at the menu she had memorized. She waited for her companions to agree with her as she admired her freshly painted French manicured nails.

"Hey, it's already forgotten. Believe me—I can't even believe I did that," Lisa replied, waving her hand across her face.

"Well, you certainly did, girlfriend, and I'm not mad at you. But I guess I can forget," Ranetta added, turning her attention back to the menu in her hands.

"Don't worry about it," Jolene interjected. "Besides, I know how you both can make it up to me. I would love for you two to join me at church on Sunday. This is Valentine's Day Sunday and you two single sisters need to be in attendance. Every single person is supposed to bring at least one single friend with them to service."

Lisa and Ranetta both looked down at their menus, pretending to be absorbed to avoid eye contact with Jolene. They should have known this was coming.

"Well, ladies? I know you both heard me," Jolene stated, determined not to be ignored.

"Yeah, I heard you," Ranetta responded, placing her menu on the table. She scanned the restaurant for the waitress.

"What's the name of your church, again, Jolene?"

"Ranetta, you remember I attend Noah's Ark Missionary Baptist Church on the northwest side of town. Anyway, services start at eleven o'clock on Sunday morning. I'll meet both of you ladies in the vestibule at ten-forty-five sharp. We need to be there on time because the church gets crowded real fast."

"Jolene, is that the small church on Kings Road?" Lisa asked, wrinkling her brow, making a peculiar face.

"Why, yes it is, Lisa," she responded with a smile. "Since you both know where it is, I expect to see you both tomorrow."

"Okay, okay," Lisa and Ranetta responded in unison. They didn't feel up to a religious discussion today and just decided to go along, to get along with Jolene. Right now, they just wanted to get something scrumptious to eat.

#

Sitting in her convertible sports car in the dimly lit parking lot with her head leaning back, Lisa listened to soft music. She was still in love with Sade's song titled, "Soldier of Love." The music made Lisa feel like she was at a live concert, up close and personal with the mellow singer who seemed to know a thing or two about heartbreak. It was full of slow melodic jams she could easily meditate to because tonight, Lisa needed to be calm. She waited for Michael to come out of the office complex so she could finally talk to him, perhaps persuade him to have a late dinner with her in some secluded bistro.

She had painstakingly planned for this rendezvous with Michael. Dressed in a satin midnight blue, low-cut evening dress with a black Victoria's Secret push up Wonder bra, Lisa wanted to remind him of the valuable assets he was missing. Sniffing the alluring floral scent on her wrist, Lisa was happy she'd splurged and bought the complete fragrance collection, Midnight Heat, by Beyonce. If she could turn out millionaire rapper Jay-Z, Lisa fantasized that she could grand slam Michael Wayne.

He's successfully managed to avoid me all week. I can't even get past that nosey secretary of his. She probably wants him for herself. Well, he's not going to be able to avoid me that easily. I'm surprised his dumb wife hasn't put him out by now anyway; but when she does, I'll be there to take him into my arms.

Lisa pulled down the lighted vanity mirror to check her flawless makeup and perfect coco red lips. She saw Michael coming across the parking lot heading towards his car. He looked so tired. He had taken off his necktie and had his suit coat draped over his arm. Michael was rushing so fast to get in the driver's seat he didn't even see Lisa approach him.

"Hey! Hey!" Michael looked startled trying to make out the outline of Lisa's face. "Don't walk up on me like that. What are you doing out here this time of night anyway?"

"Hi, Michael. I was waiting for you since I can't get within five feet of you during the work day," she pouted.

"Well, what do you want Lisa?" he asked, trying not to sound agitated with her.

"I need to talk to you Michael," she said, sternly.

"Lisa, we don't have anything to talk about. If you'll excuse me, I need to go," he said, reaching for the car door handle.

"Wait, Michael! What about what happened between us? You can just forget about that?" she asked, seductively.

"Look, Lisa that was a mistake. It's not going to happen again. Let's just pretend it never happened and try to maintain a professional relationship from now on," he said, keeping his eyes on Lisa, making motions with his hands while he spoke to her.

"Michael, I was hoping we could still be friends. After all, we do have to work together. It's late and I know you haven't eaten. Why don't we go share a table somewhere and get a bite to eat?" Lisa asked, politely.

"Not tonight, Lisa. I have to go, all right?"

"No, it's not all right, because I'm pregnant, Michael. I wanted to tell you under different circumstances but since you insist on mistreating me, I just had to get it out. I need to know how you intend on handling your responsibility."

Michael made a dry chuckle. "I don't believe for one single second you're pregnant, Lisa. This is just another one of your ploys to get my attention."

"But how can you say for sure? Are you absolutely positive, Michael? I don't remember you wearing a condom when we made love. Do you?"

Michael stopped cold as the scenes from that night flashed rapidly through his mind. Had he really been that careless with Lisa? Of course, he had. It hadn't been planned that they would spend the evening together engaged in wild sexual intercourse. Michael leaned against his vehicle for support as all of the energy seemed to drain slowly from his slumping body. Although they had only spent one night together, he recalled having more than one orgasm with her on that occasion.

"Lisa, I—I can't talk about this right now," he sputtered, sounding out of breath.

"Now is the perfect time to talk about this, Michael. We have to make a decision together. I can give you your own flesh and blood child, but you had better talk to me now."

"No, I can't. I have to get home and call my wife before it gets too late. If you want to see me again, make an appointment with Tracy. Good night," he said, quickly entering his car. He started the engine and sped away without glancing back.

Lisa stood there in shock and disbelief. She was fuming with rage beyond humiliation. There was no way she was going to let him go so easily. She stomped back to her convertible and slammed the door before starting the engine. Lisa snatched the mellow Sade CD out of the player and jammed in another CD that matched her new mood. The sounds of Jazmine Sullivan singing, "I'll bust the windows out your car!" filled the night air.

8

Home

I was glad to finally be home. I could put away my heavy coat, leather gloves, and boots, and enjoy the warm weather in Jacksonville. I pulled on a comfortable pair of blue stretch pants and a purple short sleeve cotton shirt. I even contemplated turning on the air conditioner but decided against that. Instead, I went through the entire house and opened all the curtains and windows to let the sunshine in. The cool breeze felt good and made the interior smell quite fresh. I lit a vanilla scented candle and placed it on the table in the den to add to the cozy atmosphere.

It felt like forever since Michael had kissed and held me in his arms. I had plenty of time to think about my marriage on the airplane ride from Kansas to Florida. Ma Dear, Vivian, and Aunt Lucy had certainly given me enough to think about in the romance department. I sensed it was time to handle my business with my husband. I saw that look in his eyes when he met us at the airport earlier. Besides, Aunt Lucy wasn't too far off the mark; somebody definitely wanted my man and I was determined to find out who it was. However, I wasn't prepared to walk away from Michael based on an anonymous note from God-knows-who. Whether I wanted to admit it or not, Aunt Lucy and Ma Dear were right. The devil is busy, but he's also a liar.

The dinner Michael had prepared was absolutely wonderful. I had forgotten he could cook like that. He didn't mind getting down in the kitchen whenever I wasn't there. He usually pitched in to help with the housework and the laundry without me asking him to. That was one of the reasons why I never worried about leaving him alone. He was a self-sufficient man, and I liked that.

It took a while for us to get Bianca settled down enough to fall asleep in her bed. She finally fell asleep holding her oversized teddy bear while lying in her daddy's arms. They had missed each other so much they didn't want to be separated. Bianca had talked about Michael on the plane for the entire trip home. She wanted to be sure her daddy would be waiting for them once they departed the aircraft. I had assured my daughter several times that her father would be anxiously awaiting our arrival.

After taking a long soothing aromatherapy bubble bath in the Whirlpool jet tub, I wrapped myself in a thick yellow cotton terry cloth robe. Upon reentering my bedroom, the erotic aroma of Black Love incense filled my senses with pleasure. There were tall thick candles burning on both sides of our bed. Sounds from Kem's latest CD titled, "Promise to Love," serenely floated through the air. Kem was one of my preferred male singers, and he really set the mood for romance tonight. With each slow selection, my mind filled with tasty thoughts of what would happened next with Michael.

I was sitting on the Queen Anne bench settee at the end of our bed, smoothing Burberry's scented lotion all over my body when Michael entered the bedroom. He walked over close to me, leaned over, and whispered in my ear.

"Baby, guess what? I have a surprise for you," he said, smiling from ear to ear.

"What is it, Michael? You know how I love surprises!"

"Well, go and check out the guest room before you get changed," he said, nodding his head in that direction.

My feet could hardly carry me fast enough. I moved rapidly down the hallway towards the guest room. Michael trailed behind me trying to keep up with my fast pace. I was filled with throbbing anticipation. I quickly turned the knob, opened the door, and put both hands over my mouth.

"Oh! My goodness! You are amazing, Michael!" I said, turning to give him a kiss. Michael had laid three gorgeous silk lingerie garments from Frederick's of Hollywood across the full sized bed in the guest room. There was a black lace teddy with a high-cut thigh, a white two-piece set with a short camisole and lace panties, and a long fuchsia nightgown with a low v-neck and a flower in the center.

"Oh, Michael, they're all so beautiful. I don't know which one to wear tonight!" I exclaimed.

"Well, it doesn't matter to me. I'm going to take a quick shower and meet you in bed, in ten minutes." He gave me a juicy kiss and chuckled as he walked toward the master bathroom, undressing himself along the way.

I admired his torso as he carried his long sexy body back down the hallway.

Wow! What a man, what a man, what a mighty good man. The lyrics to that song by Salt-N-Pepa played in my head.

I promptly grabbed the black lace teddy and ran towards our bedroom.

Being consumed with pent up passion, my body yearned for pleasure. Changing quickly into the silky lingerie, I pulled the comforter off the bed and lay across the blue satin sheets awaiting my man. I didn't want to feel anything against my smooth frame tonight except for Michael's fervent body. Erotic images of what we were going to do danced through my head while listening to the sound of the water running in the shower.

I could hear Michael singing in that deep throaty Teddy Pendergrass voice he liked to use when serenading me. The words to "Turn Off the Lights" echoed in the background. Whenever he played Teddy, it was time for love and I was ready.

After fifteen years of marriage, I still got excited at the idea of making love to my husband. It had been three weeks since we'd spent our one night of quick charged passion together in Kansas. I missed the spine tingling sex that was often enjoyed between the two of us on romantic nights like this. Naturally, I didn't get to keep on the teddy for long. Michael stripped me out of the sexy garment only minutes after he laid his hard, naked body beside me on the bed. I could smell the scent of Armani, my most desired cologne for men, when he embraced me.

Our tongues did a fast paced tango in and out of each other's mouths. Michael skillfully kissed and massaged every part of my pulsating body, beginning with my hot pink pedicured toes and worked his way up. I giggled as his electric tongue played between my ticklish pinkies, and then enticingly devoured each one individually. As he slowly made his way up my body, I squirmed in pleasure until his moist lips were hovering over mine again.

[97]

"Did you miss me, baby?" Michael asked in a low sexy voice.

"Yes, you better believe I did. I thought of you almost every moment I was gone."

"I don't want you to ever leave again without me. I don't care if it's only for two days, I'm coming with you. You hear?"

"I hear you, Michael."

"I miss you too much when you're gone and I don't want us to be apart anymore. I can't ever live without you this long again."

"I agree with you, baby. No more solo trips for me. Now, give me those tasty lips," I demanded, tickling the hairs on his chest. He fulfilled my wish by covering my mouth completely with his lips. He took my breath away, slowly navigating his tongue down my throat.

After almost an hour of uninterrupted foreplay, I rolled over on my stomach. I intentionally arched my back while easing up on my knees and elbows. Michael skillfully moved so that he was behind me. Sliding his wet tongue up and down the nape of my neck, he gently squeezed my tender breasts as we stroked each other to ecstasy again.

Afterwards, we were both drained and fell backwards onto the bed. Still holding on to my left hand, Michael had my fingers in his mouth and then licked the inside of my palms. Sharing a long passionate kiss, we were ready to fall into a deep coma-like sleep with our body fluids and limbs entwined. We were completely satisfied with each other and slept with smiles glued on our faces until we heard someone knocking at our bedroom window.

"What the...," Michael jumped out of bed and ran to the window.

"What's going on?" I asked, reaching for my robe.

"It's Shelly at the window. I'm going outside to see what's going on," he grumbled, pulling on a pair of pants. I slid on my robe and a pair of panties before following behind him.

I was mortified at the sight of Shelly as Michael ushered her into the living room with two sleepy-looking daughters dressed in their pajamas walking in front of her. Shelly's face was slightly swollen; she had a black eye and a bloody lip. I involuntarily covered my gaped mouth with a hand. I would have screamed, but I didn't want to upset the girls any further. Trying to remain calm, I rapidly assessed the situation before speaking.

"Shelly, you have a seat on the sofa with Michael while I put the girls to bed."

I placed a hand on each of the girls' shoulders, escorting them to the guest room. After making sure they were comfortably settled in for the remainder of the night, I tipped back into the living room.

Michael had his arm around Shelly's shoulders, listening to her sputtering words between the deep sobs. She was trying to apologize for disturbing us in the middle of the night. When I reentered the room, he eased up from the sofa and took a seat in the armless chair facing us. I assumed his position of comforting our neighbor and friend before speaking.

"Shelly, what happened? Did you and Garret get into a fight?"

"Yes—he came over late—and—we got into an argument," she said, shaking as she spoke. I tightened my arm around her shoulder and held her hand. "The next thing I know—he's hitting me—in the face with his fists."

"Do you want us to call the police for you?"

"No, he's gone. Once he realized what he had done to my face, he apologized and then left. We just need a place to stay in case he comes back tonight in another rage looking for us. I parked my car on another street and then we walked back over here."

"Shelly, I'm going to call the police right now. There's no way I'm going to let this fool get away with doing this to you." I was beyond angry. I didn't respect any man who'd put his hands on a woman.

"No, that'll just make him worse when he comes back," she said, pausing as I stared at her. "I probably said something to provoke him, you know."

"No, I don't know. I don't know how a man can hit you like that and you not want to press charges and send him to jail. How in the world could you have provoked him?"

"I—I probably shouldn't have been questioning him at this time of night. I—I should have waited until he was sober in the morning."

"That has nothing to do with it. Nothing gives him the right to hit on you like this."

"You're right, Alese, but we'll work it out tomorrow. Can the girls and I just stay here for the remainder of the night? I promise you, we'll be out of your way first thing in the morning."

"Look, Shelly, I love you like a sister. It pains me to see you going through this. You can do better than this. But of course, you and the girls are welcome to spend the night with us."

"That's right, Shelly," Michael said, standing up. "Make yourself comfortable and don't worry about a thing." He walked towards us and gave me a kiss on the cheek. "I'm going back to bed, sweetheart. If you all need anything just let me know."

"Sure," I said, returning his kiss. "I'm going to sit up with Shelly for a few more minutes."

"That's fine. Take all the time you need. Good night," he whispered, looking at me and then nodding his head at Shelly.

"Good night, Michael. Thank you," Shelly said as he left the room.

After I escorted Shelly to the bathroom and watched her rinse her face with cold water, I helped her to a stool at the kitchen counter. I reached in the refrigerator for a frozen ice pack to place on Shelly's swollen face and bruises. Sensing the embarrassment on my friend's face, I handed her the icy blue package as I rested a hand on her tight shoulder.

Shelly had been dating Garrett Landers for almost three months now and during that short time, I understood their relationship to be somewhat stormy. Even though they had argued in the past, she swore to me that he had never put his hands on her and I made sure Bianca never went over there whenever he was around.

I wanted to stay out of my neighbor's business; however, my neighbor's business had intruded on my solitude. Therefore, I had the right to speak freely.

"Shelly, how long do you intend to take this? Don't you see, every time you all argue, it gets worse, and now he's hitting on you? That scares me, girl."

"Yes, you're right. We started out doing fine, and he seemed to be the perfect gentlemen. We went out to nice restaurants on the weekends, attended several concerts together, and he even took all of us to church a couple of times." She gulped before continuing.

[100]

"He helped me with all the repairs around my house, gave me extra money for the girls, and helped me pay a few bills. But now, he's drinking heavily, stealing money from my purse, and coming to my house whenever he wants to just to pick a fight with me."

"Well, they normally start out smelling good, but roses turn to boo-boo real fast. Didn't you tell me he was a garbage man?"

"Yes, he works for the city in waste management. He's one of the department supervisors, and he makes real good money, but I can't take it anymore. I'm telling him tomorrow it's over and I'm leaving him alone," she said softly, holding the ice pack to her face.

"I really hope you mean every part of what you say. You have to think about your two daughters. You don't want them growing up thinking this is how they're supposed to be treated by a man." I just didn't understand how an educated woman like Shelly would allow herself to be abused by a garbage collector or any other man. Apparently, it wasn't for me to understand, at least not tonight.

"You're right; I just wish I wasn't in love with him so it wouldn't hurt so badly."

"I can't rationalize how you could be in love with someone you've known only three months and who's already mistreating you. I guess I'll never understand," I said, throwing up both hands in despair, not wanting to look at Shelly.

"I know you don't understand. It might sound desperate, but I'm older now and men my age want younger women. It's hard trying to compete with them." Shelly looked up at me through tear-stained eyes. "You're so fortunate to have a good husband. I know I deserve better, but there aren't any good men out there. I mean it, Alese. I've been single for ten years and I haven't dated a decent man in all that time. They're either gay, married, or they have two or three other women on the side."

"I sympathize with you, but I'm not buying that idea. I believe there are still some good single men out there looking for decent woman to date and marry."

"You're definitely wrong if you believe that. You've been married for fifteen years, Alese, and I'm here to tell you that all the good men are gone. You better hold on to your husband, and say thanks for being one of the lucky ones."

[101]

"Well, I do appreciate my husband. But the only thing that matters right now is getting rid of the dog you got coming in and out of your house. Shelly, please take your time and pray before you start dating again. God will send you the right man when He feels you're ready."

"Just let me ask you one more thing, Alese, and then we can go to bed. How did you really know Michael was the one for you?"

"I didn't know if he was the one for me at first. I believed he was a strong Christian man, and we talked about the Bible a lot. We went to church together every Sunday, Bible study on Wednesday evenings, and prayed together every day. Once I got to know his heart, I knew in my heart he was the one for me."

"That is so sweet. I'm going to pray that you two have a lasting relationship. I love to see married people who are happy together. You give me a ray of hope."

"Of course, with him being a tall and handsome brother didn't hurt matters either." Shelly and I laughed together. "But that's a good sign if I can give you a speck of hope. I'm glad about that. Let's go to bed, please, and try to get some sleep. It'll be daylight in a few hours."

"Thanks again for letting us spend the night," Shelly said, standing up. She gave me a tender hug before heading toward the guest room.

I tiptoed into the bedroom, trying not to wake Michael, so I gently closed the door and lightly stepped to my side of the bed.

"Is everything okay?" Michael asked while I was easing into bed beside him.

"I guess so. I just hate she wouldn't let me call the police on that animal. What sane man would hit a woman like that?" I retorted wrathfully.

"Come here, baby," he said, pulling me into his muscular arms. "This is not our fight," he whispered in my ear. "It's up to Shelly to report him to the police. If she let him whip her upside the head every night of the week, that's her decision to make, not ours. I know it's hard to see your friend hurting like this, but I guarantee you, she'll get tired of that real soon."

"I hope and pray you're right, Michael. Do you want to hear Shelly told me a little while ago?"

"Yes, what did she say?"

"She said all of the good men were gone, and I was lucky to have a good husband like you."

"Well, if she stops running around with that dog, she might be able to find a decent man, too. Look, let's just try to get a little bit of sleep. It's morning already."

"You're right. I love you," I said, resting my tired head on Michael's hairy chest.

"I love you, too, baby," he said, tightening his arm around my shoulders.

9

Church Folk

"Michael, get up! Get up, now! We need to get ready for church. I don't like to be late for service."

I was trying to shake Michael awake. It was already nine and we were going to be late if we didn't hurry and get dressed.

"Okay, okay. You go ahead and use the shower. I'll be up in a minute," he responded, turning over and pulling the covers over his head.

"Yes, I bet you will. I must have given you too much loving last night," I teased.

"Well, you can always give me some more this morning."

"I hardly think so because your little baby girl will be running in here any second."

"Get in the shower and let me get a few more minutes of sleep, please," he begged.

I hurried to the second bedroom to check on my overnight guests. Shelly and her two daughters had already left, leaving the bed made up as if no one had ever been there. If I hadn't been so tired from being up with them half the night, I would have probably thought I had dreamed the whole scene. As much as I wanted to believe Shelly, my heart told me this would not be the end of her relationship with Garrett Landers.

I went on to the bathroom, showered, and threw on my housecoat before waking up Bianca. Then, I fixed a quick breakfast of hot buttered toast, oatmeal with brown sugar and raisins before going to wake up Michael again. Fortunately, he was already in the shower and had his finest church clothes laid out across the bed.

It took me awhile to do Bianca's hair. It had gotten so thick, it was hard for me to comb through it good. I wished I could get her a kiddie perm for the sake of convenience, but Michael would definitely object to me doing that. So I dismissed the notion from my mind. He loved natural hair beyond a doubt. He didn't even want to hear jokes about us relaxing or straightening our hair. Of course,

Bianca wasn't making it any easier by not sitting still so I could style her hair.

By the time we made it to the church at ten-forty-five, the lobby was crowded with people waiting to get in to claim the best seats. I was somewhat uncomfortable walking down the center aisle to our seats. I felt like someone was staring holes in the back of my head after we sat in a cushioned pew close to the front of the church. When I turned around, I looked straight in the face of Lisa Bradford. I recognized her because we had met once at an office function. Michael had made it his mission to introduce us and acknowledge me as his wife.

What in the world is she doing here? I know she's not a member of this church.

Michael didn't look back once during the entire service. Every time I glanced at him, he had his eyes on the pastor as she delivered her message about forgiveness. I couldn't help but wonder if he'd seen Lisa earlier and was ignoring her on purpose.

Pastor Karema Wright looked breathtaking standing in the pulpit wearing her custom-made white satin and gold trim robe. The lightweight fabric looked fabulous against her walnut brown skin as she raised both arms out to her sides with her head just tilted upward. Her long silky hair flowed down her back as she prepared to receive the Holy Spirit before bringing the message for today. Closing her round mahogany eyes, she called on the name of Jesus to enter into this place of worship.

The altar was artistically embellished with long stem red and white roses standing in tall ivory vases trimmed in gold around the top. Pastor Wright loved flowers, especially roses. She had roses of various colors delivered to the church every Sunday morning. She probably chose red and white today in honor of Valentine's Day. Maybe that was also the reason the sermon focused on love and forgiveness.

Even though I hadn't spoken to the pastor about my marriage concerns, it felt as though she was preaching directly to me. I had a strange feeling I would need to remember this sermon. I leaned slightly forward and listened closely to the powerful message.

Pastor Wright held the Bible opened in one hand and waved the other. She paced back and forth while preaching to the congregation in a moderately raised voice.

"Church, in closing, I tell you, we should not try to remember the number of times a person has done us wrong. If they ask to be forgiven, we should forgive them. Not only should we say we have forgiven them, but we should also forgive them from our hearts." Pastor Wright closed her Bible and then paused to look around the congregation before continuing in a slightly lower voice.

"Our God is very kind. Though we all have done wrong things, He forgives us. He does not make us pay by taking our lives away from us forever. But this is the lesson we need to learn: God forgives us only if we forgive the people who do us wrong. If you were the person seeking forgiveness, you would want the other person to forgive you, wouldn't you? So, you should do the same for them. Remember, the devil is busy. And you should live your life in such a way that when your feet hit the floor each morning, the devil says, 'Oh, oh, she's up!'"

Laughter filled the church. Several older members in the audience shouted "Amen" and "Thank you, Jesus!"

Finally, she finished with, "This is the message about forgiveness the Lord placed in my heart. This is the message I have presented to you. God bless you today and every day, for the rest of your lives. Let the church say, Amen and Amen."

The crowd rose to their feet and roared with applause as Pastor Wright headed to her seat. The choir members stood when the musicians began to play the beginning chords of the popular upbeat Christian single release, "Better Than That."

Michael was in a great hurry to leave shortly after church was dismissed. We didn't even have an opportunity to speak to Pastor Wright and tell her how much we had enjoyed today's sermon. Michael usually had some comment or question for the pastor that normally led to a brief discussion on the topic she had presented. Today, we didn't do that.

We drove home in silence. Michael didn't even look in my direction. I was too wrapped up in my own thoughts to start a conversation. While Bianca slept in the backseat, I pretended to be asleep in the front passenger seat. I just prayed I'd married a man of integrity and the note was all a lie.

Later on, I was in the master bedroom changing out of my church clothes into a loose fitting denim dress when I heard the telephone ringing. I looked around for Michael. When I realized he was in the bathroom, I snapped up the telephone receiver.

"Hello," I answered. I didn't hear anything on the other end of the telephone so I replaced the receiver. About two minutes later, the telephone rang again. This time, I checked the caller identification system before answering, but it displayed "caller unknown." Normally, I didn't answer calls with that message, but I decided to answer anyway.

"Hello, this is Alese." Again, I didn't hear anything on the telephone line. "Hello, this is Alese Wayne." The caller still didn't answer. I slammed the receiver down and turned around to face Michael coming up behind me by the bed.

"Who was that, baby?"

"Whoever it was wouldn't say anything so I hung up. It's happened twice already."

"Really? Well, if the telephone rings again, let me answer it."

"Sure, be my guest."

#

Less than thirty minutes later, Michael was relaxing in his comfy chair in the den when the telephone rang again. Alese was in the kitchen heating up their dinner plates, so he answered it that time.

"Hello." No one answered. He repeated himself. "Hello, is anyone there?" Suddenly, he heard the sound of a baby crying in the background before he slammed the receiver down. Looking around the room for Alese, hoping she didn't see the anger on his face, Michael closed his eyes and tried to calm down.

"Did they answer that time, Michael?" Alese asked, peeping in from the doorway.

"Ah, no, it's probably some kids playing on the telephone," he responded, avoiding her eyes. "I'll call the telephone company tomorrow if it happens again."

"All right." Alese turned and went back into the kitchen.

\#

About two weeks later, I decided it would be a good time to drive out and make a social call on my pastor and friend since I was still troubled. After turning on the air conditioner in my silver Toyota Sienna minivan, I reached for my chosen Yolanda Adams CD entitled, *Mountain High...Valley Low*. I needed to hear the words to *Open My Heart*.

After pushing in the CD and making a selection, I leaned back in my car seat concentrating on the words flowing from my premium six speakers. Wishing I could carry a tune as well as Yolanda, I settled for humming along with the melody of the song. I listened carefully as one of my favorite female gospel singers asked God to help her make the right choices because she was afraid of disappointing Him. Yolanda was feeling it and singing it as she asked for guidance during a cloudy time in her life. I could certainly identify with the words of the song and took the time to send up my own short prayer. I asked for divine intervention today.

I felt I needed spiritual guidance before making any drastic decisions regarding my marriage. Michael and I were long-term members of the Noah's Ark Missionary Baptist Church where my best friend, Karema Wright, was the full-time pastor. When I was first hired as a teacher at Bayshire Middle School, Karema worked in the main office as a secretary. We were both single Christians who shared similar views on life. We also enjoyed the same type of music and extra-curricular activities. Honestly, we were often mistaken for sisters because we were almost the same age and height and had similar complexions. Karema and I had the same taste in clothes and spent most of our time together on the weekend browsing through the mall or thrift stores searching for bargains.

Karema decided to follow the ministry and started her own church five years ago. Eventually, she chose to leave her secretarial position at the middle school to become a full-time pastor after three years of service. Michael and I were two of the first members to join her church. We talked on the telephone daily and shared almost everything with each other.

Karema passed the sanctuary as I was rising from the altar. Nodding at me, she walked on to her office.

I knocked lightly on the solid oak wood door before entering Karema's tastefully designed office. Karema greeted me with a warm hug. Then, she ushered me to sit on the beige cloth love seat in front of her contemporary style desk.

"Alese, are you well?" she asked, leaning across her desk.

"Yes, Karema, I'm fine. I just have a lot on my mind. I told you about everything that's going on with us. I'm thankful Ma Dear is doing better, but this adoption thing is driving me crazy."

"I understand, Alese. Have you heard any more from your adoption attorney?"

"Yes, we're waiting for Ms. Riley to get back with us regarding a date for the aunt to visit with Bianca. We have to take Bianca to the State agency center and leave her there to meet with the aunt for a two-hour supervised visit. Can you believe that?" I asked, crossing my legs.

"I mean, that is really unbelievable," Karema began. "But listen, I have a feeling in my heart this situation is already worked out for you. Just be patient and wait on the Lord. He didn't bring you this far to leave you," she added.

"I know you're right, you're right, but it's just aggravating having to go through this right now with everything else that's going on in my life," I said, shaking my head.

"When we talked on the telephone yesterday, you said you had something to share with me regarding Michael."

"Yes, I do, and you're not going to believe this," I said, reaching into my black leather Coach purse. "I took some time to pray about this before coming to you."

I pulled out the folded paper I had received in my mailbox two months ago and handed it to my pastor. Karema took her time and carefully studied the note before speaking.

"Did you ask Michael about this?"

"No, I didn't. I'm not ready to do that without having additional information."

"What type of additional information do you need?"

"I don't know. I just need something more than this. I know after seeing Lisa Bradford in church last week, we got three mysterious telephone calls that same afternoon where the caller hung up every time we answered," I responded.

"Do you think it was her calling your house?"

"I really don't know. I could feel her staring at me in church and then, when the telephone rang that same afternoon, I got that same strange feeling. I want to trust Michael, but I just don't know what to think."

"Well, my advice to you, Alese, is to let it go. If you love and trust your husband the way I know you do, let it go. He's never given you any reason to distrust him. Don't do anything behind his back that might damage your relationship in the long run," she said, sounding more like a pastor than a friend.

"I'm sorry, Karema, but it's not that easy. I have to find out who sent this note and why."

"I tell you what. People do things every day for different reasons, Alese. I don't know why someone would send you a note like this. It may be true and it may not be true. But if you keep looking, you may not be happy with what you find," Karema stated sharply.

"I would rather know than to walk around looking like a blind fool."

"You need to think about what you plan to do either way it goes. There's no point of investigating if you don't have a plan for handling what might be the truth."

"I can't think like that right now. I just need to know if it's true before I can entertain what to do about it."

"Well, let's just pray about this and ask God to send us a sign from above," Karema said optimistically, touching my hand. We bowed our heads and began to pray.

A feeling of peace came over me after leaving Karema's office. We had prayed the Twenty-third Psalm together, and I felt my burdens had been lifted from my shoulders. I decided to let go and let God direct my steps. I had a good man who loved me and he proved that every day by the loving ways he communicated with me. Michael supported me in all the endeavors and failed businesses I had undertaken over the years. He loved my family like they were his own and treated them both the same. Karema was right--I had no reason to distrust Michael or suspect him of infidelity. In fact, I couldn't ask for a better, kinder, or more loving husband. So right then and there, I decided to let all my suspicions go.

10

Is She or Isn't She?

Michael had carefully avoided Lisa since their encounter in the parking lot despite her claims of being pregnant by him. He was wise enough to know that if she was really pregnant, she would be showing by now and complaining about morning sickness. They had slept together almost four months ago and he couldn't see any sign of a bulging belly on her size six frame. He had also checked her personnel records and discovered she hadn't missed any days from work within the last four months; in fact, she hadn't even been late so much as one time within that timeframe. Feeling it was time for them to finally have a talk regarding her so-called condition, he picked up his office telephone, dialed Lisa's extension, and waited for her to answer.

"Good morning, this is Lisa Bradford," she answered cheerfully.

"Hi, Lisa, this is Michael. I think it's time for us to talk," he said.

"Michael! It's about time you called me."

"Yes, I know. I just needed some time to think about our situation, but I'm ready to talk if you are."

"Of course, I'm ready to talk. I've been waiting for you to call me."

"Well, I'm ready to talk. How soon can you meet with me?"

"There's no time like the present. Let's meet at my place after work."

"That's fine with me. At least we'll have some privacy. I don't want to take a chance on talking about something like this in public."

"I was thinking the same thing. I'll go home directly after work and meet you there around five-thirty this evening."

"I'll be there. Bye, Lisa."

"Michael!" she called.

"Yes, I'm still here."

"I'm glad you called me today. I look forward to seeing you this evening."

"Me, too, Lisa," he replied, hanging up the telephone.

Needless to say, that really made Lisa's day. She spent the rest of the afternoon singing to herself as she flipped through the files on her desk. Every five minutes she would look up at the clock hoping an hour had passed. By four-thirty, she couldn't wait another second. She grabbed her Prada purse and headed for her office door.

Arriving promptly at Lisa's house at five-thirty, Michael reached across the seat of his automobile and picked up the red and gold gift wrapped box he had purchased for Lisa. He hurried to her front door and pressed the doorbell. He was anxious to see her.

Lisa was watching Michael as he pulled up into her driveway and parked behind her vehicle. Her heart was pounding from the excitement of finally being alone in her duplex with him again. When she saw him carrying a beautifully wrapped present, romantic thoughts began to cloud her mind.

I see he's finally come to his senses. It's about time he started appreciating me.

"Hi, Michael," Lisa answered as soon as she opened the front door. "Please, come on in. I've been waiting for you."

"You have? I'm not late, am I?" he asked.

"Oh, no, you're definitely not late. I was so excited about seeing you I came home a little early. Is that for me?" she asked, ogling the box in his hand.

"Yes, it's for you, but I have to ask you a few questions before you open it."

"Sure, Michael. Why don't you have a seat over there and we can talk?" She motioned with her hand towards the sofa. Michael followed her into the room and took a seat on the end of the couch as Lisa sat down beside him. "What is it you need to know?"

"I want to know why you aren't showing yet. I mean—you should be about four months pregnant, according to my calculations." He raised his eyebrows, smoothing his hand over his mouth.

"Well, Michael, some women don't start to show until they're much farther along. My mother said she didn't show with me until she was over six months pregnant."

"I see, and why haven't you had any morning sickness?"

[113]

Lisa was a little taken aback by that question. "I'm usually sick at night. I haven't had much morning sickness. Why are you asking me these questions, Michael?"

"No particular reason. I want you to open your present now." He handed the box to Lisa.

"Thank you, Michael." She gushed with anticipation. Lisa tore into the box, discarding the paper on the floor. Michael watched her facial expression carefully; he wanted to see her reaction when she realized what the gift was.

After opening the box, all of the excitement Lisa had felt quickly dissipated and she narrowed her eyes at Michael. "Is this a gag gift, Michael?"

"No, Lisa, it's not a gag gift. It's a First Response Pregnancy Kit."

"And what the hell do you expect me to do with this?"

"I want you to take the pregnancy test so I can know, right now, whether you're pregnant or not."

"You're out of your mind. I've already taken a test at the doctor's office. Why should I take another test?"

"I told you—I want to know for sure you're pregnant."

"Don't you realize these things aren't accurate? You have to have a test from the doctor to confirm a pregnancy."

"Lisa, if you're four months pregnant, there shouldn't be a problem with you taking the test. Just go in there and pee on the stick."

She twisted her mouth, giving him a nasty look.

"Pee on the damn stick, Lisa!" he demanded.

Lisa grabbed the package and stomped into the bathroom. She closed the door, turned on the water faucet, and sat on the toilet to think for a few minutes. Since Michael wasn't a fool or one to be played with, she made a quick decision.

Returning to the living room, she faced Michael. Lisa threw the test on the sofa beside him before opening her mouth to speak.

"You win, Michael. I confess. I'm not pregnant. You made me so angry that night when you wouldn't talk to me in the parking lot, I just said that out of frustration to get your attention."

"That's just what I thought, you were playing a game all along."
He stood up, heading towards the front door.

"How did you really know, Michael? I mean, you didn't use a condom," she said, walking behind him.

"I know you never wanted to have kids. You used to tell me that all the time whenever the subject came up. I remember how careful you were with the birth control, and even though I should have worn a condom, I didn't think you would risk getting pregnant by a married man."

"I've changed for real. I would be willing to have children with you right now. I can give you the child you're yearning for. I can give you your own flesh and blood, Michael."

"Oh, is that what this is about? You think I would leave my wife and daughter just because you can give me a baby?" He turned to face Lisa.

"That's exactly what I think. You deserve to have your own child, and I'm willing to do that for you because I love you. We can make a baby right now if you want," she said, reaching out to Michael.

He grabbed her hands before she could touch him and said, "I love my wife, and I will stay with her even if we never have a child together. I love Bianca as much as I could ever love any child, and I'm sure of that."

"That's what you're saying now, but if I'd really been pregnant, you'd be singing a different tune."

"Think whatever you want. I just hope you're through playing games. Are you through playing games, Lisa?"

"Yes, Michael, I'm through with you, Lover Boy. Go on back to your pitiful wife and leave me the hell alone. I hope you and Mrs. Can't Get Pregnant have a wonderful life with your adopted child."

"You're lucky I know how to control my temper, but I know what you're trying to do, and it's not working today. I won't give in to the devil this time."

"Who are you calling a devil? Are you calling me a devil?" she asked, pointing to herself.

"Well, if the shoe fits, wear it."

[115]

Lisa flew into a rage, searching the room for something to throw at Michael as he headed towards the exit again. He slipped out just in time to avoid the telephone book landing against the back of the door with a loud thud.

"Don't call my house anymore playing on the telephone! Just stay away from me and my family!" He yelled through the closed door. Michael jumped into his car, turned on the ignition, and sped away.

#

Hating himself even more after having that unpleasant encounter with Lisa, Michael wasn't ready to go home and face Alese just yet. It was eating him up inside and out trying to hide his guilt from his trusting wife. He didn't know how much longer he would be able to look her in the eyes and not confess to his one night stand with Lisa. Considering he wasn't typically a drinking man, he needed to do something to calm his nerves.

Michael had been sweating bullets prior to arriving at Lisa's place, but he had played it cool with her, and gambled on confronting her in the manner that he did. However, he just wasn't able to live with that hanging over his head any longer and decided to force Lisa's hand today. It was time for her to put up or shut up because he couldn't live any longer with the agony of not knowing whether or not she was really pregnant. Hopefully, this would be the end of her conniving ways since he made it clear that he was never ever leaving his wife for any reason. Even if she had been pregnant, he would never have divorced Alese to be with her and the baby.

Thinking hard about the possible consequences of his sinful actions, Michael thanked God for sparing him the embarrassment of impregnating a woman outside of his marriage.

Thank you, Jesus. I promise you nothing like this will ever happen to me again. Please forgive me for breaking one of the Ten Commandments by committing adultery.

Pulling out his cell phone, Michael dialed Marty's private line at the office, imagining he was still at work. He needed to share this with someone human to get it completely out of his system. Marty picked up on the second ring.

"Hello, Mike, where are you?"

"I'm riding around in my car right now. I really need to talk to you, man. Can you meet me somewhere?"

"Sure, where would you like to meet?" Marty asked.

"Anywhere—you name a place, and I'll meet you there."

"Let's meet at the Chauffeur's Bar and Lounge on Arlington Expressway. I sometimes stop by there to have a drink on my way home from work. I can meet you there in about thirty minutes; I'm almost done here for the evening."

"Good— I'll probably be there waiting on you, Marty."

"See you soon."

Michael hung up the phone. Turning around on University Boulevard, he headed towards Arlington Expressway as he remembered his long-term friendship with Marty Carlisle. They had met one cloudy afternoon when Michael was rushing to the cafeteria to get dinner near closing time. In his haste, he bumped into another young student right at the door of the student union. Michael readily apologized as they entered the building together. After going through the line and getting his plate, Mike took a seat at the table with Marty and properly introduced himself. They had a lot in common even though physically, they were nothing alike. Marty was much shorter, smaller, and darker than Michael, but they quickly became best friends. Neither one of them had any family in Jacksonville so they came to depend on each other.

Marty didn't play any sports, but they were both sports fanatics. The majority of their time spent together was either watching sports in their dorm rooms or attending the many sporting events hosted on campus. Marty was his biggest basketball fan as Michael led his team through several winning seasons. Marty seldom missed a game whether they were playing at home or away; he would stay wherever the team resided for the night.

Throughout their college careers, they maintained a strong friendship. Marty had even been home with Michael several times to visit his family in Tampa. Michael's father, Jeremiah, often teased him about adopting Marty as his son since they were as close as brothers. Michael was happy to know Marty admired Jeremiah and thought of him as the father he never had.

Michael suddenly realized he had made it to the Chauffeurs Bar and Lounge in less than twenty minutes. He initially planned to remain in his car and listen to the smooth jazz station on the radio, but decided to go inside to have a cool drink while he waited on his friend.

Taking a booth seat inside the lounge area, Michael ordered a ginger ale soda with extra ice. He didn't need to add consuming alcohol to his list of problems this evening. Before his drink arrived, Marty swaggered through the glass door looking for Michael.

"How you doing, man?" Marty asked, sliding in the booth across from Michael.

"I've seen better days," he replied.

"What would you like to drink?" the waitress asked as soon as Marty sat down.

"I'll have a double shot of vodka straight with no ice."

"That's a pretty stiff drink," Michael commented. "You must have something heavy on your mind, too."

"Nah, I've just had a rough day, that's all. But what's on your mind? You sounded pretty stressed out when you called me earlier."

"I just wanted to give you an update on this Lisa situation."

"Why, did something happen recently that I need to know about?"

"Well, I didn't tell you this before, but about a month ago Lisa approached me in the parking lot when I was leaving work late one evening while Alese was in Kansas. She tried to talk me into taking her out to dinner but when I refused to do that, she flew into a rage and told me she was pregnant."

"You've been keeping this from me for a whole month? I don't believe this, Mike."

"Man, I was too scared to tell a single soul about that. I was too afraid of the rumor mill getting wind of that to tell anybody or even discuss it with anybody. I've just been trying to live with it on my own until I discovered whether or not she was pregnant."

"Ah, what did you find out?"

At that moment, the waitress appeared with their drinks on a tray.

"Excuse me, gentlemen, I have your drinks for you," she stated, placing the glasses on the table. They both thanked the lady for their drinks and then continued talking.

"I know for sure that she's not pregnant, and she tried to play me big time."

"How did you learn she's definitely not going to have a baby?"

"I called her this morning and arranged to meet with her at her house after work. When I got there, I gave her this gorgeously wrapped present. At first, she was all excited thinking that I had bought her something nice and expensive. When she opened the box, it contained a home pregnancy test kit. Then, I demanded she take the test right there."

"What? How did she react to that?"

"Oh, she was beyond mad. But you can guess that she didn't pass the test, can't you? First, she went in the bathroom pretending to take the test. Then, a few seconds later, she came out. She threw it at me and confessed to lying about the whole thing."

"Man, that woman is psycho. I don't know how you ever got involved with her. I wish we had seen all of this coming when we first hired her trifling ass."

"I know that's right. I made my position clear to her this evening and hopefully, she's through playing games with me."

"I don't know, Mike. Women like that find it hard to give up on a man. I certainly wish there was some way for us to get her out of our company. Somebody that vengeful is not going to just leave quietly."

"Well, I know Alese is going to be crushed when I tell her about all of this."

"What are you talking about? I know you're not still thinking again about confessing to Alese after having a pregnancy scare."

"Oh, yes, I am. That's exactly why I'm going to confess to my wife. This last month has been sheer torture. The only way for me to ever have a peaceful night's sleep is to bear my soul to Alese right away and beg for her forgiveness."

"Well, it's your funeral, man. Honestly, I hope she forgives you. If it's bothering you that much, it might be best if you confessed to her after all. She'll be mad for a while, but eventually, she might come around if you're persistent with her."

"I'm hoping she won't leave me if I confess and throw myself at her mercy. Anyway, it's a chance I'm willing to take. I've prayed about it and I don't see myself having any peace until my wife knows the whole story and hears it from me."

"If that's what you've made up your mind to do. When are you planning to tell her?"

"That's what I haven't decided yet. It'll have to be perfect timing, though."

"You got that right. It'll have to be damn perfect timing. Look, I hate to leave you hanging, but I need to get home. Tina has been complaining about me coming home late every night, so we need to have one of those talks," Marty chuckled.

"I know what you mean—it's time for one of those marriage talks, right?"

"Yeah, buddy. But after listening to you, I'm not dreading my talk with Tina tonight as much as I was before."

"Very funny, Marty. Thanks for listening to me."

"It's no problem—anytime. I'll see you at work tomorrow," he said, shaking hands with Michael. Marty walked outside into the clear evening air, thinking that his friend's marriage was doomed.

11

Confrontation

It was such a lovely day outside. I decided to get a take-out lunch from China Garden Buffet. Michael and I loved oriental food. We used to order out for Chinese at least once a week, but it had been a while since we had done that. I ordered sweet and sour chicken with shrimp fried rice and pork egg rolls. I grabbed plenty of duck sauce because I loved that stuff on my egg rolls.

There was so much food in the take-out container I thought it would be great to surprise Michael and share my lunch with him. I called Tracy to make sure he was in his office before making the trip. Of course, Tracy assured me Michael was there and she would make it her duty to see that he remained there until I arrived with lunch.

I pulled the minivan into the parking space closest to the front entrance door. I was struggling to balance the food in my hands when I glanced up and saw a white convertible Corvette parked several cars over from me. I could tell from a distance it had a purple and gold JSU alumni tag, but I wasn't close enough to read the license plate number. My heart skipped a beat and I could hear myself breathing while opening the door to the reception area.

"Hi, Tracy. Girl, you look great today. I like that hairstyle on you," I said. I loved to compliment Tracy because she always looked so professional, but today, I also had a hidden agenda.

"Thank you, Mrs. Wayne. You look good today yourself," she replied, her eyes sweeping over me from top to bottom.

"Tracy, I know you're familiar with everybody who works here. Aren't you?"

"Why, yes, I think I do," Tracy stated with confidence.

"Well, ah, can you tell me who's driving that new white convertible Corvette in the parking lot? I might have seen someone nick that car on my way in and I just wanted to let the owner know. Doesn't that car belong to Lisa Bradford from the design department?" I asked innocently while trying to remain cool.

"Oh! My goodness! I don't know who owns that car, Mrs. Wayne. It must be one of the visiting clients here for a meeting. Ms. Bradford drives a red convertible Mustang."

"Well, then, please don't worry about it." I tried to play it off. "They'll see it soon enough. Thanks anyway." I was content upon learning the car did not belong to Lisa or anyone else employed at the firm. I dismissed the notion of Michael having another woman at work and enjoyed my lunch. Besides, Shelly wasn't even sure about the make of the car she'd seen anyway. There had to be over a thousand white convertibles in Jacksonville and I couldn't get suspicious every time I saw one.

We had an enjoyable lunch together. He showed me how much he appreciated me coming in to share my lunch with him by placing soft kisses all over my face. We really needed to do things like that more often. I think he noticed that I seemed to be a little preoccupied with something, but he probably figured it was just concern for Ma Dear and this adoption thing hanging over our heads. I could tell something was bothering him, too. Several times during lunch, it seemed like he wanted to tell me something but kept changing his mind. But then again, maybe I was just being paranoid.

As I was leaving Michael's office, I noticed Tracy was not at her desk and the white Corvette was gone, too.

"Oh, well."

#

It was almost two o'clock and I was going to be late for my hair appointment with Tina at *the Braids and Locks Hair Shop*. I didn't want to miss the appointment because it was difficult to get one scheduled. I usually tightened my own locks, but I wanted to be pampered today and get a new hairstyle. It had been over two months since I had seen the inside of a hair salon and I was looking forward to the feminine experience. I was also looking forward to seeing Tina today because we had not seen each other or talked since the Christmas holidays and it was already the first week of March.

Tina and I became friends through our husbands' business partnership. We liked each other from the start and got along great. Tina had been a natural hairstylist for almost the entire time we had known each other. She had started my locks about three years ago and now they were at my shoulders.

Tina was outgoing, just like Marty, and easy to get along with. She was the life of every party and the last person to leave any social gathering. Tina had a mouth made for gossiping, like most hairdressers, and she talked a lot of trash. There was always an array of people in her shop getting outlandish braid styles or getting their locks tightened up for some special event. Tina changed her braids every month to a different style with colored hair. She was the best natural hairstylist in town and had the customer base to prove it. Her styles were featured in all the popular braid magazines including, *Braids & Beauty* and *Braids & More*.

"Tina, the traffic was terrible. I didn't think I would make it in time," I said, catching my breath.

"Girl, you're fine. Come on back and let me wash your hair," Tina said, turning for me to follow her in the back to the wash basins.

"Yes, goodness, that's my favored part of the salon experience. How are you, Tina?" I asked, smiling and climbing into my seat.

"Well, I could complain, but I won't. Marty told me you were out of town again. I would have called you if I had known you were back. How is your mother?" Tina asked, reaching for the hair shampoo.

"She's much better, thank you. I still call her almost every day just to hear her voice."

"Oh, that's great. I know you must really worry about her, especially since you're so far away."

"Yes, I do. That's the hardest part about having your family so far away from you like that," I responded before closing my eyes to enjoy the luxuriousness of the lathering shampoo. I waited patiently while Tina rinsed the last few traces of shampoo from my hair, wrapped it in a towel, and sat me upright before I spoke again. "It's pretty busy in here, Tina," I commented, observing that almost every chair in the place was taken. I found a vacant chair, crossed my legs, and picked up a magazine before sarcastically asking, "How's business?"

"Hey, you see I have all I can handle. Marty has been complaining about me spending so much time at the shop lately. But

I got to make that paper while I can. Natural hairstyles are on the rise now. Plus, I have to get ready for that natural hair show they're having next month in Atlanta," Tina said, laughing and glancing around the shop at customers entering and leaving. "But he'll be fine," Tina continued. "I took a break and went by to visit him during lunch today for the first time in ages."

"Well, I went to see Michael for lunch today, too. We had Chinese food."

"Hi, Alese, we miss you at school." I looked up from the current copy of Ebony magazine I was holding to see Elaine Jackson, my co-worker and an English teacher, smiling down at me.

"Hello, Elaine. I miss you all, too. Tell me, how are things at Bayshire Middle School?"

"Well, everything is about the same," Elaine sighed. "Ms. Fulton has all your classes."

"That's great. She's a good instructor."

"She's smart, but the kids really miss you, and they ask about you all the time."

"That's good to hear. I appreciate you telling me that." I smiled.

"Thanks, Tina. I'll see you next time." Elaine paid the receptionist at the counter and waved good-bye to us before she walked out the door.

"Pardon me, Tina, but I want to dreadlock my daughter's hair. I just can't take doing her hair everyday anymore," one of her customers complained.

"You may not know this, but you still have to groom her hair every day even if you lock it."

"What? I'm trying to find something that I don't have to do nothing to every day."

"Well, locks are not the answer. It takes a long time to lock, and the hair has to be maintained between monthly visits to the salon."

"You mean she still has to come to the salon for dreadlocks? I didn't know that," she said, pulling her daughter away.

"Girl, do you believe that?" Tina asked, shaking her head and laughing.

"No, I don't. She just wants something where she won't have to do anything to that child's hair ever again. Doesn't she see that I have locks?"

"Yeah, but yours probably look better than the unkempt ones she's used to seeing. Yours are so pretty and neat, they don't really look like locks."

"Well, thanks to you, Tina," I replied. "Why do people call them dreadlocks? There is nothing dreadful about them."

"Yeah, I know that's right. They are beautiful African locks."

It didn't take Tina long to have my hair tightened and twisted up in a lovely style. She touched up my caramel colored locks and trimmed the ends neatly before styling my hair. Tina had the top section going up into a twisted topknot and the back section hung down to my shoulders. I admired Tina's work in the mirror before leaving in a happy mood.

I was fumbling with the keys trying to open the door of my minivan when I spotted a white convertible Corvette parked on the side of the hair shop. It looked exactly like the car I had seen earlier at M & M, Inc. I was in such a rush when I entered the shop, I probably overlooked it. But sure enough when I moved closer, it had purple and gold JSU alumni plates that read, "MAR TIN." She recalled the owner.

"I don't believe this," I mumbled. "I can't believe that after all this time … All this time and Tina knew about Michael and Lisa Bradford and didn't tell me. Why didn't she just come to me as a girlfriend and say something? I figured we were closer than that. I remembered that was the license plate Tina had on her old Acura RL. Tina thought it was so cute to have a personalized license plate with a portion of Marty's name and hers.

Michael had told me that Tina had bought a new vehicle near the end of the year, but I didn't remember him saying it was a Corvette. "Well, it's time for Tina and me to play catch up." I suppressed the urge to storm back into the shop to confront Tina with tears rolling down my cheeks. On the drive home, I figured it would be better to question Tina in a more private setting, away from the prying eyes of her gossipy customers. The last thing I needed was for my business to be spread all over her packed salon.

#

The next day, I called and invited Tina to my house for lunch. Fathoming I would have to bribe Tina with food, I promised to make curry chicken salad on sliced pumpernickel bread and a fresh strawberry cheesecake. Tina loved good food and I recollected her two favorites. It took me most of the morning to prepare the dishes, but it would be worth it if Tina came through with the information I wanted. It didn't take much coercion for her to agree to meet me for a late lunch, and Tina assured me that she would be there soon after she completed her twelve o'clock appointment.

Tina arrived shortly before two o'clock wearing a Donna Karan tangerine pants suit and carrying her new brown Michael Kors purse from her weekend excursion in Atlanta. Tina loved the finer things in life and lived by designer wear for herself, Marty, and her boys. She also employed a manicurist in her shop, so she kept her nails and toes done. We were sitting at the granite kitchen counter savoring our meal and drinking lemonade when I decided to make my move.

"Tina, I know you're the one who sent me the note about Michael and Lisa," I said, waiting for a reaction.

"How did you find out?" Tina asked, dropping her head.

"Well, my neighbor saw your car New Year's Day when you left the note. Anyway, that's not important. What's important is what you know. And you better tell me everything right now," I said firmly, placing my hands on my hips.

"Look, Alese," she began sadly, dropping her hands at her sides. "I heard Marty and Michael talking at my house one night before Christmas. They must have thought I had gone to bed, but I got up to use the bathroom and heard them talking in the game room. Marty asked Mike why didn't he just fire Lisa and be done with it. That's when Mike told him he had slept with Lisa one night when you were out of town. He said she might get angry and sue him for sexual harassment or something if he fired her or tried to demote her from the position."

"Tina, why didn't you just come to me and tell me this before?"

"I wanted to, but I didn't know how to approach you."

"But, Tina, we're friends. You know me better than that."

"Girl, please! I know women don't want to hear nothing from another woman about their man cheating." Tina accentuated each word as she spoke, moving her head from side to side. "I presumed you would take the note seriously and track me down sooner or later, if you really wanted to know," Tina said, averting my stare.

I felt my heart muscles tightening, head pounding, ears ringing, and my pulse rising. I touched my chest with both hands. Now, I understood how Ma Dear felt when she was having a heart attack. It was the most painful and scariest feeling in the world.

I had just received solid confirmation that my husband of fifteen years was cheating on me with Lisa Bradford. My throat went desert dry; I was absolutely speechless. I stood to get a glass of water, but my knees were too weak to help me out.

"Oh! Alese!" Tina shouted.

She stretched her arms out to keep me from falling. The room was spinning, I slipped through Tina's arms and slid down to the floor on both knees, threw my head back, and released a harrowing sound.

"No! No!" I screamed loudly but didn't hear a word.

I felt the warm tears streaming down my face uncontrollably. I was holding Tina's hands and searching her face for comfort. Tina knelt down in front of me, wrapped her arms around my trembling body and held me tightly. We remained on the floor for several minutes before Tina helped me to the sofa in the den. She stayed with me until I calmed down enough to go pick up Bianca from pre-school.

"Tina, you can go back to work now. You shouldn't be away from your shop for so long. I'll be fine," I stated, standing up from the sofa and smoothing my hands down my clothes.

"Alese, there is no way I'm leaving you in this condition."

"No, really. I have to go pick up Bianca in a few minutes and I'll be all right."

"What do you plan on doing about this?"

"Tina, if I knew that I would probably feel a little bit better than I do. But the truth is, I think I'm going to stay here tonight and confront my husband. Hopefully, he will tell me the truth. Not that it's going to make a great deal of difference."

"I know that's right," Tina interjected.

"Right now, I need to get cleaned up and collect my child."

"Do you want me to get her and bring her home for you?"

"No, no. That's my responsibility. Please, Tina, just go on back to work, and I'll call you later if I need anything," I insisted.

"Alese, please don't do anything crazy."

"Tina, I can't make any promises because I'm one mad black woman today."

"I know you're angry and beyond upset. But please don't do anything outrageous. He sounded really pitiful the night I heard him talking to Marty. It's not like he was bragging about it or anything. He just sounded regretful."

"You think I should stay with him after this, Tina?"

"I'm not telling you to stay with him. I'm telling you to listen and hear him out before you go off on him."

"Oh yes, I intend to listen, just like Mrs. Bobbitt listened to her cheating husband and then cut his thing off when he went to sleep."

#

Michael was late getting home. He had tried to call me at the house all afternoon to no avail. I also didn't answer my cell phone, which was unusual. I had all the overhead lights out in the house. Usually, I left a lamp on in the hallway for Michael whenever he was this late coming home, but not tonight. I was sitting at the table sniffling in the dimly lit kitchen area.

"Alese, baby, is everything all right? Where's Bianca?" he asked, creeping into the kitchen area, looking around for his daughter.

I was sobbing lightly into a paper towel. When I looked up at him through watery eyes, he showcased a worried expression. I wiped my face and stared coldly at Michael before replying, "Bianca is spending the night next door with Shelly and the girls."

"Okay, Garrett's not over there, is he?"

"No, I made sure of that."

"Well, what's wrong? Why are you crying?" Michael asked, sounding fearful and concerned about me. I could hear his heart beating outside of his chest.

[128]

"I know you screwed Lisa Bradford."

I spoke clearly, glaring up at his startled expression.

"What—what did you say?" Michael gasped. His head snapped back like he'd been slapped across the face. Undeniable fear flashed in his eyes.

"You heard me! I know you screwed Lisa Bradford, you dirty bastard!" I said disgustedly.

"Baby, baby," he pleaded. "Hold on, please. Hold on for just a minute, please."

"Oh, are you going to lie to me Michael and say it didn't happen?"

"Can we talk about this, please?"

"What is there to talk about Michael? Did you sleep with Lisa Bradford while I was away in Kansas or not? Tell me how many times you slept with her!" I demanded, standing up, clenching an ice pick in my right hand.

"Whoa! Baby, wait! Put that thing down!" Michael stepped back fast, stumbling over his own feet.

"Don't tell me what to do, Michael! I should stab you in your damn heart!" I glared at him with reddish eyes like I was the devil holding a pitchfork. Some type of spirit came over me and I felt like one of those murdering women from the "Snapped" television show.

"It was one time! I swear! It was one time only! Now put the pick down, please, and talk to me," he said, holding up both hands, preparing to defend himself.

"You expect me to believe that. You really expect me to believe that?" I asked, pointing the pick towards him. I could barely recognize his face through my colossal tears.

"Baby, it's not that simple. Please, let me explain. Just listen to me, please," he said, inching closer, keeping his eyes on the ice pick.

I couldn't fight the nasty bile rising in my throat any longer. Tossing the ice pick on the tile floor, I grabbed my stomach with both hands. I ran to the bathroom, dropped to my knees, and placed my face over the toilet bowl. I heaved so hard it felt like both my intestines were spilling out. My throat and stomach felt completely raw by the time I'd finished regurgitating.

Michael followed me into the master bathroom, staring down at me from the doorway as I flushed the toilet. I stared up at him, showing a swollen wet face. Slowly, I rose on wobbly legs, steadying myself against the bathroom counter.

"Michael, I just need to hear the truth. Just tell me the truth. I can handle the truth," I said, staggering towards our bed.

"Alese, I love you. You know I love you with all my heart—I want to be a man about this. I want to be a real man about this. You deserve to know the truth. I'll tell you everything, if you just promise not to leave me." Michael sat down beside me on the bed, placing his arm around over my shoulder while he continued to speak. "I mean it, Alese. I will tell you everything, but you have to promise not to leave me. Alese, do you promise not to leave me?" he pleaded.

"Yes, Michael," I spoke weakly. "I promise not to leave, if you promise what you're about to say is the truth." Those were the words from my mouth, not from my heart.

"Baby, I told you. I want to be a man about this. I promise, I'll tell you the truth about this. I just don't want to lose you, I— I can't function without this family."

"Michael, just tell me what happened, please."

"Baby, this happened back in November. I swear on my mother's grave, it only happened one time."

Michael relayed the details surrounding the night he had sexual intercourse with Lisa at her place. He was crying and shaking the entire time he spoke with his body pressed closely against mine. Michael tightened his arms around me while slowly confessing his sin. I felt his pain, but mine was much greater than his.

I listened in silence, picturing my husband in the arms of another woman. My heart was breaking for us because I couldn't keep my promise tonight. My head was aching in pain. I was finding it difficult to concentrate on Michael's words, but I had to hear everything.

Michael said, "I'm so relieved that I've finally confessed everything to you, baby. Now, there aren't any secrets between us, and we can work on repairing the damage I've done to our marriage. You don't know how many times I've wanted to tell you, but I was so afraid of you leaving me. I know you would never break your

[130]

promise by leaving me because you always keep your word. And since you're woman enough to stay with me, I promise to be man enough to never let this happen again."

I nodded like I agreed with him. He held me close as we drifted off to sleep on top of the covers.

Waking up a couple of hours later, I felt miserable, and I couldn't get back to sleep. Rolling over on my side, I remembered the promise I had made to my husband. I felt miserable about not being able to keep my word to Michael. While he snored soundly behind me, I slid out of our bed for the last time.

#

Michael awakened before daylight, startled from a nightmare. He turned towards Alese's side of the bed, extending his hand all the way to the other side to feel for her. She wasn't there. Michael leaped out of bed, running through the house calling her name.

"Alese! Alese! Baby, where are you?" he asked, rubbing his eyes.

He searched every room in the house, but she wasn't there. He looked in the garage and her car was gone. He came inside to check the refrigerator door for a message. That's normally where they left notes for each other when they had to run errands. Michael had a feeling Alese was not out running errands today, so he headed back to the bedroom to check the closet, then her dresser drawers. He checked the bathroom, too. Alese's overnight bag was missing from the closet, her underwear drawer was empty, and most of her toiletries were missing from the bathroom vanity. She had broken her promise to him and left sometime during the night. His worst nightmare had become reality.

Michael threw himself back on the bed, pondering what to do next. Rubbing his aching chest, he felt like Alese had really forced the sharp ice pick through the center of his heart and pulled it out, hoping he'd bleed to death. How could he have slept so hard that he didn't even know she was gone? How did she pull that one off without him waking up? He usually woke up at the least little sound, especially since Bianca came into their lives as a baby. He was the first one up when she cried out during the night.

Curling up on the bed in tears, Michael wondered where his family could be. Should he call her friends and try to track her down and beg her to come home? Should he wait a day or so and give her some time to calm down? Or should he just go on to work and pretend like his personal life was still intact and wait for her to call him?

Man, knowing Alese, she could be anywhere. She's expecting me to come after her if she stays in town, so she's probably in Kansas or somewhere by now.

He wouldn't dare call her family in Wichita because they would be truly upset if she wasn't there. Michael definitely didn't want to alert her family to their marital problems, if they didn't already know. He decided to stay there in the bed and cry his heart out all day long.

#

It was a glorious spring-like day to have lunch outside. I sat on the patio waiting for my lunch partner to arrive as I viewed the menu for the Flamingo's Bar & Grill. I was wearing a casual camel pants suit with beige and camel trimmed mules. I was still wearing my brown rimless sunglasses when I motioned for the waitress. I hoped I wouldn't see any familiar faces and that the staff would not notice my swollen eyes underneath the shades. We had planned an early lunch so there were hardly any people there yet.

I was the only one on the patio accept for the Team City Group, about six people, who seemed to be having some type of meeting on the far end. They all wore khaki pants and white polo shirts with the organization's logo on the front.

I leaned back in my seat to enjoy the sunshiny day. I was there on a serious mission. I wasn't interested in eating anything; I was there strictly for the conversation, and I was ready to get that over with. Just as I released a weighted sigh, I heard her voice.

"Hello, Alese," Lisa said, pulling out a chair and sitting down beside me.

"Hi, Lisa," I responded. It took all of the restraint within me not to pull every inch of her blonde weave out. "I'm glad you could make it. I was beginning to think you had stood me up."

"Oh, no. I wouldn't dare do that. However, I am curious regarding why you asked me out to lunch today."

"Lisa, I'm not here to be coy with you," I began. "I'll put all my cards on the table right now. Last night, my husband and I had a conversation about you. Michael confessed to me about his affair with you, or should I say, his one night stand with you." I glared at Lisa as I spoke.

"Is that what he told you, that it was a one night stand?" Lisa looked bemused.

"That's exactly what he said it was. What do you have to say about it?"

"I say if you believe that, you're a damn fool."

"Excuse me, ladies. Miss, may I get you something to drink?" the waitress asked Lisa.

"Ah, yes. I'll take a glass of merlot, please," she responded.

"I'll just have water with lemon," I added. "Thank you."

"I'll be back in a minute with your drinks and I can take your orders at that time," the waitress stated, turning to leave.

I just sat there, staring rigidly at Lisa. She had her elbow on the table and was holding the side of her face in one hand. Determining I couldn't trust a word out of this woman's mouth, I still needed to hear what Lisa had to say before I could move on. I never imagined I would be faced with this type of predicament. Here I was confronting the woman who had shamelessly slept with my husband, and I didn't know what to do or say. Well, I really knew what I wanted to do, but I wasn't prepared to go to jail.

I tried hard to maintain my composure by crossing my legs. I would never let Lisa see me break down and think she had conquered me, not today. That's why I chose a public place for us to meet. I would have to save face at any cost. I had to hold my hands together under the table to keep from slapping her.

"Why don't you just tell me how many times you were with my husband, Lisa?"

"All I can tell you is that it was more times than I care to count," she responded, smiling wickedly.

"I see. Can you tell me why you would knowingly sleep with a married man?"

"Please. He didn't seem to mind, so why should I? I mean it's not like I had to force him or anything," she said, slinging her bangs out of her face.

"No, I don't know. Why don't you tell me? Enlighten me. That is the reason why I'm here," I retorted.

"Look, Alese, if you asked me here to apologize to you or something, you're out of your mind. I didn't tell your husband to come sniffing behind me."

"No, you probably didn't. But I'm sure you gave him an open invitation, didn't you?"

"It doesn't matter what I did or didn't do because he kept coming back for more. Don't believe that one time lie he's telling you," she said, waving a finger.

"Lisa, it really doesn't matter if it was one time or a thousand times. What's done is done."

"Then why are we here? If it doesn't matter to you, then why are we here, Alese?"

"Because I just wanted to look in your face and see if you had the same regrets that my husband had in his face last night. But, obviously, you don't care, Lisa. This man has a family."

"He didn't seem worried about his family to me, and you didn't seem too worried about your man because you were constantly leaving him alone. Hell, I felt sorry for him."

That hurt. Still I smiled.

"I feel sorry for you, Lisa. You should have more pride about yourself than to knowingly sleep with a married man, especially your boss, or is that why you slept with him? You're trying to move up in the company or something, Lisa?"

"I certainly wouldn't have to sleep with Michael to move up in the company. I mean, he'd already experienced what I was capable of doing in the bedroom."

"Excuse me again, ladies. Are you all ready to place your orders?" the waitress asked, nervously placing Lisa's glass of red wine on the table.

"No, thank you. I'm not hungry anymore," I said standing, intentionally knocking over Lisa's glass. I watched as the blood burgundy liquid spilled out all over her white linen chemise dress.

[134]

Lisa leaped up from the table, screaming obscenities at the top of her lungs. The waitress rushed over and tried to calm her down. She offered to help clean her up, but Lisa pushed her hands away. I aimed the remote towards my van and clicked it. I just kept walking towards the parking lot without looking back. I was through with Lisa Bradford and Michael Wayne.

12

On My Own

Karema owned a lavish two-bedroom condominium in Meridian Commons Estates. It was beautifully decorated in her signature pastel colors. She had it meticulously adorned with African-American artwork and collectible figurines on every table and all across the marbled mantel above the fireplace. The pale peach European designed sofa set with sweeping rolled arms complemented the light coloring in the room. Karema had a black lacquer Steinway baby grand piano on display in the right corner of her living room, facing the entranceway. This was the prized possession she used along with her angelic voice to entertain guests on special occasions. I had been with her when she picked out the beautiful instrument for her showpiece about two years ago.

"Karema, thanks for letting me and Bianca stay with you for a while. We certainly appreciate this."

We were sitting at the breakfast table eating buttered toast and drinking orange juice. I had already dressed in a gray sweat suit and taken Bianca to preschool for the day. I needed to be on my own so I could think my way clearly through this dilemma.

"No problem. You're welcome to stay here no matter how long it takes to work out things with Michael."

"I'm not sure if that's going to happen."

"What do you mean? Of course you're going to work things out with Michael. Isn't that what you want?"

"No, it's not," I spoke humbly. "I can't ever be with him again, Karema. Not after this much hurt. I mean, I thought he was the best husband in the world and look at how he did me. That's not love."

"Alese, I know you're hurting right now. But you need to at least call him so he'll know that you and Bianca are safe. He's probably worried sick about you two."

"He needs to be sick about something, if you ask me. I don't care if he's worried sick or not. I'm not calling him."

"It's your decision, do whatever you want to. I have to get to the church. I'll be in and out of several meetings today with the advisory board and the missionary committee, but you can call me on my cell phone. You're familiar with where everything is. Just act like you're at home."

"Yes, I will do that," I responded half-heartedly, standing and walking Karema out of the kitchen.

We were almost to the front door when Karema stopped in her tracks and spoke.

"Alese, I know this is not what you want to hear right now, but I have to bring it up considering what's happened between you and Michael"

I hung my head, thinking my friend was about to bring up the one secret I'd shared with her in confidence. The one thing I had never even told my husband.

"Have you deliberated anymore about telling Michael why you've never gotten pregnant?"

"No, I haven't. I just told him the doctors said I couldn't conceive. He's never asked me to explain why. Besides, what does that have to do with what he did, Karema?" I asked, beginning to form tears in the corners of my eyes. "He cheated on me."

Karema sighed. "Sin is sin, Alese. They don't come in different sizes like small, medium, or large. Yes, Michael was wrong, but he's not perfect. I just think you should at least listen to him and share what's been burning in your soul for all these years. It might be time for both of you to heal." Karema took her thumb and wiped one long tear from my cheek.

"I've got to go. Think about what I said and call me later." Karema sped towards the front door. I walked behind her, holding the door open long after she walked down the sidewalk, got into her Toyota Camry, and drove off.

I could hear Ma Dear saying, "Let he who is without sin cast the first stone." That's why I was thinking about calling Michael regardless of what I had said to Karema. Only I wasn't planning to share my hurtful secret with him. I would never be able to tell anyone, aside from Karema, why I wasn't able to conceive a child for my husband.

Michael probably is worried about us, though, or calling around looking for us. I'm really surprised he hasn't called here already, especially since at least a whole day has passed by. Maybe he's pleased that we're gone, maybe he's ready to end our marriage, and maybe he was lying the other night after all. Could Lisa have been telling the truth about their relationship? I wondered if I'd ever know the whole true story.

#

Karema had just returned from lunch and was headed to her office to prepare for the next meeting which was scheduled to start in about thirty minutes. She wasn't surprised to see Michael Wayne sitting quietly in a pew outside her office door. Karema immediately noticed his torn jeans and a long sleeve wrinkled sweatshirt. She could tell from the stubble on his chin he hadn't shaved today and his hair hadn't been brushed. His eyes were blood shot, indicating he'd been drinking or crying really hard. Karema was not used to seeing him looking so disheveled. Obviously, he was in deep concentration—a distressed look was plastered on his face, but he snapped out of it when he saw her getting nearer to him.

"Hello, Brother Michael." Karema spoke mildly upon approaching him. Michael stood and gave her a warm hug before they turned to enter the pastor's suite.

"Hello, Pastor Karema. It's good to see you," Michael said with a halfway smile, keeping his eyes on the pastor. "You understand why I'm here, don't you?" he asked, sitting down on the love seat.

"Yes, I'm pretty sure I do." Karema took a seat in the swivel armchair behind her desk and then turned to face Michael. "Your wife and daughter are at my house, if that's what you came to find out."

"Thank you. Thank you," Michael said, sounding relieved. "I'm just glad they're safe and in one piece. I started to call your house first thing yesterday morning, but I doubted Alese would talk to me after the way she tipped out the other night without telling me."

"Yes, she and Bianca came to my door about three-thirty in the morning. Bianca was passed out in Alese's arm and we put her straight to bed."

"Karema, I need your advice today as a pastor. I messed up my life and I don't know how to clean it up. I've got to get my family back."

"Michael, to be honest with you, I don't think that'll happen anytime soon. It's going to take some time and a lot of prayer to rebuild this union. A solid marriage has to be built on trust and once trust is broken, it is hard to put the pieces together again. But now, I do believe in the spirit of forgiveness that God has placed in all our hearts," she said, keeping her voice at an even tone.

"I'll do anything, whatever it takes. It's done," he said, reassuring her.

"Have you asked her to forgive you, Michael? I'm not the one you have to convince."

"No, I haven't had a chance to ask her forgiveness. She had promised not to leave me if I told her the truth and I did that. Isn't it true that even good people can do bad things?"

"Yes, it's possible for a good person to make a bad decision. The trick is to not place yourself in a situation where you may be tempted into making a poor decision. You see, once you've already placed yourself in a compromising position, it's easy to make the wrong choice because you're in a weakened state of mind."

"I know," he uttered.

Placing his face in his hands, Michael started sobbing ferociously. Karema went to his side and put her arms around him the same way she had done with Alese the other night. She prayed with him to turn his marriage over to God and let Him work it out for them. Now was not the time to lose faith.

"Michael, don't give up on Alese. I know she loves you. You just need to give her time to digest what's happening with the marriage. Don't ever give up on your family."

He reassured the pastor that he would never give up trying to reclaim his precious family. After praying together, Michael thanked Karema for listening to him, and then made a silent exit through the office door. Praying his family was safe, he left feeling better.

#

Michael hung up the telephone with Ms. Riley. She had just informed him that the visitation with Bianca's maternal aunt was scheduled for this weekend. There was nothing Ms. Riley could do. She had fought to delay the visitation order for months. The court had approved the "relative visit," and they would have to comply with it. They were to have Bianca at the State agency's visitation center on Beach Boulevard at two o'clock Saturday afternoon. She would be allowed two hours to spend with her aunt under close supervision.

He didn't bother to tell Ms. Riley why Alese wasn't home. He just guaranteed her they would be in compliance with the court's order. If the court found out he and Alese were separated, they might take Bianca from them. He couldn't stand the concept of her being placed back in that deplorable shelter where they barely took care of the children. The baby diapers went unchanged all day, kids were not bathed, and they wore clothing that was either too small or too big for their bodies. There was no way he was willing to risk that. He would have to convince Alese they needed to put up a united front.

Finally, he thought he had a legitimate excuse to call his estranged wife.

Michael had seen them on Bianca's birthday in April for only a couple of hours, but he hadn't seen them since then. He had left in tears with his daughter clinging to his pants leg. Alese wouldn't even allow him to celebrate her fortieth birthday with her over the Memorial Day weekend this past week. He tried desperately to persuade her to come back home and let him be the one to move out, but to no avail. He tried to convince her that Bianca needed stability, and they should be the ones staying at the house. He had broken the marriage vows, and he should be the one to leave, but she wouldn't listen. She was determined to stay at Karema's house until she found a place of her own. Alese didn't have any plans for returning to the house they owned.

Alese had refused to let him take Bianca for any outings he had planned. Michael had bought tickets online for the UniverSoul Circus in hopes of taking his baby girl last Sunday afternoon. He imagined Bianca would have loved seeing the circus clowns, the acrobats, and the smart animal tricks. This was their first opportunity to see the only African American owned circus in the world. He was beyond disappointed in himself. Alese wouldn't even entertain the idea of letting him take Bianca out alone, and she absolutely refused to accompany them.

There was nothing he could do. His hands were tied behind his back and it wouldn't do any good to kick or scream. He was fighting a losing battle and that was the truth. Nothing got her attention. He had sent her a dozen roses in every color, boxes of Godiva's chocolate candy, expensive designer perfumes like Flowerbomb and Prada, an eighteen-karat gold emerald birthstone necklace set, and a dazzling diamond tennis bracelet. Michael even tried writing poetry for Alese, but she tore it up into tiny pieces and sent it back to him in an envelope through the mail.

He had pleaded with Tina and Shelly to talk to Alese on his behalf, but they both refused. Michael was tempted to call his sister-in-law, Vivian, and ask her to talk to Alese or even ask Ma Dear to talk to her. Realizing his wife would never take him back if he involved her family like that, he decided not to call. She probably hadn't even told them about their separation yet. He'd tried everything except showing up outside her bedroom window at midnight singing the *'Cause I Love You* song harder than Lenny Williams.

Michael kept rehearsing in his mind what he was going to say to Alese. He picked up the telephone several times and starting dialing the number but he hung up each time without speaking. He hadn't been able to do anything to get her attention long enough to hold a decent conversation since she left him.

Well, she would have to pay attention to him now for Bianca's sake. Trusting she would never risk losing their daughter to the state's custody, he picked up the telephone and dialed Karema's number. She picked up on the second ring.

"Hello, Karema, how are you doing?" he asked politely.

"Oh! My God, Michael! I'm so glad it's you!" Karema cried hysterically.

"Karema, is everything okay? What's wrong?" he asked sharply. Karema was scaring him because she was always real cool and even-

[141]

tempered. Something awful had happened for her to be sounding like this.

"Oh! My God! Is it Alese or Bianca?" he asked, panicking.

"Michael, we just got a call from Alese's sister, Vivian. Ma Dear passed earlier today."

"I'm on my way over there! Tell Alese I'm on my way right now!" He slammed the telephone down, snatched the car keys off the kitchen counter, and ran out the front door. His heart was pumping a mile a minute, but he had to get to his wife.

#

By the time Michael arrived at Karema's house, I was in the bedroom in a catatonic state. I was lying flat on my back with my face looking up towards the ceiling. I didn't even hear Michael enter the room. I didn't respond when he called my name or touched me. My mind wanted to respond, but my body wasn't in the mood. I just remained still, wishing I had died with Ma Dear.

I had dreaded this day my whole life. Ma Dear and I were so spiritually connected. I trusted I would be able to feel the exact moment that she passed away; that no one would have to call and tell me anything. I would just automatically feel it in my spirit and be at peace, but I wasn't.

I should have been better prepared for this death. Vivian had told her less than two weeks ago that Ma Dear was getting weaker and losing her appetite. Only I was too consumed with my marital problems to comprehend the severity of that development. Ma Dear had been in and out of the hospital with heart complications for the last three years, and she always got better. No matter how low she went, she would come back up. We just got on the main line and prayed her through whatever surgery or crisis she was facing. Now, it was over.

I realized right then that I should have gone to be with Ma Dear sooner. Maybe I could have coaxed her into eating more, but it was too late for that. I should have been there with Vivian when our mother took her last breath of air and closed her eyes for the final time. God, I would never forgive myself for not being there when Ma Dear passed away.

I still wanted to speak. I still wanted to move, but I couldn't. I heard Michael saying my name. I heard Bianca calling for me. I also heard Karema praying on her knees at the foot of the bed.

Tears cascaded down the side of my face like a waterfall. I felt my husband wiping away the tears and whispering in my ear that he was there for me.

I still could not make myself respond, but my brain was still actively in progress.

My mind had transported me back to a time when I was about six years old …

Vivian and I were in that big blue four-door, nineteen-sixty-five Buick with Ma Dear and Daddy Nate was driving. Ma Dear had on her blue shift dress with the yellow and white flowers in it. Vivian had on a yellow dress, and I had on a white dress, wide brim, straw hat with a pearl necklace, and pearl earrings. Daddy Nate had on his brown fedora hat, his brown pin-stripe suit, a white shirt, and a brown bowtie. It must have been a Sunday and we were coming home from church. I remembered looking out the window of the back seat at the beautiful countryside. We were so happy that day. Vivian and I were clapping our hands and singing the tune to some nursery rhyme. Daddy Nate was telling some joke and had Ma Dear laughing in the front passenger seat. He was always making Ma Dear laugh. I wanted that day, that happiness, that laughter, to last forever.

I couldn't digest the fact that Ma Dear was gone and Daddy Nate was gone, too. While I continued staring at the ceiling, I thought I saw both of their smiling faces looking down at me. They were wondering why I was lying there looking so sad, when they were so happy to be together again. I continued staring up at the ceiling. Suddenly, I blinked. I could move again, too.

"My daddy, my daddy. What's wrong with my mommy?" Bianca asked, looking up at Michael with a sad face. He picked her up and held her securely in his arms.

"Mommy's sick right now, baby. But she's going to be all right."

"But my daddy, she no talk to me," Bianca said sadly, on the verge of tears.

[143]

"She'll be fine, baby girl. I promise you. She'll be fine," Michael pledged to his daughter while lightly patting her on the back. Bianca buried her face in his chest saying, "I missed you, my daddy."

"I know, baby. I missed you, too. But everything is going to be fine. Daddy's here," he replied.

I slowly turned my head to face Michael and Bianca. It took a while for their faces to register in my mind. I reached out for my daughter. Michael laid her gently on my bosom.

I remembered the many days and nights that I had laid upon Ma Dear's chest and how I had been comforted by her loving touch. Yes, it was a mother's duty to comfort her child. Now, it was my turn to provide the reassuring touch to my own daughter. All the motherly advice I'd been given over the last forty years flashed through my mind. It was my time to get up and carry on the family torch. I would never disappoint my Ma Dear again.

13

Passing Away

"All things must change. With the passing of each season, comes a change. The passing away of a loved one brings a change," Reverend Johnson said solemnly, wearing his black robe with the black and white trim he always wore for funerals. "Sister Ruby Evon Dean has changed and passed on to the afterlife. Church, listen. Second Timothy, chapter four, verses seven and eight, read:

"I have fought a good fight, I have finished the race, and I have kept the faith. Finally, there is laid up for me a crown of righteousness, which the Lord, the righteous Judge, will give to me on that Day; and not to me only, but also to all who have loved His appearing. Amen."

Reverend Johnson spoke with eloquence while reciting the Scripture imprinted on Ma Dear's funeral program. He had his rectangular shaped frame reading glasses positioned on the end of his nose. Reverend Johnson leaned over his Bible, placed the program on top of it, and stood with both hands on the side of the podium. When he finished reading the Scripture, he looked up at the audience and removed his glasses.

"Yes, sir. I tell you, Sister Ruby fought a good fight. We should all pattern ourselves after Sister Ruby," he said, raising his voice.

"She was a loving wife! She was a caring mother! She had a kind spirit! She was a good and faithful servant of the Lord!" he shouted, then made a three-hundred-sixty degree turn, stomping his foot when he stopped.

Sitting numbly in the front row, I listened while Reverend Johnson eulogized my mother. He praised Ma Dear for having a good heart and trying to help so many people throughout her life. He told stories about the church members she had housed and fed on more than one occasion. He spoke of the many times he had ministered to Ma Dear and how she had been a faithful member of the New Hill Chapel Baptist Church for sixty-three years.

Reverend Johnson turned to the church choir and asked them to stand and bless the audience with a song. All the choir members looked majestic in their handmade burgundy robes with white and gold trim collars. They had the church initials NHC sewn across the front of the garments with white and gold thread. Sister Leola Johnson, the choir director, stood up first and faced the choir members before she motioned for them to stand in unison.

They started rocking from side to side with the rhythm of the music as they sung, *When the Saints Go Marching In*, in perfect harmony. Walking to his seat, Reverend Johnson said, "Come on, choir."

They slowed the music down a beat while Sister Leola took the microphone in her hand to sing before turning towards the crowd. She sang Ma Dear's all-time favorite gospel song, *Walk Around Heaven All Day*, in her sensational angelic voice. Sister Leola took her time and sang the song right for Ma Dear. She probably remembered just how much Ma Dear enjoyed hearing her voice.

Fighting back tears, I gazed around at the familiar church setting. I studied the life-sized mural of the Black Jesus and His disciples on the wall behind the pulpit. I inspected several stained glass windows donated by church members with their family's gold engraved nameplate in the right-hand corner of each one. This was the small two-hundred member church house my mother and father had attended all their lives. It was the holy place where my grandparents had worshipped until their demise. This was the church I had been encouraged to join the first Sunday after my twelfth birthday.

"Chile, you need to join the church today," Ma Dear told me while we were dressing for Sunday school.

I was wearing a yellow pleated dress with a white collar on it. I had the matching patent white purse and shoes to go with it.

"But I don't know if I'm ready, Ma Dear," I responded, being a fearful young child.

"Well, you're twelve years old now, ain't you?" Ma Dear asked, looking like she already had the answer.

"Ah, yes, ma'am," I answered, wondering if it was a trick question or something.

"Chile, once you turn twelve years old, you're responsible for your own sins. Up to now, Jesus been taking responsibility for your sins. But now that you're twelve, you have to account for your own self."

"Really, Ma Dear?"

"Yes, chile. You should be ready to accept Jesus and the responsibility that comes with that. It's time to join our family church," Ma Dear said proudly, rearing back to look at me. "I tell you what, after you join the church today, I'll give you this old Bible of mine that my mother gave to me many years ago. It has all the important family births, weddings, and deaths written in it."

"All right, Ma Dear," I said. "I think I might be ready, then," I said, smiling to please my mother.

Sitting in the front row pew, I was holding onto that same black textured Bible with the gold embossed title on the front cover. Yes, it was weathered and coming apart, but it was my legacy. Hopefully, I would be able to pass it on to my only child someday.

I hadn't wanted to believe Ma Dear was actually gone. I couldn't accept that fact until I was physically at the "Big House," and Ma Dear wasn't at the door to greet us. I ran to Ma Dear's bedroom, bursting into tears when I realized she wasn't there, and she would never be there again. I laid myself back across the twin bed in the same spot Ma Dear had lain in for the last few minutes of her life. I tried to imagine her lying there as the breath slipped from her fragile body.

It was time for me to say my last good bye to Ma Dear. I hadn't noticed Michael squeezing my hand and sobbing harder than I was. Vivian was wiping her tears with a monogrammed white handkerchief and screaming about how much she was going to miss Ma Dear. Darnell was fanning Vivian and trying to keep her in the seat beside him. Denise and Dennis were hugging each other and crying like newborn babies. Aunt Lucy and Uncle Clevell both sat there staring into space like they were unaware of what was going on right in front of them. Their daughter, Colleen, had Bianca sitting with her during the funeral services.

The church was so overcrowded, there was standing room only. I could hear people crying out from way in the back, but I never turned around to look at any of them.

Michael and I were the first to stand after they closed Ma Dear's lavender casket, which had the Lord's Prayer written on the inside top of the lining in vivid colors. The pastor led the flower attendants out of the church while reciting Scriptures. It took them several minutes to gather up the overflowing amount of lively floral arrangements and the many potted peace lilies lining the front of the church. I looked around the building at all of the old friends and family members that came to pay their last respects to Ma Dear. I figured my former classmates were there searching for my face, so I lowered my head. I didn't want anyone to see the pain I was fighting so hard to control.

We all marched slowly out of the church while the three pallbearers on each side rolled Ma Dear's casket out of the building towards the cemetery. Michael and I leaned on each other for support because we were too weak to stand on our own. Even though I was still mad at my husband, I was thankful for him being by my side.

I sat in a cushioned folding chair under the graveside burial tent with my hands in my lap. Vivian and I wore Chanel black skirt suits to the funeral. Ma Dear said to always wear black to a funeral. I never understood why some people wore white to services.

I also wore Ma Dear's pearl necklace that Daddy Nate had given her for their twenty-fifth wedding anniversary. Vivian and I clung to each other and wept tenderly together. I prayed silently as they lowered Ma Dear's sparkling silver and lavender casket, with the lovely lilac and green spray on top, into the ground.

Ashes to ashes. Dust to dust.

#

After Ma Dear was laid to rest alongside Daddy Nate with a double heart shaped tombstone, the entire group of family and friends gathered back at the "Big House." It was a good thing it was a brilliant June day. There was so much food, we had to set up three rented tents in the backyard with three eight-foot long tables under each tent. We placed all the meats under one tent, vegetables under the middle tent, and desserts under the last tent. Even though it looked like a "Soul Food" family reunion, I only wanted two things from all the food the people brought with their condolences: some of Big Mama's famous spicy chicken and dressing, and Ms. Sue's double-layered strawberry cream cake. They were Ma Dear's favorites.

#

Michael stayed by her side the whole time they were in Kansas. He never let Alese out of his line of vision for more than a few seconds. Even though she seemed to be handling the stress well now, he was certain the blood bond between Ma Dear and Alese was stronger than Gorilla Glue. At any moment, he felt she might have a total breakdown and collapse. He wanted to be there to console and comfort her, if that occurred.

"I'm just relieved you recovered from the catatonic state I had found you in shortly after learning about Ma Dear's death. I don't know what miracle happened to bring you back, but I'm grateful and thank God for His grace," he said, kissing the back of Alese's hand.

Michael wanted his wife back. He was miserable sleeping alone every night in that king-sized bed with fifteen years of marital memories between those sheets. He had cried more tears in the last two months than he thought were possible. Sometimes he felt like he was weak, or less of a man, for crying so much, but he determined that was wrong. His own father had taught him that valuable lesson as a fourteen-year old boy. Michael remembered hiding in his room weeping quietly after his golden retriever was struck by a car and died in the street. He could hear his daddy's strong husky voice seemingly speaking to him now.

"Michael! Michael!" his father yelled, opening the door to his small bedroom with the bunk beds that he and Rueben shared. "Son, why are you sitting over there by the window in the dark?" His father switched the light on and stared at Michael. "Son, are you crying?" he asked, sitting down on the side of Michael's bed.

"No, no. Dad, I'm not crying. I was just, uh, you know," Michael stammered, wiping his face with his hands.

"Son, don't you ever be ashamed of crying. I mean that," his father insisted.

"But, daddy, they say that real men don't cry."

"Son, that's nonsense. Sure, some people think you're not a real man if you cry," he began. "They call you weak or they call you a sissy. But I'm here to tell you different. You're not a real man until you do cry. And I'm not talking about no little sniffling. I'm talking about that deep down gut-wrenching crying you do when your heart's been broken for the very first time. That's when you can recognize yourself as a real man, son, when you can cry like that and not be ashamed of it."

Michael's father was right. He felt like his heart had been broken for the first time after Alese left him that night he admitted to his adultery. He was thankful for his loving father. Michael wondered what his father would think of his marital situation right now. He hadn't found the courage to call and tell him they were separated. Well, he hadn't really shared that information with anyone because he was determined to get his spouse back. Michael only believed one thing for certain; he had to talk to Alese.

Michael knocked lightly on the guest bedroom door before Alese told him to enter. She was sitting in a green wing chair by the window with her Bible opened across her lap to the book of Revelations. She had put her locks up into a ponytail, but a few stray ones framed her face. He thought she looked more naturally beautiful than she'd ever looked before. Michael knelt down on one knee and took Alese's hand within his and looked into her sad eyes.

"Alese, I know this is a difficult time for you right now. But I have to tell you this, I'm just really happy you agreed to let me accompany you and Bianca to Ma Dear's funeral. I loved your mother like she was my own."

"Yes, Michael, I know. Ma Dear loved you like her own son, too. She was proud of you. She always talked about her wonderful son-in-law in Florida."

"Well, we certainly had some good times together with her and your whole family in this house. Alese, the first time you brought me here before we were married, I wanted to be a part of this family. I felt the love you all had for one another and I wanted to know that feeling. After my mom passed from breast cancer when I was eleven-years old, we just never felt like a complete family again. When I saw your parents together, I realized what I was missing. That was the first moment I wanted to marry you." Michael never blinked once while speaking to Alese.

"Michael, I appreciate you traveling here with me and everything. But I—I can't live with you anymore. I can't be—be your wife anymore." Alese took a deep breath and sighed.

"Baby, please, don't say that. I know you don't mean that, baby," Michael said, shaking his head in confusion.

"Michael, I do mean it. Once the adoption is completed, I'm filing for divorce. Please, don't fight me on this. I've made up my mind."

"What do you mean don't fight you on this? What do you mean you've made up your mind?" he asked, trying to control the tone of his voice. "What about me? What about us? What about what I feel?"

"Michael, I can't go there with you right now. I don't have the answers. I just know I have the grounds for a divorce."

"Look, Alese. We have to talk about this. You can't tell me something like this and then not talk about it."

"Michael, I'm sorry, but it's late, and I can't discuss this any further. I will promise you this one thing though. I won't file for a divorce until after the adoption is final. We can't risk losing custody of Bianca because of this. No matter what happens between us, you will always be her father."

"I appreciate you doing that. But I don't want a divorce, Alese, and I mean that. I'm not letting you go that easily," he said firmly, rising before he turned and left the room, leaving the door wide open.

Alese rose and closed the door behind her spouse. Michael was determined to keep the marriage together, but she wasn't ready to love him again. She couldn't love him the way a wife was supposed to love a husband. There was no point in staying married to a man she couldn't trust and couldn't ever respect. He had destroyed the bond she cherished in her soul. Finally, Alese knelt down and asked

[151]

God to heal her broken heart. She needed to move on without Michael Wayne.

14

Here We Go Again

Bianca slept most of the way on the airplane ride home. She had caught a cold while we were in Kansas and only woke up long enough to cough every now and then before falling back to sleep. I had given her some children's Tylenol to keep her from running a fever, but she still felt slightly warm. I kept Bianca's head in my lap as she sat between Michael and me on the plane. I spent most of my time looking out the window daydreaming and rubbing Bianca's back.

After arriving at Karema's condo, Michael carried Bianca to the bedroom and placed her in bed without changing her clothes. He just took off her shoes and wrapped a blanket around her small body. Michael kissed her on the cheek and told her good night, but she didn't hear a word. He placed her trusted friend, the teddy bear, in the bed beside her, and tipped out of the room.

"Thank God we made it back safe. I wasn't too happy about riding on an airplane, but at least it's over, and it wasn't a bad ride," Michael said, bringing my charcoal gray luggage set into the living room.

"Yes, goodness, I'm just glad everything is over with and went well," I said.

"Me, too," Michael replied. "Alese, I meant to tell you before that it was a beautiful service you all had for Ma Dear. You put your mother away really nice, baby. I'm proud of you," he said, kissing me on the cheek.

"Thanks, Michael. I think she would have been pleased to see her own funeral. I know Ma Dear wouldn't want us to be sad about her passing. She would tell us to move on with life," I said laughing, remembering my mother's hearty laugh.

"That's true. That's true. She would definitely say that," Michael responded, laughing with me.

We were wired after having such an active day and a long plane ride home. I filled the kettle with cold water, put it on the stove, and made us two cups of hot lemon decaffeinated tea with lots of honey. Since Karema was out of town at a regional church convention in Orlando, I wasn't in a hurry to be alone. Michael would be good company for me right now, but I would have to be careful. Though we were separated, I was still attracted to my husband. There was no way a woman could make love with a man for fifteen years, on a regular basis, and not feel something for him after being apart for months. We had never gone this long without making love to each other before.

Michael had to be craving physical intimacy, it wouldn't take much to give him the wrong impression tonight. He had always been an emotional man and openly expressed his feelings. I didn't want either one of us to get hurt.

Michael and I sat in the living room on the fluffy sofa talking for hours about our families and reminiscing about the good ole times when we were a happily married couple. We talked about the feelings we shared when we were dating, the many couples we knew that had married and divorced since us, and the new contemporary gospel artists we both loved. I played the latest Mary, Mary CD in the background while we enjoyed our second cup of herbal tea.

We recalled the various places we had explored together when we were free to travel the world at the spur of the moment. Finally, we recalled the first time we saw Bianca, how we held her, how much we wanted her to be ours, and how we thanked God for making our family complete.

"Michael, are you afraid of losing Bianca?" I asked, turning to face him with one foot tucked under my thigh while holding a teacup in my hand.

"Honestly, I am. I mean, I think about that every day, Alese. I wonder what would happen if we lost her," Michael responded, placing his cup on the coffee table.

"Yes, me, too," I said. "I just hope Ms. Riley can find some way to stop that aunt from taking custody of Bianca. There has to be some way to stop that woman. There's no way she could really want this child after all this time."

"I agree with you on that. She didn't just wake up one morning and decide she wanted custody of Bianca. Something has got to be

[154]

behind this. But you know what? I can't imagine my life without her or you in it," he said, gazing at me with those innocent-looking puppy dog eyes. I was hypnotized for a second, then I abruptly responded.

"Michael, it's really late. I think it's time to say good night," I said, standing up and heading towards the door.

"Oh! Oh! So you're going to do me like that, huh?" he asked, faking a surprised look.

"Yes, we have to say good night now, Michael," I insisted. My resistance was beginning to wane. I had to get him out of the house before I gave in to his attraction.

"No problem, I'm leaving." He rose cautiously, walked over to the door, and stood close to me. I saw a glint in his eyes like he was beckoning me to come. He slipped his arms around my body and moved in closer for an intimate hug. The heat permeating from his body caused me to wrap my arms around him in return.

Michael snugly embraced me and whispered in my ear, "Where are those tender lips I've been thirsting to kiss all evening?"

I evaporated at the sound of his sexy tone. My hands travelled all over his back. I felt the tightness of his muscles as they vibrated against my trembling hands. Leaning my body against the front door, I moved both hands down to cup Michael's firm backside.

We kissed lightly at first, gently biting each other's bottom lip and pulling it between our teeth. He tasted so satisfying, I never wanted to stop. Then, the kissing became more intense as we slow danced our way back to the comfortable sofa. Michael was on top of me with his hands under my mauve knit blouse searching for the hooks on my Playtex full-sized bra. I had both hands down at his waist trying to unzip his Nautica snug fitting blue jeans. My mind was telling me to stop, stop this right now, but his lips and body were boldly calling out my name. That's all I could hear until Bianca's screaming broke our trance.

Both of us sprang from the sofa, almost stumbling over each other running to the bedroom. Bianca was sitting up in the middle of the bed crying loudly.

"Mommy!" she said, wheezing. "I can't breathe!"

#

We had been in the waiting area of the Shands Jacksonville Medical Center for over an hour and still had not seen a doctor. I held Bianca's tiny body in my arms, feeling her congested chest heaving against my breasts. Michael was over by the admissions desk asking the attendant how much longer we would have to wait because Bianca was starting to sound worse. At last, Nurse Bethany, a tall young woman with a friendly smile, came out and escorted us to one of the examining rooms.

Nurse Bethany quickly checked Bianca's vital signs, put a clear plastic mask over her face, and started her on a medicated breathing treatment machine immediately. Shortly after that, Dr. Ulomba, a small, African, middle-aged woman, came in to speak with us regarding Bianca's condition. Dr. Ulomba asked us a list of questions pertaining to Bianca's health. She asked the nurse to show us the way to the radiology department to have x-rays done of Bianca's chest. They also drew blood from her veins to test for bacterial infections.

Around two-thirty in the morning, Bianca was breathing much easier as she lay comfortably in the hospital bed. Michael and I held her hands as we sat on opposite sides of the bed talking privately to our daughter. She still had the plastic mask over her face connected to the treatment machine when Dr. Ulomba entered the examining room with the chest x-rays in her hands. She informed us that Bianca had acute bronchitis in her lungs and was still running a fever of one-hundred-four degrees. They were also waiting for the results of the blood tests to return before they would permit us to leave. Dr. Ulomba wanted to make sure Bianca had not been exposed to a highly contagious virus. If she had been exposed, our daughter would have to be admitted to the hospital immediately for a period of several days.

Nurse Bethany returned to our hospital room around six a.m. and apologized for the lab results taking so long. She explained that they were just backed up last night. She checked Bianca's temperature and confirmed that it was just slightly elevated now. Then, she happily informed us that Bianca did not have a contagious viral infection. However, she did have a bacterial infection that could be

[156]

treated with antibiotics and we could take Bianca home after the paperwork was processed. Hallelujah, I wanted to shout.

The nurse gave us a prescription for antibiotics to take once a day for five days. They also recommended giving her Pedialyte to help replace the fluids and nutrients she had lost due to her illness.

By the time we picked up the prescription for Bianca and made it back to the condominium, it was almost eight a.m. We had her wrapped up in a warm blanket and propped up on pillows to help ease her breathing. Once she was sleeping soundly, I walked Michael to the door.

"Michael, thank you for taking us to the hospital and staying with us all night," I said.

"Alese, you and Bianca are my family. You don't have to thank me for anything I do for the two of you. You and she are my life and you comprehend that, don't you?" he asked, gazing into my eyes.

"Yes, I do. But I still need some time to myself, Michael," I responded, looking down at my leopard print house shoes. Michael took a step back and slightly raised both hands apart in the air.

"Listen, I'm so tired, I'm going home. I'll call you later today to check on Bianca, and I'll be by later," he said, walking out the door.

#

When Michael made it home, he felt exhausted and wanted to go straight to bed. He stopped at the refrigerator for a glass of orange juice. Before heading to the bedroom, he noticed the light blinking on the caller identification box and the answering machine. Michael pressed the play button just in case there was something important he might need to know prior to retiring for the day.

"Mr. & Mrs. Wayne, this is Jenny Riley. I know you all had a family emergency and had to miss the last scheduled visit with Bianca's aunt. Well, that visit has been rescheduled for one week from today at the State agency's visiting room on Beach Boulevard from three until five p.m. It is extremely important that you call me when you receive this message to confirm the appointment. We're still investigating the aunt and I'm confident that something will turn up sooner or later. But in the meantime, we have to grant her a relative visitation. If you have any questions or concerns, please, call me tomorrow. Thank you, bye."

Michael stood there staring at the answering machine while that message clicked off and several other messages clicked on and off. He didn't hear any of them.

#

We were committed to presenting a united front for social services, so Bianca and I were ready when Michael picked us up promptly at two-thirty p.m. in his freshly detailed Infinity. He looked sharp wearing his casual green slacks with a black, short sleeve polo shirt. I wore a printed rayon pants suit in multiple shades of blue and green with matching flat-heeled sandals. I had spent most of the day preparing Bianca for the visit with her aunt. Since Bianca called her godmother Karema, auntie, it was a little easier to explain that she had another auntie who wanted to see her. I was careful not to give her too many details about what was really happening. We had never mentioned the word adoption in front of Bianca because even for a toddler, she was an incredibly smart and articulate child.

"Bianca, mommy wants you to be a good girl for your auntie today."

"Okay, mommy. I be good girl, mommy," Bianca responded with her widest smile, showing all her baby teeth.

I hugged my daughter as if it was the last time we would ever hold each other again. I wanted her to feel loved and wanted with all my heart. I fought back tears of uncertainty regarding the outcome of this adoption. Nothing would ever stop me from expressing love to this beautiful, special child.

Making sure to have Bianca at the visitation center on time, we pulled up to the double-story, red brick building and sat in the car looking at one another for several minutes before exiting the vehicle. Neither one of us knew what to say to comfort the other, so we just focused our attention on our daughter in the back seat. Bianca looked adorable in her pink dress with the white lace collar, white tights, and black Mary Jane leather shoes. She loved wearing dresses and pink was her favorite color. Bianca hardly wanted to wear

[158]

anything unless it had some pink in it. Her hair was sculpted into four equal sized ponytails with pink hair bows at the end of each one. Bianca loved shaking her head so she could feel the bows move with her.

Mrs. Francis, the elder social worker, met us in the reception area and coaxed Bianca into following her into the visitor's room. Michael and I were not allowed to stay with her and we were not permitted to meet the maternal aunt. Mrs. Francis told us we could wait in the reception area or we could come back for her in a couple of hours.

"We'll be back in exactly two hours," I stated firmly, locking eyes with Mrs. Francis.

"Try not to worry, Mrs. Wayne. I'll be with her the entire time. If there's a problem of any kind, I'll call you on your cell phone."

"Yes, that'll be fine, Mrs. Francis. Thank you," I responded, making sure my iPhone was turned on before dropping it back in my navy Coach cross body purse.

We drove around in Michael's car for almost an hour before we stopped downtown by the Riverwalk. We sat outside on one of the piers reminiscing about how we became parents of such a precious child. "Do you remember me telling you about the article I read in the Sunday paper about a couple being murdered and leaving behind a baby girl?" I asked.

"Yeah, I'll never forget that day. You had a whole section of the newspaper wet."

"I know. My heart went out to that baby. After dreaming about her that night, I had to contact the authorities and see if anyone wanted her."

"We were lucky that no one had come forward to claim the child."

"I guess since her parents were drug dealers, people just assumed she was a drug baby or something. But somehow, I sensed in my heart she was meant for us."

Michael glanced over at me and said, "I love the way your face lights up when you talk about Bianca."

I returned his smile and said, "You're a wonderful father." I could tell he wanted to talk more, and I knew what he wanted to talk about. However, I wasn't ready for that conversation. Whenever Michael brought up the subject of us, I would bring up something else, like a memory of Bianca.

#

After returning to the State agency building promptly at five, we greeted our daughter with hugs and kisses. This had been one of the hardest days of our lives.

"Mommy, mommy, I missed you."

"I missed you, too, sweetheart," I responded. "How was your visit with your auntie?"

"Good, mommy. She nice," Bianca uttered with a smile.

I picked up Bianca and held her for a long time before placing her in the car seat and planting a kiss on her forehead. Shortly after I was buckled in the front seat, I heard Bianca's voice.

"Mommy, I hungry."

"Well, would you like to go to McDonald's, baby?"

"Yeah! I want McDonald's! My daddy, I want McDonald's!"

"I hear you, baby!" Michael replied, laughing.

He pulled into the first McDonald's restaurant he saw. We decided to sit outside to eat, even though the sky was looking slightly overcast. It would probably rain any minute, but Bianca wanted to have fun on the large playground. Of course, she barely ate any of her Happy Meal because she was so anxious to get to the play area with the other children.

I sat in front of Michael and watched Bianca climb up the tunnel to the big yellow circular slide. I didn't know what to say to Michael, but I observed him peripherally eyeing me. I lowered my head and took another bite of my burger, pretending not to notice.

"Would you like anything else, maybe an ice cream cone or something?" Michael asked, remembering how much I loved sweets.

"No, thank you. I'm fine."

"So, where do we go from here?" Michael asked directly.

"Michael, right now I can't think about us. My only concern is Bianca and getting through this adoption process," I replied, raising my right hand in the air. I'd seen this one coming all day.

[160]

"I understand that, but at some point, we will have to talk about us," he said sternly.

"Yes, I know that. But just not today."

"Well, look." He hesitated for a second before continuing his sentence. "Can we at least spend our anniversary together? You know that's coming up soon."

"I know exactly when our anniversary is, Michael. It's over a month away. This is still July, isn't it?"

"I'm just saying...I hope I can at least see you on our anniversary. I'm trying to make an early reservation so you'll have plenty of time to process the idea."

"I'll definitely think about it. Maybe I'll fix dinner for us or something, I don't know."

"That would be great! I would love that! You can't cook like Ma Dear, but you can do well enough."

"What? I don't believe you said that, Michael." I pretended to sound hurt.

"I'm just playing. You can burn, baby, burn."

"Yeah, right. Please go get your daughter so we can go."

"Sure, just let me finish this last bite," he replied, stuffing the filet-o-fish in his mouth.

We finished our food in silence, gave Bianca a few more minutes to play, and then gathered our things before leaving the restaurant. It was just beginning to rain lightly as we pulled into the evening traffic. Bianca wailed all the way home because she never wanted to leave McDonald's.

15

Daddy's Home

"Michael, son, is everything all right with you?" Jeremiah Wayne asked over the telephone late one evening on a warm summer day in July.

"Hey, dad, everything is fine. I'm surprised to hear from you," Michael replied, sitting up in bed wearing his gray striped Calvin Klein pajama bottoms. He'd fallen asleep reading the latest issue of *Black Enterprise* magazine.

"You shouldn't be, considering the fact that you haven't called me in weeks. That's not like you, son. I know how you hate for me to call you long distance so you usually beat me to the punch. What's going on?"

"Dad, I'm really glad to hear from you. My life is in complete disarray right now," Michael mumbled after clearing his throat.

"Well, I'm listening. Tell me all about it."

"First of all, Alese and I are separated. We've been separated for about four months now."

"What are you talking about, son? Why haven't you told me about this before now? You've been calling me every week sounding like everything was fine until recently."

"Yeah, I know. I just didn't want to worry you with my marriage problems. It's been eating me alive to tell you the truth. I thought that after we spent some time together in Kansas after my mother-in-law passed last month that we might be able to work it out. But she's still talking about filing for divorce as soon as the adoption is finalized."

"Divorce." Jeremiah sounded surprised. "Lord, the devil is busy, ain't he? What did you do to that woman?"

"Dad, please, I can't tell you that over the telephone. It's too embarrassing to even talk about with you."

"Never mind, it could only be one thing if she's threatening to divorce you this quickly. Damn, Michael, how did you let this happen?"

"It wasn't something that was planned. Alese was out of town visiting her mother and someone from my past reappeared at a weak moment in my life."

"Hell, that's even worse. Your wife is out of town taking care of her sick mother, and you have the gall to sleep with another woman. Please tell me this other person is not pregnant."

"Ah, no, she's not pregnant. I made sure of that."

"I won't ask you about any more details, but you have to know how I feel about this, don't you? I mean, you weren't raised like that Michael. You didn't see me running around on your mother. I was faithful to my wife until the day she died, and she had been sickly the last three years of our marriage."

"I know, Dad. I know, and I'm sorry for disappointing you. I intend on making things right with my wife. You can believe me on that. I have no desire or intentions of getting divorced. I still love Alese with all my heart. We have a family now and I can't let her walk away from that."

"I assumed she's the one who moved out since you answered the telephone."

"Yes, she did. I begged her to stay here with the baby, but she absolutely refused to remain at our house. She's living with her best friend, Karema Wright, in a condo in Meridian Common Estates."

"I see. Well, this is a fine mess you have on your hands. I wish there was something I could do."

"Dad, just finally being able to talk to you is a big relief. I've wanted to tell you about our separation since day one, but I just couldn't bring myself to do it. You're all that I have, and I dreaded disappointing you."

"Son, you haven't disappointed me. I know you're only human; you're flesh and blood just like I am. I just hope you've learned a valuable lesson behind all of this."

"Yes, I have. This is one lesson I've learned, and one mistake I'll never make again."

"What are you doing to get your family back?"

"I've tried everything I can think of, Dad; I've sent her all kinds of expensive gifts. But she hasn't been persuaded by any of them."

"That was your first mistake right there. Instead of giving her expensive gifts, you should have been showing her your heart."

"I know, but how can I do that?"

"You'll find a way. Believe me, if you want her back bad enough, you'll find a way."

"Thanks for calling me, Dad. I promise to keep you better informed from here on out."

"And you better do just that. Good night, son."

#

The next evening, Michael returned home from work around seven p.m. When he turned onto his street, Meadow Bay Avenue, he saw an older model blue and white GMC Sierra pick-up truck parked in his driveway. As soon as Michael turned off the engine to his automobile, he saw Jeremiah Wayne sliding out of the truck dressed in his trademark Docker's khaki pants and a green short sleeved polo shirt, looking in his direction with the sunlight shining on his warm sable face. Jeremiah watched Michael as he exited his vehicle with a navy suit coat and printed necktie draped over his arm, carrying a Wilson's leather briefcase.

"Daddy, what are you doing here?" Michael asked his father, reaching to shake his hand.

"What do you think I'm doing here, son? I came to see about my family."

"Ah, man, I told you I was doing fine."

"It's not you I'm worried about. I want to see my daughter-in-law and my grandbaby."

"I'm surprised you made it here in that truck. Don't you think it's time for a new vehicle, Dad? I mean this one has certainly seen better days."

"You don't have to worry about my truck. It's twenty-years old and still going strong. I'll put it up against your new car any time." Jeremiah laughed.

"Ah, I wouldn't do that if I was you. Dad, I don't know if Alese will be willing to see us tonight or not. She hasn't exactly let me do a lot of visiting with them since the separation."

"Let's go on in the house and give her a call and see what she has to say about it. I bet she'll be willing to see me," Jeremiah bragged, following Michael towards the house.

"How long were you here before I came home, Dad?"

"I just got here about thirty minutes ago."

"Why didn't you call and let me know you were coming. I could have been prepared for your visit?"

"There's nothing you need to do for me. After we talked last night, there's no way I would've been able to rest until I saw all of you."

After they entered the house, Michael placed his black briefcase on the kitchen counter, picked up the telephone, and started dialing the number to Karema's house. While waiting for Alese to pick up, he glanced over at Jeremiah, who in return, gave him a hopeful smile. Alese answered the telephone on the fourth ring.

"Hello, this is Alese."

Michael breathed in at the sound of her voice, closing his eyes for a second.

"Hi, Alese, how are you doing?" he asked, slowly exhaling.

"I'm doing fine, thanks."

"And how is my baby girl?"

"She's doing great."

"That's good. Listen, I have a visitor here at the house who's real anxious to see you."

"Oh, really, and who might that be?" she asked.

"Well, it's your father-in-law."

"You're kidding. Jeremiah is there?"

"Yes, he's here in the flesh. I just got home from work, and he was waiting in the driveway. Would you like to speak with him?"

"Sure, I would love to speak to Jeremiah."

Michael handed his father the telephone and patted him on the back.

"Hello, Alese, how are you and my grandbaby?"

"We're doing fine. I can't believe you're in Jacksonville."

"Yeah, I drove up today just to visit my family. Michael told me about the separation, but I was still hoping to see you and the baby tonight. That is, if you don't mind."

[165]

"No, of course, I wouldn't mind. Karema is still at the church, and I was getting ready to give Bianca a bath, but tell Michael to bring you right on over."

"Thank you, sweetheart, I appreciate that. We'll be there as soon as we can. I'll see you then."

"Sure, Dad, see you shortly. Bye."

"I told you she would want to see me." Jeremiah smiled, hanging up the telephone. "Now, let's go see that wife and baby of yours."

#

Michael and his father talked the entire way to Karema's subdivision. It felt like they hadn't communicated in ages since Michael hadn't been open with him during many of their previous conversations. However, he felt like it was time to purge his soul to Jeremiah. They were normally able to verbalize their feelings with one another and talk about everything under the sun, moon, and stars.

Being a single parent to two young boys after his wife passed away, Jeremiah had encouraged them to come to him for fatherly advice whenever they needed it. He was determined to raise his sons on his own and not marry just anybody for the sake of providing them with a mother. Of course, he had many female suitors knocking at his side door for weeks and months after Margaret passed, bringing him homemade dishes and offering to clean his house. He turned every one of them down and concentrated on being a good parent until after both his boys had finished high school. He wasn't perfect, but he certainly tried to be a positive role model for his children.

When Margaret passed, it had hurt him to the core. He honestly felt he would never love again or feel any greater pain. Of course, that was the case until his oldest son, Reuben, died over three years ago at the age of thirty-nine. He was engaged to marry a beautiful Hispanic woman, Rosita, when they discovered the cancer in his lungs. He passed away only one month before his fortieth birthday. Now with both of them gone, Michael and Alese were his only immediate family and there was no way that Jeremiah wanted to see them divorced. He had loved Alese from the instant his son had

[166]

introduced her to him. As a matter of fact, he told Michael the first night he met Alese, "Son, if you don't marry that fine woman, I will. I've been thinking about getting married again anyway," he said, laughing heartily.

He was joking, but Michael must have gotten the message loud and clear because just a few months later, they were planning a wedding in Kansas. Jeremiah made sure he didn't miss it. He was so proud to finally have a daughter-in-law with a family he admired.

"Daddy, we're here," Michael stated, interrupting Jeremiah's thinking.

"Well, what are we waiting for, let's go on inside," he replied, opening the car door.

Alese was already at the front door looking radiant with her locks flowing at her shoulders, wearing a black and white capri pants set.

"Hi, Dad, it's so good to see you," she cried, hugging Jeremiah's neck.

"Oh, it's so good to see you, too," he replied.

"Hi, Michael. You two can come right on in." Alese held the front door open and turned sideways for them to pass on into the living room. Michael returned Alese's greeting as he entered the area looking around for his baby girl.

"My daddy! My daddy!" shouted Bianca, running towards Michael fresh out of the bathtub, wearing a long pink Barbie nightgown.

"Hey, baby," Michael replied, picking her up. "This old man right here is your granddaddy."

"Hello, Bianca. Come give your grandpoppa a hug," Jeremiah said, reaching out for her. Bianca went straight into his arms and gave him a tight squeeze around the neck.

Minutes later, we were all sitting down in the comfortable living room fawning over Bianca. She loved being the center of attention and she was definitely it for that night. Bianca kept going to her room, bringing out new toys to show her daddy or bringing out her papers from preschool to share with him.

"Oh, baby, these are great. You're doing great in school," he said, encouraging her.

"You sure are. I got me a smart little grandbaby," Jeremiah bragged.

"Let me go get you all something cold to drink," I offered. "Dad, what would you like?" I asked, looking at Jeremiah's smiling face.

"Oh, sweetheart, I'll take anything that's cold. On second thought, any kind of diet soda would be great if you have it."

"Sure, and Michael, can I get you something, too?"

"Yes, I'll have a regular Coke, Pepsi or whatever soda you have."

"I'll be right back," I stated, turning towards the kitchen.

Michael sprang up and followed behind me. I should have known he would take advantage of any opportunity to get close to me.

"Let me come help you with that, Alese," he offered.

"I think I can handle a few drinks by myself, Michael," I said, opening the refrigerator door. I pulled out three soft drinks, including one diet soda, and placed them on the kitchen counter.

"I know you can, but I just wanted to help and maybe have a minute to spend alone with you," he said, closing the small gap between us. He reached out and took my free hand into his and placed the palm of it over his heart.

"Do you feel that? That's my heart beating for you, Alese."

"How do I know that it's beating for me and not for someone else?" I asked nervously, avoiding his stare.

"Because I'm not in love with someone else, I'm in love with you," he responded quickly. I pulled my hand away from his chest, filled three glasses with ice, opened the sodas, and then poured them into the tall glasses. Michael stood behind me, wrapping his arms around my waist, and then pressed his genitals against my buttocks. "Umh, baby, you smell great. Is that a new perfume you're wearing?" he asked, whispering in my ear.

"Ah, yes, it's called Mediterranean," I replied softly, feeling his warm breath on my neck.

"It's different. I really like that."

"Thank you, Michael," I responded, trying to control my slightly sporadic breathing. This man was going to be the death of me.

[168]

"Are we still on for our anniversary dinner?" he asked, nibbling on my earlobe.

"Yes, we're still on for that. I'll call you with the details once I've decided what I'd like to do."

"Whatever you want to do is fine with me. I mean—being with you is all that matters to me." Alese Then, I gently pushed him away from me, turned around, and looked him dead in the eyes. As much as I adored his full sexy lips and craved the warmth of his body, I wasn't about to give into temptation.

"What do you want from me, Michael?" I asked.

"I want you to be my wife. I want to be with you the way a man is supposed to be with his wife," he uttered.

"What if I'm not prepared to do that? What if I can't do that?"

"Alese, I know you very well. And I know you can do anything you set your mind to. Do you want to be with me again or not?"

"I—I don't know, Michael. I want to be with you, but then I feel guilty for lusting after you. It's almost as if I'm the other woman now," I whispered, sounding fearful of my own words.

"That's nonsense, Alese. You're my wife and I want to make you feel like my wife. I can make you feel like you're the only woman on the face of this earth if you let me."

"Michael, please. Don't try to patronize me with your smooth lover's rap."

"My mommy, may I have something to drink, please?" Bianca asked, running into the kitchen.

"Sure, baby, I'll fix you a soda, too," I responded. I was grateful for the interruption because I wasn't sure if I could take much more of being alone in a room with Michael.

After preparing an additional smaller glass, we took the drinks into the living room and continued our pleasant conversation. Moments later, Karema entered through the front door, looking happily surprised, and spoke to everyone relaxing on her furniture. She excused herself after exchanging greetings with her guests, informing them that she was extremely tired and retiring for the evening.

"Well, Dad, I think it's time for us to go." Michael stood up.

"Yeah, son, you're right. It's getting late, and this little lady needs to be in bed," he said, grabbing Bianca again. He hugged her. "Thank you, Alese," he said, taking my hand into his. "It was good seeing you both."

"How long are you going to be here? You're not leaving right away are you?"

"I'm not leaving tomorrow, but I don't plan on being here more than a couple of days."

"We would love to see you again," I stated, picking up Bianca. I really like my father-in-law.

"In that case, I'll see you both tomorrow sometime."

"That sounds great." I embraced Jeremiah.

"Do I get one of those, too?" Michael asked, opening his arms.

"Sure," I responded, giving him a light hug and a kiss on the cheek. Michael held his baby girl for several moments, telling her how much he loved her, and then he kissed her good-bye on the forehead before leaving.

#

On their way to the car, Jeremiah told his son he only had one thing to say to him. "What's that, Dad?"

"That there woman is still in love with you, son. You have got to get her back."

"How am I supposed to do that?"

"I don't know. You're the one with a college degree. I'm sure you'll figure something out. I didn't raise a dummy," Jeremiah replied, laughing as he entered the car.

"You don't have to answer this question if you don't want to, Dad. I was just wondering, were you and mom ever separated?" Michael asked, turning the key in the ignition.

Jeremiah didn't answer right away. He pondered the question several seconds before opening his mouth.

"Michael, your mother and I had our share of problems just like every other married couple. We stayed together through thick and thin. I wasn't always perfect, but I never stepped outside my marriage for comfort, and I believe she respected that," he said, adding a slight laugh. "I could never find anyone to replace her. She was a saint."

"Yes, she was. I wish Alese could have known her. They would have been great friends."

"Well, I'm looking forward to having my daughter-in-law and grandbaby back at your place for my next visit," Jeremiah said, shifting in his seat, turning to look at Michael.

"Yeah, you and me both."

16

School Time

"Welcome back, Mrs. Wayne. We're glad to have you back with us this year. How are you enjoying your first day at school so far?" Principal Harper asked, wearing a tan Worthington suit with a white shirt and mocha printed necktie as he entered my classroom and smiled at me sitting behind my oak desk. It was mid-August, the beginning of the new school year.

"Hi, Mr. Harper. Thank you for welcoming me back. So far, my first day is going quite well. This is the first period, and I have planning." I stood and gave my big, tall, bald headed principal a warm friendly embrace. I smoothed my hands down the front of my wine colored pants suit after releasing Mr. Harper.

"You better enjoy it because all of your classes will be filled to capacity for this semester."

"That's fine with me. I'm just happy to be here considering I missed all of the previous school semester. I'm excited about returning to my position in the computer laboratory and meeting my new students."

"That's a good thing. You should have a lot of energy saved up for us, and I'm sure you're going to need every bit of it since you're mainly teaching sixth graders this year. Are you prepared for that?"

"Yes, sir. I'm looking forward to the challenge of working with them. This is their first year of middle school and I know they deserve special attention. I've planned some really fun and practical activities for them to explore at the computer stations."

"That's great. I just wanted to say we're happy to have you back. I was sorry to hear about your mother; you have my condolences, Mrs. Wayne," he said, patting me on the back.

"Thank you, sir. I was pleased with the floral arrangement you all sent for the funeral service. I need to personally thank the head of the courtesy and welfare committee."

"I'm sure Mrs. Parker will be delighted to hear from you. I have to continue my rounds. You know where to find me if you should need anything. Oh, by the way, we're having a short faculty meeting after school is out today in the cafeteria. We have a special treat for the teachers."

"Yes, sir, I'll try to be the first one there." I laughed. "You have a nice day." Then, I thought about something else as he was walking out. "Mr. Harper! I just wanted to thank you again for extending me a leave of absence for last semester. You'll never know how much I appreciate that."

"Mrs. Wayne, if the truth be told, sometimes we all need a semester off to become rejuvenated. I'd rather allow you time to rejuvenate than to have an overworked, stressed out educator on my hands."

"Yes, I understand exactly what you're talking about. I'm really ready to enjoy the year ahead of us. I have so many ideas for the class and field trips that I want to discuss with you at a later date if you don't mind."

"No problem. You can stop by my office anytime. I've got to run. You take care." Mr. Harper stepped rapidly out the door carrying his walkie-talkie in his hand on his way to visit another teacher's classroom. I could hear someone from the main office paging him as he exited my class.

Since this was my planning period, I could finally finish up with my bulletin boards and get prepared for the first incoming class. Sitting quietly at my desk cutting out stenciled letters, I looked up when I heard a familiar young voice call my name.

"Hi, Mrs. Wayne."

I looked up to see my former neighbor, Macy, standing in the doorway smiling through her new braces. She was wearing low cut blue jeans and a short Army green T-shirt with an oversized backpack on her shoulders.

"Hi, Macy, I'm so glad to see you." I ran to the door and hugged Macy as I pulled her on into the classroom. "Welcome to Bayshire Middle School. Are you in my class?"

"Yes, ma'am. I'll be coming to your class next period. I just stopped by to say hello. I asked my science teacher, Mrs. Patterson, for a pass to come see you since I finished my assignment early."

"That's wonderful. Come on in and sit down right here next to me so we can chat. I have to say I really miss you, your sister, and your mom. I haven't talked to her in months." I pulled up a chair for Macy to sit at the side of my desk. She really looked happy.

"Yes, I know, and we all miss you very much. My mom talks about you all the time and Angela talks about Bianca every day," she said, removing her backpack and taking a seat.

"Please be sure and tell Shelly I said hello. I will try to call her real soon. Let me give you my cell phone number so you all can reach me anytime." I removed a yellow post-it sheet and wrote my cell number down for Macy and handed it to her.

"Thanks, Mrs. Wayne," she said, taking the sheet. Macy placed it in her large black and blue backpack. "I really miss having you to talk to since you left your house. When are you and Mr. Wayne getting back together so you can move back home?"

"Macy, I can't talk with you about that, but thank you for your concern. All I can tell you for now is that I'm not sure when we'll be returning to our home. I do promise you that I'll bring Bianca by to visit you all real soon, though."

"That would be great. I really miss playing with her. She's so much fun to be around."

I noticed that Macy's mood had unexpectedly changed as she became quiet, dropped her head, and fiddled with her fingers. Not wanting to pressure the child, I gave her a few seconds to think before she said anything.

"Macy, is everything all right at home?"

"Some of the time, it's okay. Like as long as Mr. Landers is not around, I don't have to witness them arguing and fighting."

"Oh, so your mom is still dating Mr. Landers."

"I guess you could call it dating, but it's more like he's living there."

"Ah, do you have a problem with him being there? Has he done anything inappropriate around you?"

"Oh, no, ma'am, it's nothing like that. It's just that he treats my mom so bad. He calls her ugly names and hits her all the time for no reason. But then whenever he leaves, she starts crying. I just hate seeing my mom so sad all the time."

"I know that has to be difficult for you, sweetheart. When is your mom happy? She has to be happy sometime."

"All I know is when he's there, she spends most of the time fighting with him, and when he's not there, she spends most of her time in her bedroom crying and listening to sad love songs. I just don't know what to do anymore to make her happy."

"Have you tried talking to your mother and telling her how you feel, Macy?"

"I don't like to bother her when she's crying like that. She doesn't think we know she's in her room crying under the sound of the loud music. But we can hear her, and we don't know what else to do except leave her alone and try to keep quiet so she won't get angry with us."

"Listen to me, Macy." I leaned in closer to the child. "I want you to talk to your mother tonight. Even if she's crying, I want you to talk to her and tell her how it makes you feel to see her in that condition. I honestly believe if you tell her how sad this situation is making you, she might reassess her relationship with Mr. Landers. I dread giving you this responsibility, but as the oldest child you have to take the lead and approach your mom. I don't think she'll get angry with you once she hears how you honestly feel about her situation."

"You really think she won't get mad with me, Mrs. Wayne?" Macy asked with a glimmer of hope in her eyes.

"Yes, I do, and I feel it's worth a try. Do you think you can do that for me?"

"Oh, yes, ma'am, I will do that for you tonight."

"Thank you, Macy, and I want you to let me know tomorrow how it works out."

"Yes, no problem, Mrs. Wayne," she said, hugging my neck.

At that moment, the bell rang. I instructed Macy to choose a seat in my class before the other students arrived. Macy smiled as she stood and selected the work station closest to me, her new admirable teacher.

I sailed through the remainder of the work day with ease. I had been requesting to work strictly with the sixth grade students for the last two years. They were the ones who had the most interesting questions and were the most willing to work on classroom assignments. But as well as the day had progressed, I could still see the disappointment on Macy's face every time I had a free second to myself. My heart was hurting for that child. I pondered whether or not to call Shelly, but decided to wait until Macy returned to my class the next day.

Immediately after school, I hustled to the cafeteria for the faculty's reception. I was elated to see all of my former co-workers and cheerfully introduced myself to the new teachers. After about twenty minutes of eating from the vegetable tray, the fruit tray, and the dessert table, I was ready to pick up Bianca from preschool and head to our temporary home. I still had not found another place to stay since Karema insisted on us remaining with her until the divorce was finalized. Honestly, I think she was just praying for us to get back together and didn't want me to move into a new place yet.

Although I had checked out several condominiums and townhomes in the surrounding area, I decided to do as Karema had requested. Since I appreciated having the company of another adult, I wasn't in a hurry to leave her comfortable dwellings. As a pastor, Karema spent a lot of time at church, so we had the house to ourselves most of the day anyway.

Arriving home a few minutes past four o'clock, my cell phone started ringing upon entering the front door. After instructing Bianca to take her pink Scooby Doo backpack into the bedroom and watch television, I opened my black Claiborne bag and clicked on my white iPhone.

"Hello, this is Alese."

"I know who you are," Vivian laughed.

"Hi, sis, how's it going?"

"It's going pretty well. How are you holding up?" Vivian asked.

"Well, today was my first day back at school, so that's helping me to really keep my mind intact. I tell you what, one day with middle school kids, and you're still lucky to have a good brain. But right now, they're the glue that's holding me together."

"I take it you and Michael are still separated."

"Yes, we are. How are you and Darnell doing?"

"Actually, we're doing much better. Since Ma Dear passed, we've been spending a lot more time together and talking about our feelings for each other. We've also been volunteering a lot at the church trying to help other people. Like you said, the best way to forget about your problems is to help other people with theirs."

"That's right. Sometimes that's the only way to remain sane. If you get too caught up in your own problems, you'll definitely end up losing it. Helping those kids at school is the best therapy in the world for me."

"I'm just happy Darnell and I are finally laughing and talking again. It's not like it was before, but better than it's been in months."

"That's good news, Vivian. I'm always happy to see couples stay together and work out their differences."

"So when are you going to take your own advice, sister girl?"

"What are you talking about?"

"Alese, your marital situation is no different than mine, and my husband stayed with me."

"And I'm glad he did, but my circumstances are different from yours."

"Michael cheated on you, and I cheated on Darnell, so what is the difference? We both committed a sin."

"Well, for one thing, you told Darnell about your indiscretion the next day. You didn't practice to deceive him. I had to learn about Michael's affair from a friend of mine who was bold enough to leave a message in my mailbox. Then, on top of that, he thought the woman might have been pregnant by him. And as conniving as she seems to be, I'm truly surprised she didn't plan to get pregnant. So, the only credit I can give to him is that he did have sense enough to 'fess up when I confronted him. And then the other thing is this-- you don't have to see Paula every day. That woman is still working for Michael, so he's seeing her at work on a regular basis. How am I supposed to deal with that?"

"You're right. Paula and I aren't friends anymore and we hardly ever see each other. But I still wish you would reconsider your decision about pursuing a divorce this quickly. At least give it a full year from the date of your separation before filing for permanent papers. You never know how you might feel a year from now."

[177]

"I hear what you're saying, Vivian, I really do. I believe Michael has moved on and so should I."

"Alese, how has the man moved on when he's still strung out on you? I saw the way he held you at Ma Dear's funeral and the way he stood by your side protecting you from all evil forces after the service." Vivian laughed at her analogy.

"Yeah, yeah, whatever you say. I have to go check on Bianca; she's being too quiet back there in her room. Please give my love to Darnell and the kids. Are they still singing in the youth choir?"

"Yes, they are, and I will certainly tell them you sent your love and asked about them. You can tell my little niece I said hello, and I'll talk to you real soon. But seriously, sis, I want you to think about what I've said. If Darnell and I can get through this, then, you and Michael have to do the same. I'll tell you this, and then, I'll let you go. I'm so thankful to God that Darnell did not leave me when I told him about my one night stand. I've been praying every day for God to see us through this, and now we're finally making some progress. It's been over a year since the incident occurred."

"Well, thanks for sharing with me, Vivian. I'll call you later in the week. I have to go check on my child. Good-bye."

"I love you, sis. Bye-bye."

#

The next day at school, I was dressed comfortably in a long flowing brown skirt and a white knit top as I waited patiently for my first class to enter the room. Searching for Macy's face, I looked up each time a student swaggered in. Finally, Macy stepped into the classroom wearing a pink shirt, jeans, and a brighter smile than she did yesterday. She appeared to be much more relaxed and attentively listened to the instructions prior to beginning her computer lesson. I stopped at her computer station several times to confirm that she was progressing along with the assignment.

When the bell rang, signaling the end of the class period, I returned to my desk and waited for the child to approach me on the way out. Sure enough, Macy was the last one to leave the room and stopped at my desk before leaving.

"Mrs. Wayne, thank you for the advice you gave me yesterday. I got a chance to talk with my mom last night."

"Oh, I'm so proud of you, and how did it go?" I asked, beaming with joy, looking up at Macy.

"It went really well. She said she was sorry for crying around us so much and it was time for her to put Mr. Landers out of our lives. She said she didn't want me or my sister to think that's how a real man treats a woman."

"I'm just glad to see you wearing a big smile today, sweetheart."

"Yes, ma'am. I even helped her pack his clothes last night. My Uncle Ricky came over to our house to protect us while Mr. Landers came in to get his things. He put a gun in Mr. Landers face and told him that if he ever touched his sister again he would shoot him dead, and he wasn't playing either."

"Oh, goodness, I am so sorry you had to witness something like that, baby." My heart went out to Macy as I stood to lovingly embrace the child. I had also held her as an infant when Michael and I first moved into the neighborhood.

Macy shrugged. "Maybe now my mother will leave him alone, and I won't have to worry about her crying all the time and being so sad. Maybe we can all be happy again for a while. I just hope she don't get another boyfriend too soon and repeat the same cycle."

"Sweetheart, your mother loves you, and she would do anything in the world to make you happy. You have to trust that she has learned something from this experience, so don't you worry about her."

"Yes, ma'am. Thank you for encouraging me to tell her how I felt. I never thought she would put him out for me. I love you, Mrs. Wayne."

"I love you, too, Macy." I prayed that Shelly had come to her senses and was finally ready to leave Mr. Landers alone. She could do bad all by herself. I never understood how someone with Shelly's looks and sparkling personality could fall victim to an abusive man like Garrett. I'd seen cases where women with doctoral degrees had married city bus drivers. Certainly, there wasn't anything wrong with that, but it takes a special man to handle those circumstances. I remembered one of Ma Dear's profound sayings, "Sometimes you need to look deep before you leap."

By Friday, my computer technology classes had shaped up fine. All of the students had been assigned to a particular work station and had their major projects lined up for the next two weeks. The last class had just left for the day and after straightening up my classroom desk, I entered my office to retrieve my purse along with the stack of papers I was planning to take home and grade over the weekend when the office telephone rang.

"Hi, Alese. This is Shelly. I was calling to say thank you for talking with my daughter at school this week. She told me that you were helpful and you advised her to talk with me. I really appreciate your kindness."

"It was my pleasure to counsel with Macy. She is an adorable child and she's old enough to know what's going on in the house. It's almost impossible to fool children once they reach a certain age; I was even surprised by some of the things she said."

"Yes, I know, it was something I had to seriously think about, and once I realized how our behavior was affecting my children, I had to do it for no other reason but for them. That wasn't good for them to see me doing all that crying, walking around the house with a black eye for days and a busted lip because I was too ashamed to go to work. I just can't live like that, girlfriend."

"I don't understand how you lived with it for as long as you did. There's no reason for you to let any man abuse you like that, Shelly. You're a beautiful woman and you haven't even turned forty-years old yet. I know God has somebody good in store for you. I'm telling you, I'm not psychic, but I can see the handwriting on the wall. I'm praying for you to find happiness with or without a man."

"Thank you so much for everything. Listen, when can we get together and have lunch or dinner one evening? We have so much to catch up on and I've really missed having you so close by."

"I've missed you and the girls a lot, too. Bianca asks about you and them all the time. I feel so bad taking her away from her home like that, but I just can't be in that house right now. And even though

[180]

Michael volunteered to move out, I just can't see myself living there for the time being."

"I just find it hard to believe you two have been separated for this long. I've never seen a more loving couple with so much love and compassion for each other. Are you sure this is something that can't be worked out? Have you guys tried going to marriage counseling?"

"No, we haven't even discussed the possibility of consulting with a marriage counselor yet, but we have been counseling separately with our pastor."

"Well, that's good. That's real good. I know she's giving you both sound Christian advice. Hold on for one second, please." After a brief pause, Shelly returned. "I'm sorry, Alese, but I have to get back to work. My boss will be back any minute and I don't want her to catch me making a personal telephone call for any reason."

"Thank you for calling me, Shelly. I feel better just speaking with you."

"Well, thank you, for helping me with my child. You see these children are something else, but you have truly been a blessing to both me and my family. I'm so glad Macy is in your class. Please keep me posted and let me know if you have any problems out of her."

"I don't think you have to worry about Macy causing any problems. She's already one of my best students and I'm happy to have her in my class."

"Thank you. I'll talk to you soon. Don't forget to call me about having lunch soon."

"You can count on it, Shelly," I replied, hanging up the telephone. I truly hoped she meant every word she'd just said. Shelly didn't have any reason to be desperate for a man.

17

Love Me or Leave Me?

Lisa waited in her office until most of the employees had left for the day. She pretended to be doing Internet research for an upcoming deadline on the Keiser project as her co-workers bid her good night, one by one. Finally, everyone in her department was gone for the day. Believing Tracy left work early every Tuesday night to take a computer class at the local community college, Lisa straightened her short belted sheath and tapped down the hall to Michael's office. Assuming he was working late, Lisa tried to catch him before he left.

"Hello, Michael," Lisa said, marching into his office. She sat down in front of him, crossed her legs, showing off her yellow toned thighs, and hung her hands over the side of the armchair. "You know, you don't have to avoid me. I mean we do work together, right?"

"Lisa, I believe you're confused. We don't work together, you work for me," Michael responded, looking up at Lisa from his desk before he continued. "And why did you enter my office without knocking?"

"There's no one here and I didn't think we had to be so formal. We are still friends, aren't we?" she asked with a sly smile.

"I don't know if I would call it that. But, anyway, what do you want, Lisa?" Michael asked, trying to get to the point of her visit.

"Well, today is my birthday. I stopped by to see if you were coming to my birthday party tonight, or did you forget?" she asked, gazing at him.

"Lisa, I have no intentions of attending your birthday party tonight or any other night for that matter," he responded, staring at her in amazement.

"Michael, all of the Program Designers will be in attendance and most of the office personnel. How would it look for the boss man not to be at a birthday party for one of his top Program Designers?" she asked, eyeing him carefully. "Don't you think that might make people a little bit suspicious? Some rumors might start circulating about us."

Michael guffawed. "Like I really care what people around here think," he said, throwing his head back laughing more.

"Your wife might care what people around here think. If she heard a rumor about us being involved again, don't you think she would leave you this time?" Michael stopped laughing and looked at her seriously.

"For your information, Alese and I are already separated so don't waste anymore of your precious time worrying about my wife. That's my responsibility."

"Oh, I'm sorry to hear that," she said sarcastically. "Then, she wouldn't be surprised if I filed a sexual harassment suit against you? I mean, if it came to that?" she asked, raising both hands to pull her long hair back and let it fall over her shoulders.

"Are you trying to blackmail me, Lisa?"

"No, Michael, I was just joking," she said with a short giggle. "All I'm doing is asking my boss to make a guest appearance at my birthday party tonight at eight, at Café Pierre in the back party lounge," she stated, emphasizing her words.

"Yeah, whatever," he responded. "Good night, Lisa."

"Michael, I'm really sorry about your wife. I wouldn't do anything to jeopardize your relationship with her. You have to believe me about that. I'm finally over you and I haven't tried to communicate with you in months. Besides, my new man is going to be there tonight and I just don't want to have a big party and neither one of my bosses show up. I mean, Marty is out of town until Friday. Everyone will be looking for you there for real."

"The only thing I know right now is that you need to leave my office. I believe I've already said good night once."

"Fine, Michael. Don't say I didn't try to help you maintain a front with your employees. If you start hearing any rumors around the office, don't try to blame me," Lisa said sweetly, swinging her hair back. She trekked out of his office.

\#

It was almost nine o'clock before Michael arrived at the restaurant. He had second thoughts about attending this event but since he was the president of the company, he usually attended birthday parties, especially for the Program Designers. Even though he agreed with Lisa about arousing suspicions, he didn't want her to know he was in agreement with any part of what she said. That little sexual harassment joke she threw in there wasn't funny. All he needed was the hint of a sexual lawsuit being filed, and his reputation and marriage would be long gone along with any chance of adopting a child. Keeping all that in mind, he decided he would go and make a guest appearance, as Lisa had put it, speak to a few employees, and be on his way.

Michael felt strange entering the restaurant; he didn't see any sign of a party. But then he remembered she said it would be in the back lounge room. Passing the long bar area, he assumed he recognized a face with oddly colored eyes, but since they didn't look up again in his direction, he didn't bother to speak. There was definitely a party going on in the back area, although he couldn't identify any of the people. He stepped further into the area, searching the setting for familiar office associates.

There, in the corner of the room sitting at a table alone, was Lisa. She had put her hair up and changed from her work clothes. She was wearing a designer red sequin evening gown with thin straps and a plunging neckline. When he approached her table for two, she sprang out of her seat, wrapped her arms around his neck, and held her face against his for several seconds. Michael reached up and pulled her by the arms away from him, staring her in the face.

"What is this, Lisa? I understood you were having a birthday party tonight?"

"Well, there is a party here tonight, and it is my birthday," she responded, pointing in the direction of the party crowd and then looking back at him with a huge grin on her face.

"Oh, so you're playing games again, Lisa?" he asked, using a dangerous tone.

"Michael, please, just sit down so we can talk," she said pleadingly, grabbing him by the hand. She pulled him down beside her. "Please, don't make a scene. This is the only way I could think

[184]

of to get you here. All I want to do is talk to you. Just sit down for two minutes, and then you can leave. I promise."

"Look, Lisa," he said, sitting down at the table. "I told you before, there's nothing to talk about. I don't know how to make myself any clearer than I already have. I don't need your games or your threats. I can't fire you because I know you'll file a frivolous lawsuit just to ruin my name, but I don't have to play your games. Now, get a life and leave mine the hell alone!" Michael stated angrily, storming out of the restaurant.

#

I was simply ecstatic Michael had asked me out to dinner on Saturday night. I felt like a teenager going to my first prom. Even though it was our sixteenth wedding anniversary, I wasn't ready to take him back. But I was finally ready to talk with him about our marriage situation. Regardless of what he'd done, my heart was saying he still loved me and Bianca more than all the tea in China.

It was early September and we had been apart now for six months already. Although I agreed to go out with him, I had decided I would prefer cooking a meal for us at the condominium. Michael loved my cooking and he had never turned down the opportunity to taste one of my homemade specialties.

Karema had volunteered to take Bianca out to see a new children's movie. That would give us at least two hours together to enjoy our dinner and conversation. I wouldn't have to worry about things going further than I intended like they had before because there was a time factor involved. I asked Karema to give me a call before they left the theatre and to bring Bianca home directly after the movie. I still didn't quite trust myself being in Michael's company for that long, especially knowing the power he held in his strong hands and tongue.

It took all day for me to pick out on the perfect outfit to entertain my husband in tonight. I didn't want to appear too alluring, but I also didn't want to look homely either. I eventually decided to wear something blue, Michael's preferred color. I had bought this dress before we separated and hadn't had a chance to wear it for a special occasion. It was a cloud blue, full-length, jacquard print caftan with three-quarter sleeves, and gold embroidered trim around the v-cut neck. There were deep slits on both sides to show off my shapely legs. It came with a matching head wrap, but I thought that might be a little bit more than I wanted for this occasion. I left it out on the bed just in case I changed my mind.

After I chose the perfect outfit, I walked to the kitchen and started preparing our evening meal. I chose to make my delicious lemon pepper baked chicken, Italian green bean casserole, buttered new potatoes, and pecan candied yams. I also made a fresh pitcher of sweet tea with sliced lemons and placed it in the refrigerator to chill while I finished working on dinner.

As I prepared our meal, I managed to control my desires to sample the dishes after I took them out of the oven and placed them on the counter. Immediately after the pecan-candied yams were done, I wrapped things up in the kitchen and headed off to take a hot bubble bath before getting dressed. I was eager to open up my new two-piece perfume set, Sensuous, by Estee Lauder with the shimmering body lotion. I loved myself some good perfume, and so did Michael. He made sure I was always stocked with the best designer fragrances on the market. I didn't wear many designer clothes, but designer perfumes were my trademark passions. I visited the Dillard's fragrance counter on a regular basis to sample the newest scents upon their arrival. All the sales women greeted me by name and with pleasure whenever I entered that department.

I scanned through my CD collection case and pulled out Helen Baylor's, *The Live Experience*, and placed it in the CD player. I wanted to hear the uplifting live version of the song, *God Is Able*. As I closed the door to the guest bathroom, the doorbell ring.

Oh, my goodness. I hope that's not Michael here already. He's got at least another hour before he's supposed to be here.

Peeping through the door window, I saw the mailman standing there with a brown manila package in his hand. I wondered who would be sending me a package, but it really didn't matter because I actually loved surprises.

"Hello, may I help you?" I asked, opening the door and smiling at the postman.

"Hi, how are you today? I have a special delivery package for Alese Wayne. Is she available?"

"I'm fine, thank you, sir. I'm Alese Wayne," I responded.

"Oh, great," he said. "I just need you to sign right here, and you can have your package," he said, passing her the clipboard to sign.

"Thank you, sir. You have a nice day," I said, smiling.

"You're welcome, and you have a nice day, too," he said, turning to walk away.

I thought Michael had sent me some new token of love to show his appreciation for me making dinner for us tonight. He had sent me so many nice gifts over the last six months until I barely had enough space to keep them all at the condominium. Not to mention all the presents he sent for Bianca; he bought for that child like every toy store was having a going out of business sale and giving it away almost for free. He even bought the baby jewelry and diamond bracelets, too.

I pulled all the tape off the flap of the envelope, reached inside, and pulled out a stack of eight-by-ten photographs. At first, I assumed they were pictures of Michael and me together. But then, I didn't recognize the setting or the red-bone, half-dressed female with her arms wrapped around my man and all up in his face. I quickly flipped through the stack and glanced at all the other pictures. They were all of Michael and—wait a minute—Lisa Bradford!

There were a total of ten photographs in all. Each one was a shot of Lisa and Michael at some restaurant together either embracing or sitting at a table for two holding hands and gazing at each other. I was absolutely livid; I tossed the photographs across the room where they scattered to the floor.

"How dare that...," I couldn't say it. I would not let his disloyalty turn me into committing blasphemy again. I had already repented for that sin.

Running to my bedroom, I slammed the door shut, fell across my bed, and wept into the pillow. Our marriage was over for real. I would not wait for the adoption to become final to file for divorce from Michael. I couldn't and wouldn't live like this for the rest of my life. Just when I was beginning to think maybe we had a chance and maybe he was really sorry, I found out he was still involved with her. He would have to suffer the consequences of his adulterous actions this time.

I was suddenly awakened by the sound of the ringing doorbell. I rolled over, realizing I had cried myself to sleep and almost an hour had passed.

That must be Michael at the door this time.

Scrambling out of bed, I gathered up all the pictures. Placing the photographs back in the mailing envelope I had received them in, I walked stealthily to answer the door. I threw the door open to see Michael standing there neatly dressed in taupe trousers, a taupe printed shirt, and freshly polished black leather shoes. He was holding a dozen red roses wrapped in green foil paper in one hand and a huge box of Godiva's assorted chocolates in the other hand.

"Hello, baby," he said. "What took you so long to answer the door? I was about to call you from my cell phone," he added.

"Hi, Michael. Come on in. I need to talk to you," I said, turning away from him quickly, walking into the living room.

"I have something to show you, Michael," I said, handing him the package. "This came in the mail for me today as a special delivery."

"What is this, Alese?" he asked, eyeing the package with a puzzled look on his face. He placed the flowers and chocolates on the coffee table.

"Just open it and find out, Michael," I retorted, standing with my arms crossed.

Michael held the large envelope with one hand and pulled out the large pictures with the other one. After viewing the first photo, he instantly dropped the whole stack on the floor, and jumped back like he had touched a hot iron.

"What in the world is this?" he asked, staring at me in horror.

"I don't know, Michael, you tell me. The date I see stamped on those photographs is August 31, which means they were taken just four days ago," I said. "Surely you can remember where you were four nights ago."

Michael didn't answer; he was too busy picking up the pictures and viewing each of them in total astonishment with his mouth gaped open. He wondered out loud, "How did someone take these photos of me?" Suddenly, I could tell he remembered something.

"Alese, baby, this is a misunderstanding. I can explain this, baby. I really can," he begged.

"Save it, Michael!" I snapped. "One picture is worth a thousand words! And right now, I don't need to hear one word from you!" I shouted, burning with rage.

"Alese, please, it's not what it looks like."

"Get out Michael! Right now! I mean it!" I yelled at the top of my lungs that time, grabbing his presents.

"Alese, let me explain, please!" He yelled back at me.

"I said get out Michael! And just for the record, I want a divorce—happy anniversary!" I shouted, opening the front door, throwing the flowers and the candy outside as far as I could.

After he left, I slammed the door and stood there on the other side holding myself with my head leaning back against the door. I slid all the way down until my bottom hit the floor and cried out in pain. "Why me, Lord? Why me? Oh, Jesus! Why me?"

#

Michael was steaming when he slid the keys into the ignition and started his car. First, he clutched the steering wheel and tried to control his temper but then started hitting it with all his might.

"I can't believe I let that crazy woman set me up like that!" he shouted, brimming with anger. "How could I have been so stupid? I should have known Lisa was up to something. I really should have known she was up to something. Well, I got something for her head, I tell you that. Oh, I got something for that head!" he screamed, driving away.

When Michael arrived at Lisa's house approximately thirty minutes later, the lights were off, and her car was gone. Even though he was calmer by now, he still got out, ran up the steps, and banged on her door. He considered maybe she was in there and didn't want to face him right now. But more than likely, she had sense enough not to be there after doing what she had done to ruin his life. Michael stood there for a few minutes looking around for any sign of Lisa

[189]

before he headed back to his car and drove off again towards Marty's house.

"Marty, man, I got to talk to you. I need to talk to you right now. Man, you are not going to believe this," Michael said, entering Marty's side door leading into the game room.

"Mike, man, what in the world happened to you? You look like you're ready to wrestle a live dinosaur, man. Have a seat," Marty commanded, closing the door and turning to face his friend. In all the years he had known Michael, he had never seen him this angry. He was even scaring Marty.

"Marty, man, you're just not going to believe this. It's so unbelievable I can't even get it out," he said, shaking his head and looking around the room for Tina.

"Ah, man, don't worry. Tina is still at the shop and the kids are at one of the neighbor's house for a sleep over. We're alone, so get it on out," he demanded, sitting down beside Mike on the upholstered cloth ottoman.

"I told you about the other night, how Lisa tricked me into thinking she had a birthday party going on at the restaurant while you were out of town. I told you how she hugged me and clung to my neck when I arrived, then, she grabbed me by the hand and pulled me down in the seat beside her. Well, anyway, I go over to Karema's place to have dinner with Alese tonight for our anniversary, and she hands me these pictures," he said, pulling out the photos to show Marty one by one.

"Damn, man. How did she do this?" Marty asked, leaving his mouth opened wide.

"I don't know. She probably had one of her little tramp girlfriends take the pictures for her. I'm sure it was just a set up. She had it planned long before she even invited me to the fake party," he said with disgust.

"Yeah, that's probably the truth right there. She set you up big time," he said. "I guess I don't even have to ask you about how Alese reacted to all this judging from the way you look," he commented.

"Yeah, you're right about that. Alese freaked out on me. She told me to get out and asked for a divorce," Michael said flatly.

"What? Didn't you explain to her how this was a trap, Mike?"

"I tried, I tried, but she wasn't trying to hear that. She said a picture was worth a thousand words. It's over, Marty. My life is over."

"Come on, now. Don't say that. Look, just give her a little time, and she'll be able to view the pictures from a different angle."

"Yeah, right," he said. "You don't really believe that and neither do I. But I tell you what, if I could get my hands around Lisa's neck tonight, it would be over for both of us. I mean I'm willing to go to jail."

"Mike, don't even think like that. Don't let her ruin your life and any chance you have of getting your wife back."

"I mean, Marty, come on. What chance do I have right now anyway? Absolutely zero is all I have."

"No, that's not true. I don't agree with that. Alese is a reasonable woman who's just upset right now. You can understand that, can't you? I mean, if you saw pictures like this of her right now, what would you think?"

"I don't know. I just give up, that's all I can do." Michael looked crushed.

#

Lisa was sprawled out on the peach fabric love seat in Ranetta's two-bedroom apartment on Duncan Street. Ranetta was laying on the matching sofa eating popcorn and Planters chocolate covered peanuts. They felt relaxed wearing stretch jeans and rayon jersey tops. They were watching the video, *For Colored Girls Only* starring Janet Jackson, as they laughed and joked with each other.

"Ranetta, girl, thanks for everything," she said. "I owe you one for the good job you did on producing those pictures for me so quickly," Lisa said, laughing with her friend. "Hey, thanks for also letting me stay here with you for a few days. I don't think it's safe for me to be at my place tonight."

"Yes, you are right about that. I can just see Michael at your door right now, and I bet it's not a pretty site. That black man is probably mad, thirty-eight hot, and out of his mind," Ranetta joked, stretching her eyes.

"Well, I know a girl's got to do what a girl's got to do. All's fair in love and war," Lisa said, laughing evilly like the devil himself, slapping Ranetta on the shoulder.

"I know that's right, girl. For a second in the restaurant, I thought he recognized me from that day at church. Then, I turned away like I didn't know him and didn't want to be bothered. Anyway, he walked by so fast, he didn't even see me get up and follow him into the lounge area," Ranetta stated. "There were so many people taking pictures at the party, he didn't notice the flash either. Lisa, you really outdid yourself on that one, buddy."

"He probably didn't recognize you with that wig you had on, but he might have remembered your hazel eyes," Lisa said, giggling again. "I have to admit, though, it was the perfect set up, and I am good," she bragged. "I know that dumb wife of his fell for it hook, line, and sinker. I bet you I won't have to worry about her pitiful ass anymore after tonight."

"Yeah, you're right. Anyhow, it's too late now, even if he did recognize me. His little life has been turned upside down. Unh, unh, unh," Ranetta grunted, shaking her head, almost feeling sorry for Michael.

"That's cool because I'm just the one to help him get it turned right side up, again. Ain't I girl?" Lisa asked with a sly grin.

"Now that you are, girlfriend," Ranetta answered. "But, I tell you what, you better not ever tell Jolene what we did. She's so crazy, she'll have us in church every Sunday for the rest of our lives."

"I know that's right," Lisa said. "No, I know better than to ever tell Jolene about that. I only agreed to go to church with her that Sunday because I wanted to see Michael with his little "so called" happy family. I broke that union up real fast, and that's real," she added.

"Girl, you're so funny. I hope you never get mad with me," Ranetta stated. "By the way, how did you know where to send the pictures to his wife?"

"Everybody at the office knows they're separated, and that preacher woman is her best friend. I just got the pastor's name and address from the good ole telephone directory. I sent them to her "special delivery," and I wish I had been there to see her face," Lisa said, laughing at herself.

"You were bold to do that, girl."

Yeah, I am a bold beast. But it won't be long now, and I'll be Mrs. Michael Wayne for sure. Alese will divorce him for real now. All I have to do is bide my time. Yeah, that's all I have to do. He won't stay mad at me forever. Once his fat, ugly wife is out of the picture, it'll be smooth sailing for me.

"Lisa, what's your next step?" Ranetta asked.

Lisa snapped out of her trance and blinked her eyes. "Well, let's wait and see what happens. Let's just wait and see what happens after tonight."

"I know you'd better do your best to avoid Michael for a while. There's no telling what he might do to you. But you're welcome to hide out here longer if you like."

"Yeah, I plan to avoid him for a while, but only for a little while," Lisa responded.

18

Something, Something

Lying back on the floor with his feet kicked up on the ottoman in front of the stone fireplace, Marty enjoyed being home on a Monday for the Labor Day holiday. He watched ESPN-TV on his Sony sixty-inch plasma television set and waited for Tina to finish grilling the T-bone steaks outside on the patio. She enjoyed the splendid day outdoors with the boys, Malique and Jordan, while he preferred staying inside, lounging around the house in his black sweats.

Marty held his hands behind his head while he recalled his conversation with Michael on Saturday night. Being flabbergasted from the information his friend had shared with him regarding his marriage, Marty shook his head in disbelief. He was never really fond of Lisa, even in college; he just tried to get along with her because Michael was so in love with the woman. Marty had no idea Lisa was that evil.

Man, something ain't right about that girl. Tina never liked her either. I should have known then that woman was trouble. I got to help Michael get out of this situation and get his life back together, but what can I do?

He wanted to call Alese and explain things to her himself but decided against that. Marty had a hunch, and he had already anticipated the arrival of tomorrow morning so he could follow up on it. It was certainly worth a try.

Tomorrow is another day. You never know what might happen. I've got to think of something.

\#

Early Tuesday morning, Marty was sitting at his solid cherry wood desk looking over reports for the Prudential Corporation accounts when he realized the best way to follow up on his intuitions. He picked up the telephone and starting dialing.

[194]

"Good morning, NuWay Software Designs. How may I direct your call?" the receptionist asked with a foreign accent.

"Hello, this is Mr. Martin Carlisle, co-president of M & M Software Development in Jacksonville, Florida. I'm calling for a reference on one of your former employees who has applied for a position with our company. May I speak to Mr. Raymond Gomans, please?" he asked in his most masculine professional voice.

"Sir, Mr. Gomans hasn't worked here in over ten years," she stated firmly.

"Really, are you sure?"

"Yes, sir. I've worked here for almost twenty-five years, and I remember Mr. Gomans well," she commented.

"All right, then, do you remember a former employee named Lisa Bradford? She just left your company last year."

"Why, yes, I do remember Ms. Bradford. She worked in the Planning Department with Mr. Gomans, but she left over ten years ago, about the same time as Mr. Gomans."

"What are you telling me? Are you saying that Ms. Bradford has not worked there in over ten years? Her application says she was employed there for seventeen years until last year when she moved back to Florida."

"I'm sorry, sir. I'm sure about that because I remember when they closed out that department approximately ten years ago. She and Mr. Gomans were both let go," she said firmly.

"Thank you, thank you very much," Marty said, hanging up the telephone.

Michael and he had never discussed checking out Lisa's reference since they had attended college together and NuWay Software was a well-known company. They were so happy to have a former classmate join their team, it didn't dawn on them to verify anything.

Why would she lie about where she worked?

Marty decided not to question Lisa about her application because he feared that would make her suspicious. *No need to tip her off if she's hiding something.*

Marty felt deep within his spirit she definitely had a secret and he was determined to have it exposed.

He didn't want to upset Michael any further either, at least not until he had all the facts. There was no reason to rock the boat unless he had solid proof about Lisa's lies. Marty decided he would have to get his dirt on her the old-fashioned way.

Flipping through the yellow pages, Marty came across the business advertisement of one of his fraternity brothers who used to be a police officer. There he was, Jonathan Payne, private investigation services. The ad read, "We can help you find whatever or whoever, you're searching for."

"Hello, this is Marty Carlisle," he said cheerfully.

"Hello, Marty. Man, where have you been? I haven't heard from you in I don't know how long. How are you doing?"

"Well, the business is doing great. But, look here, Johnny. I've got a problem I need you to help me with. I need a background check on one of my employees. Can you help me out?"

"Ah, what kind of information do you need, Marty? I mean, give me some idea of what I'm looking for."

"First of all, her name is Lisa Laraye Bradford, and I need to know everything about her life in D.C., especially where she worked and also about her personal life. You know, the type of men she had. Just get me any dirt you can find," he said.

"What makes you think she's dirty, Marty?"

"I can feel it, man. I can just feel it," he replied.

"Brother, if there's any dirt to be found, I'll find it. I promise you that," Johnny boasted.

They spent several more minutes talking and updating each other about their lives and their businesses. Marty told Johnny everything he recalled about Lisa and faxed him a copy of her personnel file after they were disconnected. Johnny had assured Marty that he worked fast, and he would be back from D.C. within a week with all the history he needed on Lisa Laraye Bradford.

#

I had spent the last five days fighting the on-set of depression. I was in turmoil from the realization that my marriage had collapsed and I could possibly be losing my daughter to some woman who cared nothing about children. I didn't have to meet her to know

[196]

Varnisha Grant was up to no good. Our attorney had hinted that the aunt seemed to be an unsavory character, but she hadn't found anything they could use to discredit her. Time was running out for them. If their investigations didn't turn up something soon, Bianca would be gone forever. I couldn't handle the thought of that as I broke down into tears.

The telephone rang at least six times before I answered. I wiped my face and cleared my throat before picking up the telephone. I didn't want anyone to think I might be coming unglued.

"Hello, Mrs. Wayne, this is Jenny Riley. How are you?" she pleasantly asked.

"Hi. Ms. Riley. I'm fine, thank you."

"Mrs. Wayne, I have some good news for you regarding your foster daughter," she said, sounding even happier.

"Yes, ma'am, I'm listening. Please continue."

"Well, it seems that the aunt has a felony arrest record after all. It took us so long to find it because she had a felony drug conviction in another state and under a different name. She served five solid years in Texas on more than one drug charge, and she was also arrested out there several times for prostitution. She didn't think we would ever find out about that considering it was another state and fictitious name. But, anyway, she's been terminated as a candidate for relative custody and adoption."

"What does that mean?" I asked, not wanting to get too elated too soon.

"That means that you and Mr. Wayne are free to pursue the adoption of Bianca. In fact, I've already requested a finalization court date be set at the earliest date possible. I just couldn't wait any longer to tell you," she added.

"Oh! My God." I screamed with happiness. "You mean it's over? We can finally adopt Bianca?"

"Yes, ma'am. That's exactly what I mean. Whenever we get a court date, I'll call you back with the time to be there."

"Ms. Riley, thank you so much. God bless you for all your hard work. You don't know how much this has uplifted my day."

Finalizing Bianca's adoption would be a bittersweet victory. I was overjoyed that this episode in my life was over. I could now live in peace knowing that no one would ever be able to take away the child I had grown to love as my daughter. On the other hand, I was also free to file for divorce papers from Michael. I had kept my promise not to file for divorce until after we were cleared for the permanent adoption order. I resented him for putting me through this extreme agitation and I didn't know how or if I would ever be able to forgive Michael for that.

While thinking about my marriage, I was still haunted by Karema's words.

"Have you deliberated anymore about telling Michael why you've never gotten pregnant?"

Truth was, I thought about it all the time. It hurt me to the core that I hadn't shared my secret with my soul mate. I should have been able to tell him anything. And I had, except for this. I wanted to, but I didn't know how I'd be able to deal with the pain I'd see in Michael's eyes if he learned the truth about my past. Now, it was too late to share with him because our marriage was coming to an end.

"There's no reason for him to ever know now. What good would it do?" I asked myself.

In tears, I got down on my knees and prayed to God. I thanked Him for making this day possible and for all His goodness, kindness, and mercy. I also asked God to forgive me for keeping a devastating secret from my husband for over sixteen years. I closed my prayer by saying, "Father, please heal me and give me peace of mind as I continue through this life. In Jesus name, I pray."

I had many friends and relatives I wanted to share my good news with. But first, I would have to call Michael at his office. He would be even more ecstatic than I had been.

"Alese, that's wonderful! This is the best news I could possibly get today! We have to go out and celebrate tonight as a family. Where would you like to go?"

"Ah, I'm just as happy about this as you are, Michael, but we're not going out with you," I said. "I just called to give you the news regarding the permanent adoption and to inform you that I've contacted a divorce attorney."

[198]

"Alese, you can't be serious. Why would you contact a divorce attorney so soon? Let's try to work this out."

"Michael, it's been over six months since we have lived together as husband and wife. I think it's time to move on. Besides, you already have someone else."

"No, I don't. I told you those pictures were set up. There is nothing going on between Lisa and me. I was only with her the one time that I told you about. She set up those pictures to break us apart."

"We were already apart, Michael, so it doesn't matter. I'm filing for divorce. You can work out the details with my attorney when she contacts you. Bye, Michael," I said, hanging up the telephone. I was hurting inside like the world was coming to an end.

#

Michael hung up the telephone with Alese and quickly walked out the door of his office heading to his car. He had to get away from there. How could God do this to him? Why was his life in such a mess? He pondered these questions before he entered his vehicle.

While Michael was driving around, he decided to stop by the church to see Karema. She had always been a friend to both of them and strongly supported their marriage from day one. Karema and Alese were closer than any two friends he had ever known. If anyone could help him reach Alese, it would be Karema. She was their pastor, Bianca's godmother, and a devoted friend for many years. She would know what to do.

Karema was in her office meditating on the Word when Michael lightly knocked at her door. She sat behind her desk with the Bible opened in front of her as she told him to come in. Michael entered slowly and carefully closed the door behind him after he and Karema greeted each other. As soon as he noticed how calm and peaceful it felt to be in the house of the Lord, he relaxed himself and slid down on the love seat across from Karema's desk.

"Michael, I was beginning to wonder when you would be back to see me. You look better than you did the last time you were in my office. How have you been, brother?" she asked, showing concerned for him.

"I'm, well, I'm not too good right now, pastor," he mumbled.

"Tell me what's wrong," she said encouragingly.

"Pastor, I just don't know what to do, where to go, or where to turn in my life right now. I never dreamed Alese and I would be separated for this long. If I could just go back in time and erase that one night, I would be a happily married man today. Can you believe that?"

"Yes, that is easy to believe. We all have done things in the past that we are not proud of, Michael, and would like to have erased forever," she stated.

"What can I do? I mean, what in the world can I do?"

"Have you asked God for forgiveness, Michael?"

"Yes, I have. I did that before I ever confessed to Alese. I know I'm guilty and unworthy of my wife, but I still love her. We deserve to be a family again."

"If you have asked God for forgiveness with a true heart, then you are already forgiven. He's cleansed you and washed you in the blood never to remember your sin anymore," she said, smiling and continuing with her hands folded on the desk. "Have you asked your wife to forgive you, yet?"

"I don't think I did. I just remember asking her to promise not to leave me that night before we separated," he said frowning, trying to remember what happened that evening. "It's such a blur to me, I can't say for sure."

"Okay, this is my advice to you, Michael. The first thing you need to do is ask your wife to forgive you. Then, you need to keep lifting up the name of Jesus in prayer. You also need to trust in the Lord that things will come out according to His will and not your will. That way you'll be covered, no matter how things work out," Karema said plainly.

"Thank you, Karema. You always make me feel better. I appreciate you taking the time to minister with me like this. I need to ask you something. Will you please ask Alese to meet with me and talk before we head to divorce court?"

"Michael, I can't interfere on your behalf. I'm there for Alese, just like I'm here for you, but I can't tell her what to do. May I ask you a question?"

"Yes, of course, you can ask me anything you want."

"Are you still seeing the woman that you were involved with on any level?

"No, I don't see her at all. She hasn't even returned to work since she sent Alese those pictures. Why would you ask me about that?"

"Because, you need to pray for her just like you pray for yourself," Karema solemnly said.

"Pastor, I don't know if I can do that. It would be kind of difficult for me to do," Michael uttered, standing and hugging Karema good-bye.

"You just try it, Michael. It might make your burdens a little easier to bear. Just try it," she said, hugging him back. Karema escorted him to the office door, watched him walk down the hallway, and exit through the church doors. She prayed silently for her best friend's marriage before returning to her desk.

19

Revelations

A full week had passed and Marty hadn't heard from the private investigator, Jonathan Payne, he hired to investigate Lisa's past. She had called in last week to request at least a week of emergency vacation, and it was a good thing she had done that, too, because she would have had a real emergency if Michael had seen her. At least, she had sense enough to hide out for a while and let the brother calm down. Marty had kept his eye on Michael all week, expecting him to lose it at any minute. He wasn't behaving like himself at all lately; his partner came in late two days during the week and seemed absent minded during several meetings. Accepting that Michael was on edge waiting to confront Lisa, he grew even more concerned about his friend.

Marty had begun to doubt that Johnny had found any evidence they could use against Lisa. *I know Johnny. He would have called by now if he had something worth reporting.*

Maybe it was time to find another angle for releasing Lisa from their company business. They needed some way to get her out before she caused any more trouble. Maybe it was time to develop another strategy before she returned to work. Anyway, Marty picked up the telephone on his desk and dialed Johnny's office number.

"Hey, Marty! I'm glad you called! I just got back to Jacksonville this morning."

"Hello, Johnny. I was about to give up hope of hearing from you. It's been a week today, man, and you hadn't called me. Did you find anything on my girl?"

"Yes, I sure did. You won't believe what I found out about your Ms. Lisa Bradford."

"Well, don't keep me in suspense, let me hear it." Marty was on the edge of his seat.

"No, man. This is too good. I need you to come by my office this morning and see this file for yourself."

"No problem, brother. I'll be there in a few minutes," Marty said, hanging up the telephone.

Marty jumped into his black BMW X5 and hurried off to Johnny's office on the west side of town. His heart was pumping extra fast, filled with anticipation. He wondered what could be so shocking that Johnny didn't want to share it over the telephone. Whatever it was, he just hoped it would be enough to get Lisa out of their lives.

He was in a hurry to get across town, so Marty turned west on Riverplace Boulevard, thinking he was taking a shortcut.

"Damn!" Marty shouted. It was just his luck the traffic was at a standstill. There had been an accident with three cars right at the corner; the police had the street blocked off where he couldn't get around anybody and since other vehicles had pulled in behind him, he couldn't turn around. Picking up his cell phone to call Johnny back, he realized the battery was dead. Marty was so frustrated by this time, he needed something to help him relax. He reached up and tuned the radio dial to WSOL for the Tom Joyner Morning Show with Sybil and J. Anthony Brown. They always gave him a good laugh when he needed it most. It was almost time for the show to leave the air, but at least he would hear the tail end of it before changing to the smooth music station while he waited for the traffic to clear.

Marty saw several police officers taking statements from pedestrians and other motorists. People were everywhere trying to see who all was involved in the accidents. Some drivers had left their cars unattended to get a closer look at the scene. Marty was wondering how much longer this would take when he noticed two Southern Wrecker's towing trucks backing in to load up the damaged vehicles.

Finally, the police cleared the way for the tow trucks to depart and motioned for the waiting vehicles to pass. Marty hoped Johnny had waited for him since he had gotten held up in traffic and had taken longer than he expected. Anyway, he was almost there now.

Johnny's office was on a west side street with a row of small older wooden homes that had been converted into office buildings. He had a one-man operation except for his young secretary, Lizzie, who answered the office telephone and kept the books for him. She was talking on the telephone when Marty arrived but waved her hand for him to go on back to Johnny's office.

"Hey, Johnny!" Marty exclaimed, Johnny grabbed his hand and pulled him into the office.

"Hello, Marty! Man, it's good to see you. You haven't changed a bit since I saw you last," Johnny joked.

"I know that's a lie, but thanks anyway. I'm sorry it took me so long to get here. I ran into a traffic jam and had to wait it out. What you got?" Marty asked, looking Johnny up and down.

"Have a seat, and I'll get my file folder for you," he said, walking to his desk. Marty took a seat in the worn armchair and waited.

Johnny reached into the middle drawer of his pine wooden desk and pulled out an expandable manila file folder and handed it to Marty. He went to the door and asked Lizzie to hold his calls until this meeting was over. Then, he returned and sat on the edge of his desk to watch Marty close up while he opened the folder.

Marty scanned through the documents reading at his fastest speed. He flipped through the pictures in the folder with his eyes bucked and mouth opened. Johnny was hunched on the edge of his desk grinning at Marty's facial expressions.

After viewing the entire file, Marty looked up at Johnny with a huge smile on his face thinking this was better than he had imagined.

"Thanks, man. You came through for me. You really did," Marty said, shaking his hand.

"Anytime, brother. Anytime at all," Johnny said, still grinning.

"I've got to run, Johnny. Please put me a bill in the mail, and I will take care of you real soon." Marty stood as they did their secret fraternity brothers hand slap.

"Okay, Marty. But tell me, what are you going to do with this package?"

"Ah, I'm not sure right now. It's definitely more than what I anticipated. It's going to work for me, though, it really is."

"I'm glad I was able to help. I'll put your bill in the mail tomorrow, man."

Marty floated back to his car with the folder in his hand. He tucked the file in his glove compartment drawer for safe keeping. After driving around for almost an hour, he decided what his next move would be. There was only one honest way to get Lisa out of their lives. But first, he needed to call Tina. He wanted to let her know how thankful he was for their marriage. The problems they were having seemed small compared to what Michael and Alese were dealing with.

When Marty made it back to his office desk, he dialed Tina's number at work.

"Hey, babe," he said.

"Hi, where are you?" Tina asked.

"Ah, I'm at the office right now. I have some business to handle and I'll be home later this evening. I'll have some major news to share with you then."

"No problem. I'll be home by eight o'clock tonight, Marty."

Closing his eyes, Marty spoke softly into the mouthpiece. "I love you, Tina. I'm so thankful for our marriage."

"I love you, too. I'll see you later," she replied, hanging up the telephone.

Marty locked the door and eased back in his office chair. He needed some time to devise a good strategy. He dialed the extension to Michael's office, but there wasn't an answer. Then, he dialed the extension to Michael's assistant, Tracy.

"Hello, Tracy. Do you know where Mr. Wayne is?" he asked calmly.

"No, sir. I'm sorry, but I don't know where he is, Mr. Carlisle. He left the office almost an hour ago without saying a word to me."

"Thank you. Please let me know when he returns."

"Yes, sir," she replied, clicking off the speakerphone.

Lisa resolved it was time for her to return home. She had hung out with Ranetta for a whole week and that was long enough. Hopefully, Michael had calmed down by now and would not be waiting for her. She had tried to avoid him by not going to work for a week. He always presented a cool exterior, but knowing how every man could lose control of his anger when pushed to the edge, she kept her distance.

She felt good talking with her friend about their college antics and the unholy things they had done between then and now. Lisa had even felt comfortable enough to confide in Ranetta regarding her life for the past ten years. Of course, once Ranetta got over the initial shock, she thought it was amazing. Hell, she would have done it, too, if she reckoned she could have gotten away with it. But everybody was not as bold as Lisa.

"Lisa, are you sure it's safe for you to go back to your apartment already? Michael is probably still waiting to confront you," Ranetta said.

"Girl, please. That man has probably cooled off by now. He's somewhere soaking his wounds and waiting for me to come and lick them dry," Lisa said, wetting her lips.

"Lisa, you are too crazy. Do you ever give up?" Ranetta asked, laughing quickly.

"No, I always keep my eyes on the prize until I get what I want," she responded with pride.

"You better be careful and keep your cell phone close by just in case you need to call me," Ranetta said.

"Thanks, again. I'll call you later tonight once I get settled back in," Lisa replied, hugging Ranetta good-bye.

Daylight had almost filtered away by the time Lisa arrived at her duplex building. She pulled up in her red Mustang convertible, making sure to let the top up before getting out. As she exited the vehicle, she took a careful look around for any sign of Michael before reaching in the back seat to retrieve the packed duffel bag she had carried with her to Ranetta's apartment. There was no trace of Michael's car as she neared the door, so she turned the key and cautiously entered her side of the duplex.

Lisa walked straight to her bathroom and turned on the hot water in the shower stall. Suddenly, her body froze upon hearing the doorbell ring and her heart kept beating double time. Her first inclination was not to answer the door, but quickly remembered that her car was parked out front and the lights were on in the living room. Lisa speculated she would have to confront Michael sooner or later so she might as well get it over with right now. She snatched her Samsung phone off the bed, jammed it in her front pants pocket, and stomped to the door wearing a frown on her face, ready to show some attitude. She yanked the door open while he was still standing there ringing the doorbell.

"Marty! What are you doing here?" she asked, looking stunned.

"Lisa, I need to talk to you, and I mean business," he said, entering her living space.

"Look, Marty, this has nothing to do with you—just go. I'm not talking to you; it's none of your business," she said angrily, pointing at the door.

"Lisa, you can talk to me or you can talk to Michael after I show him what I have in this package here," he stated, holding up the manila folder he received from Jonathan Payne.

"What is that?" she asked, looking scared.

"Why don't you look inside and see for yourself. I understand you like having your picture taken, Lisa. Yeah, that's what they tell me. Take a look at some more of your pictures and tell me what you think of these," he said mockingly.

Lisa jerked the envelope away from Marty, stormed over to the sofa, and plopped down. Marty followed behind her and sat in the chair beside the sofa and waited for her reaction. Lisa rapidly glanced through the pictures in the folder before throwing them on the floor at his feet.

"Where did you get these pictures, Marty?" she demanded, glaring at him through fiery red eyes.

"Don't worry about how I got this information. Are you ready to talk now? Tell me why you did this, Lisa. Tell me why you worked at Marcino's nightclub in D.C. as a stripper for ten years," he stated boldly, watching her closely.

Looking at the pictures on the floor, Lisa felt her body becoming more enraged with anger. She hadn't planned on revealing her sordid past to them. This was supposed to be a new beginning for her with an old flame, and now it was all falling apart. Her past had caught up with her, now she felt like a caged animal that desperately needed to break free. But she presumed she was smart enough to play one more card and that it might work on an unsuspecting man.

"Marty, I know you don't understand that I love Michael. I just wanted to be with him again," she began tearfully. "When I first moved to D.C. eighteen years ago, I was employed at NuWay Software Designs. I worked with them for six years, and then they decided to downsize, eliminating the Planning Department. I spent almost a whole year searching for another job, to no avail. I mean, I applied everywhere, and no one was hiring at that time. Finally, a friend of mine, Tameka, told me she was working at Marcino's three nights a week to make ends meet. Well, I didn't know what else to do. All of my savings were about to run out, my rent was behind, my car was broken, and I had no family in D.C. to live with. I went to the club for an interview and the manager hired me on the spot because I looked young. I wanted to be a server at first, but he wanted me to dance and take off my clothes. Anyway, the more I did it, the more I realized how much I enjoyed doing it," she said, glancing up at Marty through teary eyes.

"Lisa, why didn't you just move back here then? At least you had a lot of contacts here, and we already had the company started then."

"Marty, I wasn't ready to give up on my dream and move back here. I wanted to stay there and make it work for me. I had planned to make just enough money to get out of debt and leave. But the money was so good. I just couldn't let it go," she said.

"What happened? Why are you here?" he asked, looking puzzled.

"Marty, look at me! I know I look good—but I can't pass for twenty-five anymore!" she shouted hysterically. "The manager came to me one night and told me that was it! Just like that, I was out of the business! I wasn't prepared for that and hadn't planned on it. My body is still in good shape. I'm the same size and everything. But no, he told me I was too old to work up the crowd like I used to, and he needed the 'pretty young thangs' to make real money," she said in disgust.

"So what, you decided to just come here and screw up Mike's life? The man you profess to love so much. I mean, I don't get it," Marty said, wringing his hands and shaking his head.

"Marty, I do love Michael. I came back to rekindle what we had. He's the only man who has ever loved me and treated me right. He's a real man and I need him to be mine," she retorted.

"Lisa, the man is married and he has a baby girl. They have been together for sixteen long years. That man loves his wife. I mean, he truly loves her, can't you see that?"

"I don't care about that. I loved him first, and he should be with me," she pouted.

Realizing it was useless trying to talk sensibly to Lisa, Marty decided to play his trump card. Since she was truly deranged and needed psychological help, he had to move on with his program and get her away from his friend before it was too late for Michael to save his marriage.

"Look here, Lisa. You need to leave town tonight or you are going to be arrested first thing in the morning," he said seriously. Lisa looked at Marty like he had lost his mind and was speaking in tongues.

"What—what the hell did you say?" she snarled.

"I spoke to the company attorney earlier today, and I'm going to file charges against you for fraud and falsifying documents. All of the credentials and experiences you presented to us were falsified. Even your State professional license was a fake, Lisa. Fortunately for us, that's damn illegal," he snapped. "Now, you can keep your pretty ass here and go to jail or you can move the hell on, Lisa. The game is over. I don't want you anywhere near Mike or his family, do you understand me?"

"Marty, I don't believe that you're going to have me arrested. You can't be serious," she gasped, breaking into more tears.

"Oh, I'm very serious. You see, I also know about you and Mr. Gomans and why they shut down your department in D.C. That's the real reason you haven't worked in this business in over ten years. You both were about to be fired for embezzling funds, but the company didn't want a major scandal like that on their hands. So don't try to scam me, Lisa. Besides, I'm taking this information to Michael tonight, and you really don't want to be around here when he gets his hands on this package. I strongly suggest you pack some bags and I'll take you to the airport myself," he said, bending to pick up the pictures and putting them back in the folder.

"You can have one of your girlfriends to pack up the rest of your things and ship them to you wherever you want to go. I'll tell the employees at the office that you had to leave town indefinitely due to a family emergency. That's all they need to know—like I said, Lisa, it's over."

Lisa cried about how sorry she was, hoping to convince Marty to at least let her stay in town a little while longer. Pouring out her heart, she said, "I just want to be loved. I've never had a man to love me for me. My father abandoned us when I was a little girl. Marty, please try to understand. I'm sorry, I'll leave him alone, I promise." She sounded like an innocent teenager.

For the first time, Marty felt like Lisa might be a human being and actually have a conscience. Only he wasn't going to be fooled by her words or her tears. "I'm sorry, too, Lisa. You gotta go."

#

Michael was having a really rough day; nothing seemed to be going right for him. He had just returned from a meeting across town regarding one of their major projects. He sat quietly at his desk contemplating how to tell Marty they didn't get the Berber-Jamison account due to a missed deadline that was his responsibility. He had let his partner down because of his personal crisis and he felt terrible about it.

It was time to get himself together and maybe move on with his life. He had been praying for a miracle with his marriage and so far nothing had happened. Alese was just waiting on a final court date for the adoption so that she could formally divorce him. He hadn't been able to see her or Bianca since that incident with the pictures. She wouldn't communicate with him at all, and he had to wait for the courts to set up some type of visitation with his daughter.

He was so exhausted; he finally decided to call it a day around eight-thirty. Michael closed his briefcase as he continued looking around his office for anything out of place. He stopped when he thought he heard someone entering the building. Before Mike made it to the door with his attaché in hand, Marty came rushing in looking paranoid.

"Hey, Mike. I'm glad I caught you before you left, man. Look, I really need to talk to you before you leave," Marty said.

"Marty, what's going on? You look like you just saw a ghost or something," he said, staring Marty down.

"Mike, please, just sit down and let me talk to you for a minute. I have something to tell you and it's dreadfully important," he said, stressing his words.

"Okay, okay," Mike said, sitting down and placing his briefcase on the desk before rearing back in his chair.

"Well, after Lisa set you up with those pictures the other week, I got real suspicious of her. Something just told me to call D.C. and check out her history with NuWay Software. Anyway, when I called there, the receptionist told me Lisa left there over ten years ago. That made me even more suspicious, right, because that meant she had lied on her résumé. So I'm thinking, what else has she lied about?" Marty explained.

"Marty, wait, wait. Where is this going? What's in that package you got?" he asked, looking curious.

"Let me finish, and then I'll show you the package. You remember my frat brother, the private investigator, Jonathan Payne. I hired him to go to D.C. and investigate her past and this is what he turned up. Take a look at what he found," Marty said, handing the package to Mike.

Michael took his time reading the documents and viewing the photographs. All at once, the universe slowed down for him. His mind and body went to another place where his deepest anger lived. Suddenly, springing from the chair, he bolted towards the door without uttering one word. Marty jumped up from the seat just in time to block him from opening the office door. Swinging both of his arms around Michael, he struggled to hold him back.

"Let me go! Let me go!" Michael yelled, wiggling underneath Marty's grip.

"No, man. I'm not going to let you go," he said.

"She tried to ruin my life! Now, I'm going to ruin hers!" Michael shouted.

"No, I'm not going to let you go until you calm down," Marty uttered, tightening his hold. "She's gone. She left town about an hour ago. I took her to the airport myself," he said.

"What do you mean she left town?"

"I confronted her and gave her a choice of going to jail or leaving town for good," Marty said, releasing his hold on Michael when they both relaxed.

"You're joking, right? You were going to have her arrested?"

"Well, that's what I told her. I didn't think she'd be crazy enough to risk her pretty ass going to jail," Marty responded.

"I just can't comprehend this. Why would Lisa come here to deliberately destroy my life?"

"Mike, she was just crazy. That's all I can say. She really believed that she was still in love with you. I tried talking to her and she just couldn't see the light. For a minute, I envisioned maybe she had a conscience, but I couldn't trust her. I had to come up with something to get her to leave town," Marty replied. "I told her she definitely needed to be gone before you saw that file and came after her yourself."

"Marty, thanks for having my back, partner. You really saved my life tonight," he said, pausing and thinking for a second. "I never conceived that Lisa would do something like this to me."

"Next time, be more careful about who you get involved with," Marty said.

"No, man. There won't be a next time," Michael stated seriously. "I'm going to get my wife back." Walking out the door with renewed determination, he was ready to reclaim everything he'd lost in the past few months. Believing that God was surely on his side, Michael's spirit felt revived. Nothing would stand in the way of him being with his family tonight.

"I hear you, man. Tina and I will both be praying for you all. I'm on my way home to let her know what's going down. Give me a call if you need me."

"Thanks again, Marty. I've got to get out of here," Michael replied, heading for the door with his car keys and the file folder in his hand.

20

Whatever Will Be

Sprinting through the rainy parking lot, Michael pressed the remote control button to unlock his car doors before he jumped into his automobile and started the engine. Reaching up to turn on the windshield wipers, he realized how desperate he was to see Alese. He didn't want to waste any more time being separated from his family. Surely, she would be able to understand he had been manipulated into being unfaithful by a conniving and unscrupulous person. Lisa had set out to destroy their lives and their love, but she had drastically failed. Now that she was out of the picture, they could be happy once more and raise their daughter together.

Nothing would ever come between them again. They would bury this episode of their lives and build a newer and better one together. He would never commit adultery again because his faith in God and his marriage was renewed. Michael was determined to gain her forgiveness, even if it meant staying on his knees all night long begging and crying. It would be worth that and more to have his life back like it was before this horrible nightmare began.

Michael was only ten minutes away from Karema's condominium as the rainy downpour increased. He picked up his cell phone, calling Alese to let her know he was on his way. Then, he changed his mind and clicked off his iPhone. He placed it in the seat with him.

I better not call her this late. She definitely won't answer if she knows it's me. It'll be best if I just show up there and beg Karema to let me in.

Michael was confident he would be able to persuade Karema to let him in the house. She had been praying for their reunion and counseling with them both since they were first separated. Karema would most likely sympathize with him and maybe even convince Alese to hear him out tonight once he told her everything. Then, it would just be a matter of getting Alese to listen to him long enough to explain his case.

[213]

His mind was so filled with thoughts of how he would convince Alese to listen to him tonight that he didn't see the homeless man stumbling off the slippery curb in front of him until it was almost too late. With only a few seconds to react, Michael instinctively pressed down on the brakes and swerved the car abruptly to his left. The vehicle crossed the median, jumped the curb, and hit a huge oak tree on the other side of the road, knocking Michael unconscious upon impact.

The homeless man, dressed in dingy jeans and a black T-shirt with a khaki jacket, went rushing to Michael's side, grateful that the automobile had missed striking his frail body. Michael's face was bloody and drooping to one side while the stranger went yelling for help. He ran out to the edge of the street and frantically began waving for drivers to stop. Finally, a young man dressed in a business suit driving a new Toyota Highlander, pulled over with a cell phone and dialed an ambulance for him.

Arriving quickly after receiving the nine-one-one telephone call, the paramedics immediately begin working on removing Michael from the car. The homeless man, who identified himself as Marvin Simms, had remained with Michael and was anxious to communicate with the emergency care workers. Shortly after the paramedics' arrival, two male police officers, identified as Hackett and Brown, appeared on the scene. Marvin calmly told the officers what happened. He was on his way to the Rainbow Homeless Shelter for the night, he explained, when this driver showed up out of nowhere speeding down the street. He had waved down another driver, Robert Keyes, who called the ambulance on his cell phone.

Michael was still unconscious when they pulled his long limp body from the Infinity automobile, carefully placed him on the stretcher, and firmly strapped him in. The female paramedic reached in Michael's back pocket, pulled out his wallet, and passed it to Officer Hackett. The other policeman, Officer Brown, walked over to the ambulance driver. They were wheeling Michael in the back of the vehicle and pulling out the oxygen mask to place over his marred and swollen face.

"He's still out of it. Do you think he's going to make it?" the officer asked the ambulance driver.

"He's hurt pretty bad, and his pulse is actually low. We'll start him on oxygen, but we won't know much more until we get to the hospital." He looked over at the other paramedic and then turned back to the officer. "I suggest you try to contact his next of kin immediately," the driver stated, passing Michael's iPhone to the officer before running to jump into the opened door of the ambulance. He turned on the flashing red siren full blast before they zoomed down the wet street.

Officer Brown looked at the small cell phone in his hand. Reviewing Michael's last call on the list, he was hoping to reach someone who related to the victim. He waited patiently as the voice of a female answered the line.

#

Sleeping soundly, I was awakened by Karema's persistent tapping on my bedroom door. I wiped the sleep from my eyes as I turned to see the red numerals on the digital alarm clock displaying eleven-ten. Then, I bolted out of bed, opened the door, and stepped in the hallway so I wouldn't wake up Bianca.

"Karema, what in the world is going on? Why are you knocking at my door this time of night? I was sleeping hard," I whispered.

"Alese, it's the police on the telephone. They want to speak with you," Karema said, handing the telephone to me.

"What?" she asked, grabbing the telephone from Karema, "Hello, this is Alese Wayne."

"Yes, ma'am, this is Officer Brown with the Duval County Sheriff's Department. Ma'am, are you related to Michael Leron Wayne?"

"Yes, sir, I am, that's my husband," I responded, crinkling my forehead.

"Ma'am, I'm sorry to inform you that Mr. Wayne was involved in a one-vehicle car crash on North Jackson Street, almost an hour ago. He is in route to the Jacksonville Memorial Hospital as we speak."

"Oh! My God! Oh, my God! Officer, how is he? What is his condition? Is he still alive, officer?"

"Yes, ma'am, he was alive when they left with him in the ambulance, but he was unconscious. His face was pretty damaged, and he barely had a pulse."

"Oh! No! Oh, Jesus, please help me!" I shouted.

"Ma'am, do you have someone there that can drive you to the hospital?" the officer asked.

"Yes, I do. I mean, no I don't. My friend is here, but she needs to stay with my little girl."

"Well, ah, give me your address, and I'll send a car to pick you up."

"Oh, thank you, officer. I'm at thirty-four-fifty-five Meridian Court."

"I'll have a car there for you in about five minutes, ma'am."

"Thank you, officer," I said, hanging up the telephone.

Karema reached out to comfort me. We embraced each other in tears for only a few seconds. I abruptly pulled away, wiped my face, and hurried to dress myself. I grabbed a pair of blue jeans from my closet, pulled on a white sweatshirt, and quickly laced up my Reebok tennis shoes. I also pulled a lined windbreaker from the closet; I was expecting the weather to be cool at night since it was so close to the fall season. Besides, based on my experiences, hospitals were usually extremely cold.

I was barely finished dressing when I heard the police car pull up outside and saw the flashing red light shining through the window curtain. I kissed Bianca's warm forehead, hugged Karema at the front door, opened my compact umbrella, and slipped quietly out into the rainy night. I thanked the female police officer for holding the car door open while I slid in the back seat still trying to maintain my composure.

Oh, God, please forgive me. I left so fast I forgot to ask Karema for prayer. But if I know my pastor, she's already sent up several prayers for Michael and me.

While sitting in the moving police car, I bowed my head. I whispered the Bible verse that Ma Dear had often advised me to remember for times like these, James 5:15:16:

And the prayer of faith will save the sick, and the Lord will raise him up.

[216]

And if he has committed sins, he will be forgiven.

It was time to call on the Lord. I had called upon Him many times to save my mother's life and He had delivered her each time. I remembered the last time I had been in the hospital with Ma Dear in Kansas, how the doctors had given up all hope, and how I had prayed all night long for a healing miracle. I asked the Lord to give me just a little more time with her, and He answered my prayers, just like He had done many times in the past. Now, it was time to pray for my wayward husband, the man I needed more time with for my own daughter's sake. Bianca deserved to have a loving father helping to guide her into adulthood because there was one thing I never questioned; Michael loved his daughter and his wife.

After the police car screeched to a halt at the Emergency Room entrance, I bounded out of the cruiser and rushed through the hospital doors seeking the night attendant. The young man sitting behind the admissions desk looked up at me and asked, "May I help you?"

"Yes, I'm Alese Wayne. I believe my husband, Michael Wayne, is here."

The attendant stood up, opened the side door, and then motioned with his right hand for me to follow him down the hallway. Although I stepped briskly, it was difficult to keep up with the tall attendant's lengthy strides. We walked down a long corridor, then turned left, and passed two opened doors before reaching Michael's room. The distinct smell and ambiance of the hospital created uneasiness in the pit of my stomach.

I almost fainted when I entered the room and saw my husband lying there profoundly unconscious with an attentive, plump nurse on one side of his hospital bed and a tall heavyset physician on the other side. Michael had an IV in his left arm; he was connected to a heart monitor and oxygen tubes ran through his nostrils. His face was so swollen until I scarcely recognized him. However, I was able to identify the body as one I was exceedingly acquainted with.

As I slowly entered the room with parted lips and eyes stretched in fear, the doctor and nurse both glanced up at me at the same time. I must have looked like something from a scary movie.

"Are you Mrs. Wayne?" the doctor asked sternly.

[217]

"Yes, I am," I answered, noticing how my voice cracked.

"Mrs. Wayne, this is Nurse Kelly and I'm Doctor Walters. Your husband has sustained massive trauma to the head and neck area. We must perform surgery immediately to relieve some of the pressure around his brain in order to prevent any possible brain damage from occurring."

I covered my gaped mouth with both hands while I gazed at the doctor's moving lips. I forced myself to concentrate on his words; although I was actively listening, his voice sounded as though it was traveling through a water tunnel before reaching my ears. I felt suspended in time.

"Mrs. Wayne, I have to go prepare for surgery on your husband. Nurse Kelly will give you the proper surgery release forms and escort you back out to the waiting area. They will be moving Mr. Wayne to the surgery wing in just a few minutes. Nurse Kelly and I will give you a little bit of time alone with your husband now," he stated, motioning with his head for the nurse to follow him out of the room.

I affectionately squeezed Michael's hand while I knelt down beside his bed and prayed. There was nothing else I could do. He was now in God's unchanging hands.

When I raised my head from prayer, Nurse Kelly was entering the room with several papers for my signature. I didn't want to release Michael's hand, but I had to take care of business. He was still my husband.

"Mrs. Wayne, I need you to sign the admissions form and the surgical authorization form," she said, handing the papers to me on a clipboard.

My hand trembled reaching for the clipboard. I wiped the tears from my eyes, signed the papers, and handed them back to the nurse. "Thank you, Nurse," I said, forcing a smile.

"Does your husband have a living will, Mrs. Wayne?"

"Yes, he has signed a living will before."

"Are you aware of his wishes in case he goes into cardiac arrest or other problems occur during surgery that may leave him incapacitated or comatose?"

"Yes, I do. He does not wish to be placed on any life support or be resuscitated in case of heart failure," I whispered.

"Mrs. Wayne, I need you to follow me to the waiting area while the orderlies take Mr. Wayne to the surgery wing on the third floor."

After reentering Michael's room, I turned to speak to Dr. Walters. He was standing in the doorway, propping it open with one hand and directing the orderlies with the other.

"Doctor, what are my husband's chances for survival?"

"Mrs. Wayne, I can't say because there is no way to tell what type of damage has been done. We just really need to go," he said, swiftly walking away from me.

"Yes, doctor, I understand."

When I turned the corner, returning to the waiting area, I spotted Marty and Tina running to greet me with open arms. We clung to one another in a three-way hug, weeping and wiping each other tears away. Apparently, Karema had called them soon after I left in the patrol car heading to the medical center. We found a vacant sofa, sat down leaning against one another, and prepared ourselves for the long miserable night ahead.

Early the next morning, I awakened to Doctor Walters calling my name and lightly touching my forearm. I had fallen asleep in Tina's arms while Tina slept in Marty's arms. They both rose up when they felt me move. I rubbed my eyes and then quickly wiped my mouth before speaking to Doctor Walters.

"Yes, good morning, doctor," I said.

"Mrs. Wayne, your husband is out of surgery. He's in the recovery room right now. He'll be transported to a room in a couple of more hours. You'll be able to see him then."

"Thank you, Dr. Walters. What can you tell me about the surgery? Is he going to fully recover? Is there any brain damage?" I asked, speaking rapidly.

"Well, Mrs. Wayne, the surgery was a success. However, we won't know if there has been any brain damage until the swelling has gone down a lot more. I don't know about a full recovery yet, but we do expect for him to gain consciousness sometime today."

"Oh, thank you, doctor. God bless you."

"You're welcome, Mrs. Wayne. The nurses will contact me if you have any further questions. Take care, and I'll be back to check on him later today," he said while walking away.

#

Michael was in and out of consciousness for almost a week before the swelling began to go down significantly. His lips were still too sore and swollen for him to speak clearly, but he was holding my hand and mumbling something whenever he was awake. I had been by his side praying both day and night. I'd only been home a couple of times to shower, change clothes, and play with Bianca for a little while before returning to my spouse's side. Karema made sure we joined together in prayer each time before she left the house. Even Bianca joined us in saying a prayer for her daddy and always added her "Amen" at the end of each one.

Heading back to the hospital on this clear day with the front windows half-way down in my minivan, I felt really positive for the first time in what seemed like ages. I had my crinkly locks hanging down and flowing right at my shoulders. I had taken a long hot shower and was wearing one of Michael's favorite outfits. It was a marble blue Lycra and rayon pants suit with wide legs and long bell sleeves. He said that he loved the way the material felt and how it delicately adhered to MY body, showing MY curvaceous shape when I walked.

Without warning, I was inspired to listen to something upbeat by a popular female duo. When I stopped at the next red light, I reached down for my black music case and removed the Mary Mary CD. I pressed the fast forward button four times before reaching the desired song. With the music crisply drifting through my speakers, I leaned back in my seat and sang along to the beats of, *God in Me.*

Driving along the highway, I began to remember the dream I had last night about Ma Dear. It had been haunting my memory for most of the day, but I hadn't taken the time to review the entire dream since awakening this morning.

Ma Dear and I were in a valley of tall green grassy hills. But we were on top of the tallest and the greenest hill in the valley, lying on our backs, and looking up at the beautiful blue sky above us. Ma

Dear had on a long white robe and I was wearing blue jeans and a white T-shirt. As far as we could see, we were completely surrounded by grassy hills. Anyway, Ma Dear cautiously rose up on one elbow and looked down at me smiling proudly as she said, "Baby, you know you got a good man, don't you?"

"I—I don't know, Ma Dear, I guess so," I responded, sitting up and raising my knees upward while wrapping my hands around my ankles.

"What do you mean you guess so? Honey, I know you got a good husband. He loves you, and he treats you right. Now he's not perfect, but he loves you, and he has a good Christian heart. Baby, the first time you brought him home, your Daddy Nate and I knew it wouldn't be long before you two tied the knot."

"Ma Dear, how could you and Daddy Nate possibly have known that?"

"Well, he hardly took his eyes off of you for one thing, and he followed you around that house like he was a lost soul looking for Jesus himself."

"Ma Dear, you are so funny. You can always make me laugh."

"I ain't trying to make you laugh today, baby. I'm just here to help you see that you got a good man who deserves a second chance. If God has forgiven him, who are you to judge him and withhold your forgiveness? Do you know how many times the Bible says we're supposed to forgive someone who sins against us?"

"No, ma'am. What does the Bible say about that?"

"It says that you're to forgive a man seventy times seven. Every time he asks for forgiveness, you must forgive."

"But Ma Dear, what if he keeps committing the same sin against me?"

"Well, the Bible says you're supposed to forgive him every time."

"Ma Dear, how can he love me then, if he keeps hurting me?"

"You see now, that's the key, baby. If he really loves you, he will never hurt you like this again. If he truly loves you, he has learned his lesson. God has already dealt with him on that."

Ma Dear stood up and raised both arms towards the clear blue sky while her feet began to leave the ground. I flew into a panic and

[221]

started shouting to her, "Ma Dear! Don't leave me! Please, don't leave me, Ma Dear!"

"Chile, please. All my work is done here. There is no need for me to come this way again. I told you, the devil is busy, now you need to get busy, too," she said serenely, continuing her ascent into the heavenly sky.

I stood there and watched until Ma Dear completely disappeared. Then I remembered thinking, "How am I going to get down from this hill?"

#

When I returned to Michael's hospital room late in the afternoon, he was gone. Panicking, I ran to the nurse's station to inquire regarding his whereabouts. There was only one nurse available behind the counter, and she was talking on the telephone. I stood there peering down the halls for any sign of Michael or his physician. I nervously tapped my right foot while drumming my fingers on the desk. Finally, the nurse hung up the telephone and asked if she could assist me.

"Yes, Mrs. Wayne, how may I help you?"

"Ah, I was looking for my husband. He's not in his room."

"Oh, yes, ma'am. They took him down to x-ray shortly after you left. He also had to have some other tests done, but he should be back soon. You're welcome to wait out here, if you like, or you can wait in his room."

"Thank you, I believe I'll just wait inside his room." I was honestly relieved to hear that.

"That's fine, Mrs. Wayne."

I returned to Michael's room and smelled the array of floral arrangements we had received from family, friends, and employees. The small room, resembling a mortuary, was covered with plants and floral compositions of every kind. I pushed the morbid idea of a funeral parlor out of my mind and quickly replaced it by imagining I was in the center of a fragrant blooming flower shop. Not knowing how much longer I would have to wait for my husband, I decided to sit down in the green recliner located in the corner near the window and read. I pulled out the small book, *Secrets of the Vine*, which was tucked in my purse. I had been meaning to read this book ever since my neighbor, Shelly, had given it to me as a Christmas present nine months ago.

After reading only five pages, I was interrupted when Michael returned to the room in a wheelchair being pushed by an attractive nurse. He was beginning to look like himself again since most of the swelling had subsided. There were only two small scars on his face; one was across his forehead, and the other one was across his left cheek. One corner of his mouth had a tiny cut on it. His speech was much better, but he still slurred some of his words.

"Hi, baby. How long have you been waiting for me?"

"I haven't been back that long. I just started reading this little book I brought with me today." I put the book down while standing to help Michael get back into the bed.

"Oh, thank you," he said, leaning back against the pillows propped up high in the bed. "You didn't have to rush back here for me."

"I just wanted to get back in time to see your doctor before he left the hospital for the day."

"He said he would be in here in a minute. I was just with him in the x-ray room."

"How do you feel, Michael?"

"I feel fine. I just have a bit of a headache that I'll probably have for a while, I guess."

Before I could respond, Dr. Walters waltzed in with the x-rays in his hands. When I saw the serious look on the doctor's face, my stomach did a miniscule flip. I tried to maintain an expressionless face while prudently eyeing Dr. Walters.

"Mr. and Mrs. Wayne, I'm glad you're both here right now. I have the test results and the x-ray results back on Michael," he stated, gazing back and forth between the two of us. "I have carefully reviewed the lab work and the complete set of x-rays, and there are no signs of any type of brain damage or infection in any areas of your body," he spoke evenly while looking at Michael. "We need to keep you under close observation for one more night, and you'll be released tomorrow. However, you'll be on some heavy

[223]

painkillers, so you'll have to be careful even after you're released from the hospital," he added.

"Oh, praise God! Praise God!" Michael and I chanted in unison. Our prayers had been answered.

#

I slid on a comfortable hooded pink terry spa suit and Rockport tennis shoes to pick up Michael from the hospital the next day. I chauffeured him home in my minivan so he would have plenty of leg space in the front seat.

After being in the hospital for two weeks, Michael was ready to go home wearing his navy warm-up suit and blue corduroy house shoes. We mostly talked about how Bianca, smiling in the back seat, had grown in height and vocabulary over the last year. She was speaking in complete sentences now, dressing herself, and reciting the alphabet with ease.

Walking through the front door together, I felt remarkable being in my own house again. I hadn't realized how much I had missed this distinctive place we had lived in for over ten years. I admired the many special touches I had added to the house that made it feel unique to me. The compatible beige colors on the walls we had painted with our own hands; custom made paisley printed curtains we hung together over the patio door; and limited editions of artwork hanging in the double-wide foyer were all special to me. This was the home we had created for our family, and it was filled with many happy memories.

Noticing that the red light was blinking on the answering machine, Michael continued easing down into his reliable cloth recliner. The caller identification revealed he had received a total of six messages from Jenny Riley, our attorney, over the last five days. Michael punched the button to replay the last message left that day.

"Hello, Mr. & Mrs. Wayne, this is Ms. Riley. I've been trying to reach you all week. They had to reschedule one of our cases, and we have a court date reserved for you all on Friday, October first, at eleven a.m. for the final adoption decree. Please call me whenever you get this message. I truly hope that everything is fine with you all. If I'm not in my office, please call me on my cell phone. This could all be over with this week, if you all can make it. Thank you, bye."

Michael and I were so happy we just stared at each other for a few seconds, and then, we embraced with joy.

"Thank you, Jesus," I said, releasing Michael from my arms. "Let me call her back, right now, before they cancel the date."

"Yeah, that's a good idea," Michael said, handing me the cordless telephone.

"Hi. Ms. Riley. This is Mrs. Wayne. I'm calling to inform you that we will definitely be in court on Friday."

"That'll be fine. Is everything going well?"

"Yes, ma'am, everything is great. Michael was in the hospital, but he was just released today."

"Oh, well, I'm glad he's out. I look forward to seeing you all on Friday."

"Thank you very much, Ms. Riley. Good-bye." I smiled, handing the telephone back to Michael.

"What are we having for dinner tonight? We have two major reasons to celebrate, don't we?" Michael asked, smiling with joy.

"I don't know but let's let Bianca decide." I looked down at Bianca and asked, "Sweetie, what would you like for dinner tonight?"

"Ah, I don't know," she replied.

"Well, how about pizza?"

"Yeah, pizza, mommy," she said. "I like pizza."

\#

Michael and Alese stood with Ms. Riley in the family court chambers' before Judge William Hunter. The seasoned judge leaned forward, tilted his head upward, and focused his eyes on Ms. Riley as she spoke directly to him. The couple waited patiently while their skillful attorney presented their uncontested case for adoption. Michael stood tall wearing a tailor-made warm brown suit with a beige shirt and a printed tie with a matching handkerchief tucked in the breast pocket. Alese was gleaming in her platinum jacquard long sleeve pants suit with a long jacket top and a mandarin collar, showcasing her white gold heart charm bracelet and matching earrings for this memorable event.

"Your honor," Ms. Riley stated, pulling on the jacket bottom of her professional black striped suit with a short skirt. "Mr. and Mrs. Wayne have come to love the child, known as Bianca Elyce Grant, as their own. They are legally married and willing to adopt this child and provide for her until she becomes of legal age. In addition, they request that her last name be changed to Wayne. Therefore, I am officially requesting on their behalf that you grant them a final adoption decree and a name change at this time, your honor."

Finally, it was almost over. These were the words they had waited almost three years to hear. Alese and Michael squeezed each other's hand as the judge struck his gavel and said loudly, "I hereby declare on this day, that Michael and Alese Wayne are the legal parents of the minor child, Bianca Elyce Grant, hereafter to be known as Bianca Elyce Wayne. In addition, I declare that they will have all the rights and privileges thereof as the natural born parents. A new birth certificate shall be issued in their names and filed with the court at the earliest date possible. That is the final order of the court." He struck his gavel again and closed their case file.

"Congratulations, Mr. and Mrs. Wayne. I wish you both many years of successful parenthood," Judge Hunter spoke into the microphone. "The court is always happy to see a loving couple like you accept a child into their home. I wish we had more citizens willing to help more foster children. The State of Florida is in dire need of good solid homes for the many children we have to place. We appreciate you all very much for coming forward and taking some of the responsibility from us."

"Thank you, judge." They both spoke at the same time before they turned to leave the courtroom. It only took about fifteen minutes for the bailiff to give them the signed court document. At last, they were an official family.

Alese and Michael walked out of the county courthouse holding hands and laughing together, appearing to be a newlywed couple who had just received a marriage certificate. The joy they both felt at this moment was indescribable.

#

Michael was thankful Alese and Bianca had moved back home with him. They truly felt like a family again and now that it was official, he felt even better. He had an adorable wife and daughter by his side whom he loved from his soul. He couldn't even bear thinking about how he had almost ruined all their lives through one regrettable act. Michael thanked God every day for sparing his life and giving him hope for saving his family.

While Bianca napped, he relaxed on the sofa in the family room with Alese in his arms. Suddenly, Michael realized there was one thing he'd meant to ask his wife.

"Alese, the night I had the accident, I was on my way to see you. I had just gotten this news about Lisa and…"

"I know about that already, Michael. Marty told me everything while we were at the hospital praying for your recovery."

"Baby, can you—I mean, will you please—can you forgive me for what I've done?"

"Michael, you're already forgiven. I've already forgiven you."

"What? I mean, you have?"

"Yes, I have forgiven you, and God has forgiven me. I never should have left you alone for weeks at a time when you really wanted to be with me in Kansas. So, I asked God to forgive us. When you were lying unconscious in that hospital bed, mumbling my name every night, I accepted that my life would never be complete without you. He showed me that our love is greater than anything that could ever come between us. I just need to know you love me as much as I love you."

"Oh, yes. There's no doubt about that," he said, passionately kissing her curved lips.

Breaking their burning kiss, Alese shook her head, causing Michael to ask, "What's wrong? Why'd you stop?"

Wiping the tears forming in her eyes, Alese sighed heavily. This was going to really hurt their relationship even though they'd just declared their love for one another, but it was time to share the truth with her husband.

"Michael, I've been keeping something from you for so long I don't know how you're going to take this."

Michael sat up straight. Alese hadn't looked this serious since she'd held the ice pick in her hand and threatened his life.

"What is it, baby? You can tell me anything."

"I—I never told you why I couldn't get pregnant."

Michael took one of her hands and gently stroked it. "Yeah, and I never asked."

"Thank you for that," she began the same time as the tears flooded her face. Somehow, she continued. "The reason I'm not able to conceive is because I was raped in high school and got pregnant. My parents made me get an abortion from this whack doctor, and he scarred me for life. Doctors told me later on, before we were married, it would take a miracle for me to ever get pregnant again. And I'm sorry, Michael. I'm sorry I never told you the truth, but I was scared you wouldn't understand. That you wouldn't love me if I wasn't perfect."

Feeling his wife's throbbing pain, Michael pulled her into his arms and held her tightly against his heaving chest.

"Baby, you don't ever have to worry about me not loving you because that's just not an option. I regret what happened, but it could never affect the way I feel about you. If you were perfect, I'd never have a reason to complain, and that would be a pretty boring life."

Inhaling his manly scent, Alese giggled through her tears. He always had the ability to make her laugh regardless of how sad she got. Michael waited patiently for several minutes while Alese got her laughter and tears out before continuing, "Baby, I really hate to ask you this. What happened to the guy who raped you? Do you even know who he was?"

Alese nodded. It would be difficult to recall the details of an event she'd fought so hard to forget.

"I was a senior, and he was a young new teacher. We all thought he was handsome, but I didn't like him like that. Anyway, I stayed after school to work on a science project and. . ." The tears took over again.

Michael pulled her closer, saying, "You don't have to do this right now."

"Yes, I have to get it out," she stated between sobs. "When Daddy Nate found out, he was livid. He and Uncle Clevell hunted

[228]

the teacher down and beat him within an inch of his life. After that, he disappeared and no one ever heard from him again. Ma Dear told me what they did and made me promise to never speak about it again."

"Wow! That's unbelievable, why didn't they report it to the authorities?"

"It was a small town. Daddy Nate was embarrassed and believed in handling his own family affairs. He said there was nothing the police could do that he couldn't do himself. He was going to shoot the man, but Ma Dear begged him out of it. She was afraid Daddy Nate would go to prison for life."

"And you've never told anyone?"

"The only other person who knows is Karema. Not even Vivian knows about it because she'd already left home for college."

Michael saw how it was hurting Alese to talk about this, and since there wasn't any sense in reliving her complete past tonight, he changed the subject back to them.

"Alese, this whole year I've felt like we were on a soap opera. Almost every day has been some kind of drama for us. Baby, I just want to put this year of our lives in the past and start a brand new day. I want this Thanksgiving and Christmas to be the best one we've ever had together. I love you. I'd never hurt you again, and I'm going to spend the rest of my life making it right."

"Well, Mr. Wayne, Mrs. Wayne does not have a problem with that."

"Alese, I have one more thing to ask you," he said, sliding off the sofa and landing on his knees.

"I'm listening," she replied softly.

"Alese, will you marry me? I mean—will you marry me again?"

Epilogue

New Year's Day
(One Year Later)

"Welcome to the Royal Palm Crowne Plaza Resort, Mr. & Mrs. Wayne!"

The hotel's gentleman concierge, wearing a fabulous royal blue uniform, happily greeted us as we arrived in a white Lincoln Navigator stretch limousine. Michael and I exited the vehicle dressed in all white Gucci suits and overflowing with joy. We held each other's hands wearing matching custom-made platinum and diamond wedding bands. Noticeably, our eyes squinted in the bright sunlight beholding the elegant Art Deco architectural structure of the first Black-owned hotel on Miami Beach. I had yearned to visit there ever since I had read about the extravagant resort hotel in an issue of *Essence* magazine.

"We hope you will enjoy your stay in Miami. My name is Hector Gonzales and I'll be here to serve you during your visit in our city," he stated, extending his hand to Michael in a warm and friendly handshake as he smiled and tipped his head at me.

"Thank you, thank you." Michael responded with pride. "Believe it or not, we're here on our second honeymoon."

"That is wonderful! Let me know if I can be of assistance to you in any way. I'll get a bellhop to show you to the receptionist desk."

Hector motioned for one of the young male employees to come assist them with their gray Samsonite hard body luggage. He stepped away to greet another couple that was arriving in a black Bentley.

Michael and I felt ecstatic entering the lobby of the handsome hotel complex that included a curved receptionist desk and a circular upholstered banquette. The Royal Palm was actually a superb blending of two hotels--one had Old World glamour and the other was a contemporary chic model. However, they blended well together to provide one splendid site to behold. Being connoisseurs of fine food and music, we were looking forward to dining on wonderful seafood specialties, lounging by one of the hotels' two swimming pools, and enjoying cocktails in the lobby's sleek jazz bar.

Before entering the elevator, we observed the terrazzo on the main floor and the masterfully designed courtyards between the old and new sections of the hotel. As the door closed, we embraced each other and French kissed, oblivious to our surroundings.

The elevator finally stopped at the seventeenth floor on the top level for our honeymoon suite while we were still engaged in a lip lock. Several people exited the elevator chuckling and smiling at us. An older couple, sporting matching Hawaiian shirts, purposely waited to be the last ones to leave. The small gentleman lightly tapped Michael on the shoulder before he exited and said, "Congratulations." Michael thanked him, politely apologized for our overt rudeness, and then followed them into the entranceway.

After we located our room at the end of the hallway next to the exit sign, Michael punched in the code to enter our suite before he swept down and picked me up. I couldn't see my face, but I was surely a blushing bride. I wrapped my arms loosely around his neck while he carried me over the threshold.

"How you like me now, baby! This suite is the bomb!" Michael exclaimed, racing to the window to take in the dramatic ocean view setting. I walked up behind him and placed my arms around his midsection and gently squeezed his barely there love handles. I had predicted we would fall in love with this place from the detailed description I had read.

"Well, you're not bad for a penny pincher," I whispered teasingly in his ear.

"Yeah, yeah, but there was no penny pinching on our wedding or our honeymoon," he bragged. "You know I'm the M-A-N, baby!"

Smiling gracefully at him, my mind flashed back to what an incredible day the wedding ceremony had turned out to be. We had decided to renew our wedding vows at Noah's Ark Missionary Baptist Church where my best friend and pastor performed a lovely ceremony. She had ministered to us and prayed with us regarding our decision to renew our vows. Karema was overjoyed we had decided to stay together and cherish our relationship with renewed faith in God.

The impressive wedding had taken us almost three months to plan, but it was worth it. The modest sized church was elegantly garnished throughout with lilacs, cream tulips, and green floral arrangements. I selected an ivory, off the shoulder, chiffon Vera Wang wedding gown with a beaded bodice, long silk skirt, and a ten-foot train. Angela and Macy were the cutest flower girls I had ever seen in their smaller versions of my dress. Bianca was the precious ring bearer as she smiled strolling down the aisle for her daddy. Shelly, the matron of honor, was purely stunning in her sparkling champagne sleeveless dress with a sheer scarf wrapped around her shoulders in the same color. Not to be overshadowed, Michael and Marty both looked like exceptional gentlemen in their black ducktail tuxedoes with satin trim on the wide collar and down the side of each pant leg.

I was overjoyed that Vivian and Darnell had decided to come to the wedding at the last minute, and they brought Denise and Dennis with them. Vivian was glowing in a spectacular gold satin two-piece dress suit. Darnell even resembled his old charming and lovable self, dressed in a mocha brown Brooks Brothers suit. Vivian had happily confided in me three months ago that their lives had finally returned to normal since rededicating their lives to Christ. Participating in the married couples' ministry at the church had also helped them through some of their own problems. In addition, Vivian had started working outside the home as a part-time teacher's aide at the local school in Wichita. They appeared to be a contented couple again. Vivian and Darnell gave us a long hug at the end of the wedding ceremony and wished us well as a renewed couple.

Michael and I felt fortunate to also have his father in attendance. Although it had taken some cajoling to get his daddy to wear a black short coat tuxedo, he certainly wore it well. Jeremiah wasn't quite as tall or nearly as handsome as Michael, but he was a decent looking man who had aged gracefully. Ms. Flossie, his father's friend, an exceptionally well-groomed older lady wearing a silver dress with a coordinating pillbox hat, smiled throughout the entire ceremony. She couldn't stop gushing about how much she enjoyed the ride to Jacksonville with Jeremiah in his brand new red Chevrolet Traverse that Michael and I bought him for Christmas.

Both of our families were sitting together on the front row looking proud and thrilled about this special occasion. I made a mental note to make sure the professional photographer captured all of us on film immediately following the ceremony. I wanted to remember our two families sitting together in perfect harmony for the remainder of my life.

The majority of the two-hundred wedding guests also attended the lively reception held at the Grand Embassy Hotel Suites in the heart of downtown Jacksonville. Elaborately designed, circular, and well-constructed, the hotel provided the perfect atmosphere for celebrating this memorable event. The top floor was enclosed in glass on all sides to provide a panoramic view of the city for miles around. The entire place was enhanced with the wedding color flowers with marvelous elongated beige and gold centerpieces at each table. Pictures of us beaming with our daughter were placed at each table in heart-shaped sterling silver and gold frames. Twenty tables were also set up around the perimeter of the room with a circle cleared in the center showcasing a raised platform that served as a dance floor.

Everybody jammed to the live music while the "Raw Soul" band played a mixture of jazz, neo-soul, and rhythm and blues until midnight. The lead singer, Jerome White, had an amazing voice range and sang a combination of the O'Jays, Teddy Pendergrass, and Luther Vandross love songs. He even did a beautiful rendition of their trademarked song, *Love Ballad*, by Jeffrey Osbourne. Mr. White had the single ladies squirming in their seats, crossing and uncrossing their legs.

Oh, yes, what a dynamic day it had been and what an erotic night it would be. I was absorbed in the memory from earlier in the day when I felt Michael's hot wet lips and tongue roaming the nape of my neck causing me to shimmy. Feeling even more encouraged, he leisurely moved around to nibble on my ear lobe before whispering sweetly in my ear.

"I love you, Alese. All that I am and hope to be is because of you." I turned to face Michael. I took his hands into mine and firmly squeezed them while gazing into his charming bedroom eyes.

"Michael, I love you, too. This has been the most magnificent day of my life. I never dreamed we could be so happy."

"Well, is there anything I can do to make it better?" he asked, grinning slyly.

I eyed him suspiciously before replying, "There is absolutely nothing you can do to make it better, sweetheart," I paused, "but I..."

"How about this?" he asked, reaching into his front pants pocket and pulling out a small navy blue velvet jewelry box and opening it right in my face. I was instantly consumed with overwhelming emotions after seeing the one-carat diamond stud earrings I had often longed to buy sparkling in my eyes. I cupped his smooth face in my trembling hands and batted my tear stained eyes, but I still could not will my mouth to speak.

Patiently pulling me to him, Michael wrapped his arms around me in a loving embrace. I felt the warmth of his tender body spreading throughout me.

"You don't have to speak, I understand, just let me hold you," he uttered.

He took his long slender fingers and lightly wiped away my tears before placing the velvet box on the nightstand. Then, we began quietly undressing each other, maintaining constant eye contact while affectionately stroking the familiar areas of each other's bodies. We moaned with contentment while time stood still for both of us.

I eased down and slowly leaned back against the silky white bedspread. Michael deliberately slid down on both knees and began licking between my heated thighs. Every nerve in my body was tingling with sensations, and I was praying that he wouldn't stop.

"Oh, Michael, baby, that feels—that feels..." I moaned, slightly raising my pelvis.

The pleasure was too intense for me to complete the sentence. Biting down on my lower lip, I suppressed screams of excitement. I ran my fingers over his short wavy hair, gently pushing his face deeper into my moistness.

#

Michael's mind was reeling with emotions as he prepared to soar beyond any boundaries they had ever explored before. He wanted to show his wife how much he appreciated her believing in him. No woman had ever made Michael feel this intoxicated with love; he wanted her to be the recipient of his exploding passion.

He was fully aroused with the fantasy of tasting every inch of Alese's scented body and feeling her twitching beneath his moist lips. All of his senses were intrigued as he inhaled the subtle fragrance of her Pleasures perfume. Tonight he would take his time, do it right, and bask in the joys of pleasing his woman.

She will be my wife for the rest of my life.

Holding Alese in his arms after an hour of making sweet amorous love, the man was ready for rest. He was about to nod off like a drug addict on his first high.

"Michael." He heard Alese softly calling his name but was too weak to open his eyes. He felt her gently placing his right hand on her tummy.

"I got so caught up in all the excitement of the day, I forgot to tell you the good news I've been saving for our honeymoon night."

"Oh, yeah, and what could that possibly be?" he asked, sexily.

"I'm pregnant."

Both his eyes popped wide open.

The End

Barbara Joe Williams is an Amazon bestselling author, indie publisher, and motivational speaker. She has published multiple novels and non-fiction books including, *A Writer's Guide to Publishing & Marketing (Volume 2)*. She is the owner of Amani Publishing, LLC, and the co-founder of the Tallahassee Authors Network. You may visit her interactive website and subscribe for updates at: www.barbarajoe.webs.com

Other Titles from Barbara Joe Williams

Upcoming titles:
A Cup of Barbara Joe (January 1, 2015)
First Class Love Affair (February 14, 2015)

Current titles:
First Class Love (February 2014)
You Don't Even Know My Name (novella, January 2014)
A Writer's Guide to Publishing & Marketing
 (Volume 2, December 2013)
Double Proposal (August 2013)
Losing My Soul (March 2013)
The 21 Lives of Lisette Donavan: Anthology (2012)
A Man of My Own (2011)
A Writer's Guide to Publishing & Marketing (2010)
Moving the Furniture:
 52 Ways to Keep Your Marriage Fresh (2008)
Courtney's Collage (2007)
How I Met My Sweetheart: Anthology (2007)
Falling for Lies (2006)
Dancing with Temptation (2005)
Forgive Us This Day (2004)

All titles are available on Kindle and Nook devices.

www.barbarajoe.webs.com

CPSIA information can be obtained
at www.ICGtesting.com
Printed in the USA
LVOW12s1938170118

563091LV00002B/278/P

9 780983 366690